The Storm Cloud

By the Same Author

SOUTH OF HEAVEN

The Storm Cloud

BY

LETTIE ROGERS

RANDOM HOUSE · NEW YORK

FIRST PRINTING

 PUBLISHED IN NEW YORK BY RANDOM HOUSE, INC., AND SIMULTANEOUSLY IN TORONTO, CANADA, BY RANDOM HOUSE OF CANADA, LIMITED

MANUFACTURED IN THE UNITED STATES OF AMERICA
BY KINGSPORT PRESS, INC., KINGSPORT, TENNESSEE
A.B.

To Robert N. Linscott

The Storm Cloud

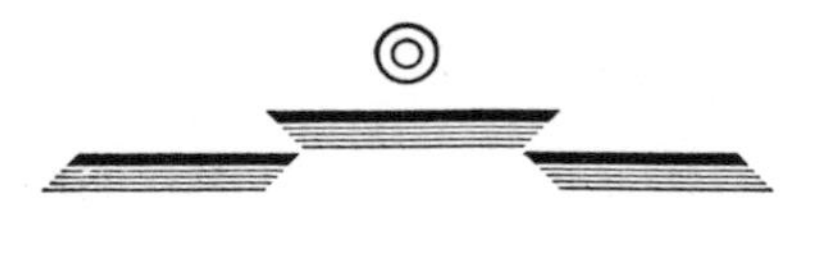

1

I

THE fallow land was the scar most visible to the eye, since it was spring and since the paddy fields, divided by the narrow dyke paths, should have been brightly green and twinkling with water. The farmers should have been working from dawn till dusk, and over more yielding tasks than watching over a few poor weeds, lest some brat or beggar steal them. There were those who insisted that not even the skinny cocks dared crow too loudly, these mornings, for fear of over-announcing themselves and thereby forfeiting their skinny necks.

The weather was glorious—an added mockery. If there had been any crops, those crops would certainly have burgeoned. As it was, the farmers were waiting for a set of promises to burgeon, instead. Which was something new under the Chinese sun, the year being nineteen hundred and twenty-seven, when a revolution was young.

In the midst of the fields, the small provincial city sat, like a second darker scar, with its black-tiled roofs running into each other and spilling over on every side of the ancient creneled wall that marked its original boundaries.

It was to the city that the farmers went, day after day. Gathering in the public squares and the teahouses and the market places, mixing with the shopkeepers and the mill workers—for the city had three silk mills—all of them restless and weary with waiting, all of them asking when the new revolutionary government was going to make good. The farmers had been promised the land for their own if they would not till it. The mill workers had been promised shorter hours and better pay if they would strike. The farmers were thinking that if the land were not soon parceled out, promises might prove to be an airy thing to live on. The mill workers were already hungry, while the mills stood idle.

The revolutionary leaders called meetings and made speeches. Two months had passed since their singing army had triumphed. They begged the people to be patient. It was perhaps both a blessing and a curse that there was one leader among them that the people continued to believe in. One was better than none. But it was very disturbing. In the first place, she could not be everywhere at once. In the second place, without any sort of invitation or encouragement, the people had transformed her into a more modern edition of the Goddess of Mercy—this when the revolution was strictly opposed to any such foolishness. They let it be known that she alone could pacify them and give them faith. Another difficulty was that she was young and beautiful in a haggard and unorthodox sort of way. It was the opinion of many of her fellow leaders that if these qualities did not render her undependable, then her sex must. The people called her the Third Koo Girl. Symbolically she pleased them because she was the daughter of Old Koo, the one who had set the usurious rates of rent on the land and was responsible for the ruinous taxes and who had owned, besides, all three silk mills. Old Koo had been the Big Man of the entire district, and it was Old Koo whom the people had been most interested in driving out. They liked it because this Koo daughter had broken with her family and taken their part; they were deeply impressed when Old Koo fled, well in advance of the army, and were quick to contend it was on her account. Oh, yes. They composed songs about her. One began:

Third Koo Girl, Third Koo Girl,
Tall Girl, Tall Girl;
Born in a garden home was she,
In the red silk bed of luxury.

While another:

When Koo Girl called the peasant brother,
Father, Mother spat upon her,
Opened gates and drove her out,
Locked the gates and turned about;
Left her out in the cold, cold world.

There were many songs and many verses and variations. Children made up games around her instead of playing shuttlecock or "Hunt the Tiger." Old men and women mixed her name with drool and spittle. . . . As the days passed, as the troop trains continued to rumble and roll toward unannounced destinations, as the rumors of what was going on in Shanghai and Nanking and Hankow became more and more confused and garbled and weighted, the more arduously did the people shift the burden of their hope (or their despair) to this Third Koo Girl, let heaven help them. What could she do? They did not ask, "What is young General Chiang Kai-shek about?" Or, "What is this talk of a split in the new revolutionary party—is it the Right Wing that will purge the Left? Is it that the Communists are wicked?" Or, "How will what is happening elsewhere affect us here?" Nothing like that. They said, "*She* will save the day." As simple as that.

. . . Nineteen hundred and twenty-seven—when the attempt to scramble four thousand years into one was being seriously made.

The temporary headquarters of the new revolutionary government were situated in a two-story building on Black Fish Way. Except that it flew the blue flag of the Kuomintang and that there were two guards flanking the main entrance, it was not a sight to impress, being indeed the former house and shop of a grain merchant, requisitioned upon his death at the hands of a mob composed of his own employees and their kin.

Upon this particular day, in April, the headquarters had a deserted air, with the guards leaning on their rifles, and no couriers or messengers hurrying in and out, and no sounds emanating from within—no typewriters going, no committees in session. But in a central room, which might be described as being more bare than barren, the titular head of the new provisional government—Yang Koh, by name—was sitting on the edge of a table and talking to another of the leaders named Huan-li who was walking slowly back and forth, in front of him, with his hands clasped behind his back. Every so often Huan-li would stop at a wall telephone, grind the crank, lift the receiver off the hook and try to get through a connection with Shanghai. He had been trying it, off and on, all morning.

"And the wireless is cut," Yang Koh was saying. "It is dead, at least. Nor is the trouble from *our* end. . . ."

Huan-li nodded. He did not waste words—he used them as most men use money—as the medium of exchange.

Yang Koh said, "For the past three days the orders that have come through from the Central Executive Committee have been contradictory. It is a crying pity we cannot move ahead on our own but must toady to these bastards who suppose they know so much better than we do—what is what. Wait—wait—wait. What are they waiting for? And what are we waiting for? And these orders—these contradictions and evasions—bode no good for us, my friend. You will see."

Huan-li sucked at his teeth, while he continued his walking back and forth, and said nothing.

Yang Koh lowered his voice. "Listen," he said. "And leave off that damnable walking, can't you? We have promised the people the land. We have promised them a government concerned with their welfare—and schools. . . . To give them less is treason. Do I make myself clear?"

"Perfectly," Huan-li said. "They are in no mood to accept less."

"No, they are not!" Yang Koh said darkly. "Comrade, do you not taste fear and treason, both, in the back of your mouth?"

No answer from Huan-li. However, he went to the phone and, once again, tried for a connection. Nothing doing.

"Just suppose," Yang Koh said. "Let us just try to predict what this Shanghai business is about. What it is that they would put over on us. Do they make a deal that will write off the peasants and the workers? Is that it—for the sake of money and gain and foreign approval? And is it that they plan to force the landlords and the gentry back down our throats? Old Koo and his friends? Is that the game? Do they really expect that they can fool these people into welcoming back with open arms the very ones who have bled them to death for generations, and who have been got rid of at such expense? *They* should masquerade as reformers? May their mothers rot! In that case the revolution becomes the counterrevolution. What else?"

Yang Koh was much excited—his eyes glittered and a whole series of muscles in his face and shoulders were twitching. Huan-li, who was older than Yang Koh by fifteen years, merely grunted. Yang Koh went on.

He said, "Consider our position, please. The people are aroused—they are organized, thanks to us, and they know what they want—but they are not armed."

"No," Huan-li said.

"We have been allotted—to garrison this entire area—two companies of troops, since the army had to move on and since we could assure the C.E.C. that we were secured by popular support. Consider. These few poor troops. And I am not even sure we can count on them."

No comment from Huan-li, which was a bad sign. Yang Koh had formed the habit of unloading his anxieties and his doubts onto Huan-li because he could trust him and because Huan-li, blunt and awkward and matter-of-fact, usually disagreed with him and was usually right. Huan-li was a rickshaw puller who had gone to college in order to learn how to go about saving the world. He was a man whose character had held up under hardships. He was not like Yang Koh—all action and passion and regrets. Yang Koh's face was hollowed out like an empty bowl, while Huan-li's was calm.

"We are being sold out!" Yang Koh said. "You know that we are! We are being betrayed from the top down and —who knows?—from the bottom up, more than likely, since there must ever be a fine, close spirit of co-operation. You and I can talk. But I am wondering how many there are in our ranks here of whom we can say the same."

Huan-li made a sudden move toward the phone. "You mean there are others among us who are in touch with Shanghai, while we are not."

"I mean exactly that."

"Perhaps," Huan-li said.

A pause.

"Well," Yang Koh said, "I did not labor all these years for this."

"No," Huan-li said. "Nor did I."

"We may be expendable," Yang Koh said more quietly, almost musingly.

"Yes."

"It's the people I am thinking of."

"I know," Huan-li said. "In the case of betrayal, it will be important for them to know that there *are* those who have remained true to a purpose—ourselves."

The two men looked at each other. They were aware that one thought was uppermost in both their minds.

"It is not us they have come to care for," Yang Koh said slowly, putting the thought into words. "That is to say, there is the one who has come to stand for us, whether we like it or not."

"The Third Koo Girl."

Silence. Yang Koh groped in his pockets for cigarettes. Huan-li stared at the wall telephone.

"She is her father's daughter," Yang Koh said. "It is Koo blood that runs in her veins. It would be interesting to know, would it not, whether she isn't in touch with Shanghai?"

"There!" Huan-li said. "Bury your jealousy. She is more trapped in this than the two of us rolled together. . . . Our concern is the people's attitude toward her, since they are so sure that she is the one who will save the day."

Yang Koh said, "Maybe they will turn on her, eh? Maybe they will hold her entirely responsible—if the day should be lost?"

"Maybe," Huan-li said. "I daresay they will—if they should feel—or be persuaded to feel—that she has gone over to her father's sort, at their expense—that she could be capable of turning her coat. It seems to me it is our duty to see to it that they are not persuaded to feel that—under any possible combination of circumstances. It is she, above all, who must appear to remain true to their purpose."

"You know what you are saying?"

"I think so."

"And do you think she has that courage?"

"If she does not have it, we must have it for her."

"And so everything will happen around her," Yang Koh said bitterly. "France had its Joan of Arc. We have our Third Koo Girl."

"Yes," Huan-li said.

"Maybe Shanghai is not aware of her significance."

"I imagine there have been informers."

"And will they try to buy her or kill her?"

"That's it. That's for us to discover. *She must not be bought.*"

"God help her!" Yang Koh said.

"Well," Huan-li said, "let us hope that we worry unduly. We are not sure what is going on in Shanghai. And we have not lost yet."

"No!" said Yang Koh. "And I suppose you are going to try again with that damned telephone!"

"As a matter of fact," Huan-li said, "I am."

II

Into another room of the headquarters a courier was ushered. Rather than saluting, he bowed to the woman who was seated at a desk with a window behind her. There were three other desks (all vacant) in the room and redwood chairs sitting not quite straight against two of the walls. The courier closed the door. So this was the Third Koo Girl—and she was alone. What he had to impart to her was written down on no paper, nor would it have been transmitted by wire. He carried it in his head and his head was very dear to him, in the last analysis. . . .

The woman was waiting for him to speak. The light from the window was reflected in her hair, but the rest of her face was in shadow and the courier could not make it out, which bothered him. He said, "I was instructed to report directly to you, without going through—uh—channels."

"Which is to say, you have not seen Yang Koh or Huan-li or—the others." Then, abruptly, "Who sent you?"

"That is not important," he said.

"Isn't it?"

It was the way she lifted her head—the sudden movement that revealed her face to him—and he realized that the hollows under her eyes and the gauntness of her cheeks had collected the shadows. Disturbing—the face. But more so than the face was the bearing and that negligent Koo pride which she had not apparently abandoned. Too much breeding, too much pride, he thought. He had not expected to understand her in her role. What sort of woman she was and why they had set a woman up—who knew? But that she was no mere figurehead or mouthpiece he was prepared to admit—she was appraising him, now, more coolly than he was her.

"Your father is back," he said, handing it out to her without further preamble. "The Family of Koo has arrived in houseboats. Last night, this happened."

A pause.

"If it is my father who has sent you," she said, "you may leave."

"I do not come from your father."

"That is just as well."

"You have been posted about troop movements?" he said.

Silence. Pregnant silence.

He said, "Those troops who are at present quartered here—two companies, I believe?—are to be taken care of, as it were, by General Ma."

"I see," she said, and there was the slightest suggestion of a smile about her lips. "And General Ma and my father are such *dear* friends."

"That is so," the courier said. "The revolution benefits by such as they. It assumes new scope."

"It does," she said. "The revolution becomes the counter-revolution. You make it official. Have you any more to say? And why did you come directly to me, rather than going to Yang Koh?"

The courier preferred to consider that she had not spoken. He said, "Naturally you understand that everything is in readiness—now—already."

"Naturally."

"That your ranks . . ."

"That our ranks are rotten," she said. "Yes."

". . . That your ranks number those who are prepared to *welcome* your father's and his friends' return and will be most happy to run this government according to terms that others—like Yang Koh—are not expected to agree to. You see, there is to be a little purge of Communists and radicals."

She said, "You still have not explained why you come to me."

They stared at each other. So she supposed he was offering her the chance to flee or recant? She supposed he was representing the high authorities of the Central Executive Committee and stood ready to make her some inviting proposition—perhaps in conjunction with her father, whose return was indeed not possible without the C.E.C.'s approval, support and protection? Piecing this obvious conclusion together with a haunting memory . . . She had at one time been a great favorite of her father's and he had lavished upon her every luxury and opportunity that money could afford. . . . Now, upon his return, was her father's attitude toward her one of forgiveness or revenge? Or did she suppose that the paradox of her popularity with the peasants and workers and her connections with the gentry rendered her very nearly untouchable? In that case, she would not be so far wrong!

Not, at least, in the opinion of the one who had sent this courier, of the one who privately considered it too great a risk, at this juncture, for either the gentry or the people to be allowed to make any move either toward or against her and who would much prefer that she make a move herself. And at once! He glanced at his watch. He might have told her, for comfort, that she resembled a bomb sitting in the middle of a narrow road, obstructing travel, with the travelers viewing it suspiciously, hesitant about attempting to pass, fearful of the risk implied in removing it. How much better if the bomb should explode of itself, harmlessly, into the air, before the travelers should have come too close! But time was passing, passing. And the C.E.C. had its own courier, in the form of a colonel, traveling with sealed orders, who was also on his way to these headquarters, as this courier well knew. His duty was to make his proposition with the speed of lightning and to get out before the colonel should arrive. For his employer had "inside information" to the effect that the C.E.C., at the distance of Shanghai, and with a thousand more major problems under consideration, had decided how to settle this one.

He said, "Those who have been labeled dangerous are to be executed—by a special squad, under the command of Colonel Shu—on the way here, at this moment, I believe, from Shanghai."

He took a step toward her—reached his hand in his tunic and saw her right hand move instantly to a drawer of the desk. He stayed his hand—she stayed hers.

"I have brought you a gift," he said, "from the friend who sent me to you. But before I offer it, at his request, perhaps I should explain."

"Yes?" Her hand was not deflected by so much as a fraction.

"It was not for a revolver I was reaching," he said, his voice as quiet as hers. "It was for a packet of cyanide. . . . But perhaps you carry it already?"

"Thank you," she said. "I neither carry it nor want it. Do you understand? You should not fail to tell your friend that."

"He is *your* friend."

The courier was breathing rapidly but had the impression that she had ceased to breathe, she was so motionless. It was her eyes alone that consumed him. He was again made acutely aware that those who would receive his credentials with favor were not in this room; he was aware that his presence preceded—no matter by how little time—the "taking over"; nor had he been led to believe that his mission could fail so completely. On this slender margin of time, she might still shoot him or have him shot—as a traitor. And his revolver—the only one he carried—was in its closed holster, as out of reach of his hand as destiny itself.

He touched his lips with his tongue. "A public execution would be most humiliating to you—and awkward to your father. Do you not comprehend?"

She said, "I comprehend that when a thief comes in the night and in disguise, it is well to sound the alarm."

He said desperately, "Should you allow me to give you the cyanide, you should swallow it *now*."

Her lower lip curled. She said, "And should I open this drawer, I should turn the gun to my own temple. Is that it?"

He was drenched with sweat.

She repeated her question. "Who sent you?"

Then both heard the commotion out in the hall, both judged the commands, the shouts, the angry retorts.

"Will you come here?" she said to him.

He went—but like a man in a trance. When he was close, she opened the drawer. It was empty.

"Good morning," she said.

The knock on the door, the door opening. Colonel Shu stood in it. He looked the courier over briefly. The courier saluted and gathered his wits enough to use the password that had been agreed upon and circulated in advance to those who were "co-operative." The colonel dismissed the courier with a motion of his hand. He addressed the woman behind the desk.

"Koo Three?" he said.

"Yes."

"You are under arrest."

Out in the hall the courier touched the papers in his pocket designed to explain his presence without, at the same time, revealing the identity of his employer—who would not be pleased about the failure of his mission, but who would be still less pleased to have it come out that he had tried it.

III

And in a small court in the rear of a blacksmith shop on Pu-tang Street Christopher Blair, a young half-caste surgeon, was facing his servant and waiting for him to speak. Blair had stood up—it was as if some secret sign had passed between them—when the servant had entered a moment before. . . .

Dressed in a pullover sweater and gray-flannel slacks, Blair hardly looked as if he belonged in the small, dingy court. He was tall, dark, and had that beauty of face and form so often peculiar to the Eurasian half-caste and which, more often than not, becomes confused in the mind with the very condition of being inferior and despised and is therefore treated without respect. (A reversal: that in his daydream he might conceivably wish that he were heavy-set, square jawed, and ugly.)

(He kept looking at his servant.)

Blair had been living here in the room that opened off the court of Wang the Little's blacksmith shop ever since the "occupation"—ever since the wealthy and the foreigners had fled and (he was tagged as being both "foreign" and "wealthy") it had become necessary for him either to do likewise or else hide. His house and the hospital where he had been Assistant Surgeon had been seized by the new revolutionary government and were being used as barracks. Seizing the property was "policy"—in this case pragmatic since, at the time, a mob had been intent upon burning it to the ground. . . . Blair had friends among the revolutionary leaders. He was torn between being grateful to them for having saved it and angry that the buildings had been put to such wretched use. He was also insistent upon their return, although his sympathies were pro-revolution.

The servant coughed.

"Yes," Blair said. "So something has happened. . . . What is it?" Then, sarcastically, "Is it time for tea?"

"No, Master."

"Perhaps some medical supplies have come through."

"No," the servant said. "Nothing like that."

Blair lighted a cigarette.

The servant said, "Old Koo is back."

It didn't penetrate, at once. He stood there pulling

stupidly on his cigarette, staring off into space, remembering his own feud with Old Koo who for two years had tried everything he knew to break him professionally because his oldest son had died on the operating table under Blair's knife.

"Is this rumor?" he said.

"No, it is fact."

"Did Huan-li send word?"

"No," the servant said, "but I have it straight."

"Then tell me what you know, for the love of Buddha, and be quick about it, can't you?"

The servant looked down at his feet. "According to my informant, Old Koo and many of the others who fled have either already returned or are on their way. There are rumors of troop movements but there is nothing definite, as yet, about them."

"Whose troops?" Blair wanted to know. "My maternal uncle's, I suppose?"

"Perhaps. That is the rumor."

"My God," Blair said, under his breath. His "uncle" was General Ma—General Ma Chi-djen, his Chinese mother's fourth brother-in-law. He was a warlord and his tie-up with Old Koo was one of long standing. It was this same General Ma and his troops who had "defended" the city two months before against the revolutionary army. This was the counterrevolution, undisguised!

"Go on," Blair said. "What else?"

"Well, your friend, Huan-li, is under arrest, along with several others. They are charged with being Communist—radical."

"I see."

"There is to be a public execution in the morning, so it seems."

He saw. He saw his servant with his hair standing

straight up off his head, giving him that perpetually startled air; he saw his servant's eyes telling their perpetual lie of guilelessness; he saw his servant's feet, looking like two oblong blocks of solid wood, planted about four inches apart. He saw the whole, stagnant, dirty, still-born scene: the court.

"And the Third Koo Girl?" he said over-casually. "Is she one of those to be executed?"

"So it is said. The news of it is getting around—in trickles. The jail is heavily guarded." The servant's voice lost its dispassionate quality: "It will be a time for gentlemen to bar their doors and remain inside."

So saying, the servant left, closing the shop door softly behind him. Blair walked over to his chair. As a doctor he understood that men never believe in their own deaths, remaining to the end secretly convinced of their own immortality. He had first known Huan-li in college, in Peking, where—clothed in rags—he had gone to learn how to go about saving the world. Blair sat down and covered his face with his hands.

The Third Koo Girl. But he never thought of her by any name—just "she" or "her." He and she had crossed the barriers that the feud had erected between the Koo Family and himself; in their own ways they had both broken with their traditions—she much more dramatically than he—and they had it in common. As a gesture, she had gone out of her way to protect his life in those first few days of anti-foreign uprisings, so much more violent than anyone had foreseen, it was she who had ordered the blacksmith shop guarded by the men dressed as beggars and it was she who had sent him the chit—"Under no circumstances should you go out. Koo Three." All of this when they had never met, although twice they had set a place and time and both times she had been unable to come. And of course if the myth had interested him, the woman had interested him more. More than a few times he had been on the verge of attending meetings at which she was scheduled to speak. So—now—he could ask himself why he had not. He could examine, at leisure, his reticence, his niceness of feeling—that was not the way he had wanted to see her. . . . Had he been waiting for some propitious and divinely appointed moment? He would let no servant say it for him, with hair and eyes and tone of voice! "The woman you have dreamed your idle dreams about is condemned to die." Huan-li had promised to arrange a meeting but had put it off. "You would complicate her life," he had said. "Wait. There will be time enough for that."

He could go to the execution. No one would prevent him. And had she made of herself much too willing a sacrifice? He looked up at the sky that was blue and cloudless. Out in the street some minstrel was singing:

"Third Koo Girl, Third Koo Girl,
Tall Girl, Tall Girl . . ."

IV

The House of Koo was situated in one of the better residential districts, though only a practiced or Chinese eye could have told that it was—the walls were merely longer than others. It was this section of the city that had been most gutted by fire but (nor was it an accident!) the street the House of Koo was on was untouched and, in the late afternoon, quiet.

A man of indeterminate age, dressed in the rough blue cotton clothes and the straw sandals of a peasant, entered the street, walking rather fast, turning his head neither right nor left. He had his hands in his sleeves. There was something about his carriage that was at variance with his dress. About thirty paces behind him came six peasants, chatting and laughing together, looking nothing at all like a bodyguard.

The first man stopped at the Small Gate of the House of Koo and knocked. The six peasants found something to loiter over. Someone called from within. Instead of answering, the man repeated his knock and the gate was opened a crack by an ancient man with a face given over to brownness and wrinkles.

"Ai," said the old-old. "And what is this?"

The man handed the gatekeeper a card and said something apparently very significant under his breath, for the gatekeeper peered at him, then opened the gate much wider and began bowing. Immediately the man had entered, the gate was closed behind him.

Outside, the peasants continued to loiter—swapping jokes and leaning on their carrying poles.

The House of Koo was an establishment—it was a "large-family" home, numbering over sixty mouths, which number did not include the lesser servants. It was called a "garden home" because it had an elaborate and formal garden. It also included reception halls, ancestral temple, library, courtyards divided by ornamental gates (moon gates—peach gates—gates shaped like vases) and one-story living quarters that opened into the different living courts. It would take no astrologer to predict that such a household—made up of wives, children, concubines, daughters-in-law, nephews, nieces, grandnephews and nieces, great-uncles, servants, slave girls—could not just arrive without a deal of confusion and turmoil. But because of the management of Madame Koo, who was the First Wife of Old Koo, the confusion was limited mostly to the children's crying and to the unpacking of baskets and pigskin trunks. The courts were swept, the furniture was in place, the bedding was distributed, many of the less valuable curios had been brought out of their hiding places, the kitchens were operating. . . . True, certain servants had been sent on ahead. Other trusted servants had not evacuated the House of Koo, two months previously, although that fact was not noised abroad. They had remained the whole time the House of Koo was supposedly standing vacant, waiting for the new revolutionary government to convert it into a modern primary school for the children of workers.

So . . . Although the Family of Koo had been back less than twenty-four hours, the women were already complaining that "the routine of their days" was upon them, they felt overly settled, and now that the excitement of arrival was waning, they began to wish they were back in Shanghai. It was perhaps curious that most of them considered their stay there "a vacation." And while—if anyone had asked them—they would have nodded their heads wisely and answered, "Ah, yes, we fled trouble, political trouble," they nevertheless had almost no notion as to what that trouble was about. They had left so well in advance of the army that they had encountered no mobs and heard not a single shot fired; in Shanghai, furthermore, they had stayed in the French Concession. When one of the servants, who had remained behind, sang "The Song of the Third Koo Girl" to some of the ladies, they were mildly shocked but hugely delighted. The Third Koo Girl had not reached the crest of her fame until after the Koo Family's departure—it was the departure that had precipitated it.

"Imagine!" they said.

"Such boldness."

"Vulgar—yet romantic."

They commanded the servant to sing the song again. They

noted that it was highly inaccurate: nobody had *driven* the Third Girl from home—she had *left* home (run away, if the truth could be given a name, for once, to keep from marrying the man of her family's choice. And she had only her father to thank that she had not been officially disowned but had been counted instead, all this time, as being "away for a visit."). The scandalous creature. What she must have gotten into! The ladies said they would surely call in a minstrel or a big-drum story teller—to hear more.

Some said, "Where is she, do you suppose?"

Others: "How diverting."

Old Koo was a man of proportions—a matter for dispute, how many chins, how many rolls of fat in the region of his belly, he had. . . . When a servant came to inform him that General Ma Chi-djen was waiting to see him, he was installed in his inner room with his latest "Shanghai concubine" who wore quantities of rouge and had a snake-like walk. Old Koo was teaching her some manners.

The servant, who could go no farther than the outer room, insisted upon sending in a message by a slave. Ordinarily, it was not considered safe to bother Old Koo when he was "closeted"—it put him in a dangerous mood. Yet on this occasion, he absently patted his concubine's buttocks, told her to go no farther than the second court if she wished to continue to avoid a fate worse than death (Madame Koo), and himself waddled out, selecting the shortest way to the Inner Reception Hall, with the servant in his wake.

"The General and I," he said to the servant, "will have a few minor trivialities to settle between us. . . . Do you serve the tea and keep everyone else away."

"Yes, Master."

"Especially those with long, pointed ears—the females."

"Yes, Master."

By the time Old Koo had reached the hall, he was panting. He paused in the entrance. His silk gown billowed down, making a tightish transition out over his paunch, then billowing on in triumph, almost to the floor.

"Ah, General!"

They bowed deeply to each other—did Old Koo and General Ma. They went through all the ceremony of who should sit where—tugging and pulling and expostulating—with high seriousness and only the faintest suspicion of uneasiness and mockery.

When, at last, they were seated, Old Koo sighed. He assured the General that his new full-dress uniform, particularly the footgear, was magnificent beyond all powers of description. It rendered him, he said, speechless. Tea, sweetmeats, and melon seeds were brought.

"The times are delicate," General Ma said.

Old Koo agreed that the times were delicate. The General put his hand into his peasant's garments and took out a carved ivory holder into which he fitted a cigarette with his long, delicate fingers. The sight pleased Old Koo—it pleased him that General Ma, who because of his elegance went by the nickname of "the Gentleman General," had had to come calling in this rude attire rather than in the style for which he was famous. Anything that smacked of paradox or irony always pleased Old Koo—it was one of the weaknesses of his nature—the trait that made him highly unpredictable even to those who supposed they knew him best.

He said, now, "I take it, you have not quite 'arrived' as yet?"

"True, true," said the General. "I 'arrive' at six o'clock tomorrow morning, when the city gates will be thrown open. I and my troops make our entrance then."

"Indeed," murmured Old Koo, whose eyes had almost disappeared into the creases of fat that surrounded them. "I seem to be imperfectly informed, do I not? Is it then that the purge—the public execution—is to light the fuse—is to touch everything off?"

"It is," murmured General Ma.

"I had thought that the arrests were to have been made today," Old Koo said, sipping his tea. "I had been expecting you before this, somehow."

"The arrests have been made today," the General said, studying the two Sung calligraphy scrolls on the opposite wall. "But quietly. Today is the day for the leakage of rumors and the activities of propagandists. Tomorrow—theatricals."

"So."

General Ma shifted his attention from the scrolls to the glowing tip of his cigarette. He said, "My dear friend, we are not quite the omnipotents we used to be."

Old Koo said, "It is true that in Shanghai we were the little fish in the big puddle. . . . But now that we are back, we need not be too grateful or too humble, either. The C.E.C.—the revitalized Kuomintang Party—Chiang Kai-shek . . . Well, they would find it difficult to get anywhere without us, in this area, now that they have so kindly returned us to it, eh?"

"But we are so corrupt," the General said sadly, "so greedy, so mistrusted by the populace . . ."

". . . which is not armed," Old Koo said pointedly.

"Which is not armed," the General echoed. . . . "It is a shame, is it not, that these people are offered only the two alternatives—Communism or us? Too bad that Chiang Kai-shek—in his anxiety to be rid of the one—has been forced to take the other to his bosom. We will corrupt and undo any program of reform he may have in mind. We *are* awful."

The two men laughed—but uneasily.

"Let us not get overly philosophical," Old Koo said. "It may be bad for our digestions. . . . We can offer the few 'moderate' reforms that these high authorities insist upon—these authorities who are so anxious to impress and dupe the foreign powers into supposing that we are modern—the democratic continuation of the revolution rather than what we are. . . .We will offer the reforms. That is what we have agreed to do. Very well. We lower the rents but levy new taxes. Reforms can be painless enough."

"Exactly so," the General said. "Of course. Once we have taught these stupid people their lesson, I have no doubt that we will get along well enough—as long as we continue to pay in the percentage of taxes agreed upon. But . . . Well, while it is certainly true that the C.E.C. has bargained with us, it would seem that it does not *quite* trust the Koo-Ma combination."

Old Koo opened his eyes.

The General said, "Colonel Shu, who is in charge of making all arrests—who is also in charge of the execution tomorrow—is not under my command, my dear friend."

"Not under your command!" Old Koo blurted out.

General Ma nodded and while he was apparently absorbed with putting out his cigarette, he was actually watching Old Koo intently.

"Who is this Colonel Shu?" Old Koo wanted to know. "Where did he come from? When did he arrive? Why have I not been informed? What is he doing here?"

"Colonel Shu is a Whampoa man," the General said. "He is one of the 'favored sons' of the C.E.C.; he has no local connections here whatsoever and he has an odd streak —he cannot be bribed."

"Merciful Buddha!" Old Koo cried. "You cannot mean . . . You . . ." He stopped. But that was why he had not broached the matter of the fate of that worthless Third Daughter of his—in Shanghai. It was why he had tactfully held it in abeyance, avoiding all mention in his transactions. Because he had known he could count on General Ma, with whom he had ever had such a beautiful understanding. Because he had been so sure that between them they could "fix" anything, once they were back in their own element. The idea that his daughter's antics could be taken seriously by others was in itself a little strange to Old Koo who rather preferred to believe she was one of those extravagant and freakish jokes that is visited upon one—usually in one's dotage. Had he lost all his fortunes, all his lands and all three of his factories forever, and people had screamed at him until their throats were dry that it was every bit her doing—Old Koo would still have laughed, half-believing, half-not. Oh, he had every intention of punishing her—it would be his pleasure to tame the rebel, to put her most definitely in her place. Oh, yes. He planned for her to eat her words, three times a day, for months to come, but at his table. He could not help it that he happened to love the wretch. It was, again, one of those ironies of fate which so intrigued Old Koo: that this female, of all his children—and he could not have said with any absolute certainty, without pausing to count, how many he had sired—that this particular female had to be the one he had lavished his love upon. This one! It was a mystery of the heart. Because she had learned to count by counting his rolls of fat, he supposed, or because she had laughed at his tantrums when others had fled. He did not know. He stole a look at General Ma. What he wished he knew, at this moment, was whether Ma spoke the truth and had been given no opportunity to touch the business—or whether, for fear of offending, he had not adroitly passed it off on some other—on this Colonel Shu! Old Koo was not one to stoop to argue: that since they were so unpopular, there might be great advantage to keeping one around who was *very* popular and for whose future conduct he would gladly go guarantor. Old Koo's mind was prouder. How dared they—anybody!—contemplate (if *that* was what dear General Ma was trying to put across) touching a hair on the head of one of his!

General Ma was looking into his teacup. Who knew better than he how Old Koo had to be placated and catered to at every turn, since Old Koo did virtually own the city! Had it been up to him . . . But unfortunately the C.E.C. did not feel the same need to placate Old Koo, and the C.E.C. had also to be dealt with. . . . General Ma might have said, "Do you not understand that the C.E.C. can afford to be high-handed if it pleases? Do you not understand that the C.E.C. has decided to take no chances with this daughter of yours who has inflamed the masses and might again? The masses must remain voiceless; the future is dependent upon it. The C.E.C. is killing many well-educated young ones who have so seized the people's fancy. There are other families, greater than the Koo Family, in Shanghai and Nanking and elsewhere who are being asked to pay the same price: the riddance of those sons and daughters considered radical. They are not objecting, they are too grateful for their own survival and re-entrenchment."

"This Colonel Shu is not to be handled?" Old Koo said.

"Dear friend and most august personage," the General said, "would that my journey on foot through these streets were not to bring you tidings and confirmation of so sad a fact."

"Well," Old Koo said, "continue. Who is to be executed? This fellow, Yang Koh, of course. Who else?"

Almost imperceptibly, the General shrugged.

"Go on!" Old Koo said. "Let me hear what other names will pass your lips."

"Spare yourself," the General said quietly.

"She is to be put to death, side by side, with common swine?" Old Koo roared. "Someone will pay for this!"

General Ma did not say, "She has been working, side by side, with common swine. It is a part of 'the lesson.' "

Old Koo turned abruptly away. "Leave me," he said.

"You understand. . . ."

"I understand," Old Koo said.

The General rose and bowed. He cleared his throat in preparation for his farewell speech, but thought better of it when he saw the face that Old Koo turned toward him. Without another word he took his leave.

V

The General had gone. Old Koo called out, "I am not to be disturbed!" and sank back into his chair, neither swearing nor groaning. He did not know how much time elapsed before a plan began to take shape in his mind, but darkness had fallen. And it seemed to him, as he sat there, that all the blood of his body was churning and thudding and that all his thoughts were blood-dark.

General Ma was a chicken-breast; Colonel Shu was not to be handled! Very well. So be it. His daughter was therefore to be murdered? It hardly followed.

Old Koo had not seen his daughter in two years—not since she had left the house, in defiance of him. She had caused him to break his best Tang vase (the feast of his eyes!). He had thrown it at her, in his rage, when she had walked out. So she was to depart forever—she was to leave the earth before Old Koo should be given the chance to even the score? But it was also Old Koo who had forbidden her feet to be broken and bound when she was five. He had not been able to endure her screams. Well. And so. They said he had ruined her life, since in those days all females of any breeding had had their feet bound. They said none but a coolie would have her in marriage. Well. And so. He had seen her clopping about like a beggar's brat, stumbling over her feet, hiding them under chairs. . . . Of course he had named her his favorite. He had given her everything, including an education in that land of big-footed females—the United States of America. (Old Koo himself had made a journey to the United States of America; it was one of the great events of his life.) The times had changed, furthermore, and with her feet she was to become the envy of her sisters. But, still, the rebel in her was born out of the hurt—Old Koo knew. To save her hurt, he had hurt her. Perhaps their score was nearer even.

She *deserved* to die—wanting to give away the Koo lands! (She was overflowing with foolishness.) Old Koo recognized that his joke: "It is a family affair, I bleed them to death—she saves them," had ceased to be funny. She ought to be made to suffer; if death were not so final she ought to die, and Old Koo would order it.

He had never been so close to himself, in darkness. The affair was serious. He could not afford to throw the whole House of Koo into the lion's mouth—for her sake. Not possibly. It was unthinkable. And all this while, his plan was maturing—developing. Old Koo heaved a great sigh.

The plan pleased him. Nor did it involve too great risk. He had known when to keep quiet—in Shanghai. Let Shanghai maintain its distance, then. He also knew that, locally, he was the man of the hour. A man of weight, power, influence. To be reckoned with, he was. So. Damn General Ma and Colonel Shu. Stricken pride and loss of face must combine, as motives, with his inconvenient love. No Koo was going to die a common death. Old Koo heaved a second, enormous sigh. Then he clapped his hands softly and a servant—the same servant he had had his earlier conversation with—appeared with a lamp in hand.

"Put down the lamp and come close," Old Koo said.

The servant did as he was told. Old Koo looked at him. He was to be trusted; he was one of the servants who had never left the house.

"Under the cover of darkness," Old Koo said, "I will be going out."

The servant inclined his head.

". . . To the Wang Widow's Bridge Mill," Old Koo said.

"Yes, Master."

"I have been informed that the women workers are still living in the dormitory. Is that correct?"

"Yes, Master. A few have grown weary with waiting for the promises that have not been fulfilled and have either returned to their homes or run away. But the rest are there—even though they have struck."

"Good," Old Koo said. "The trust I place in you is that of life and death. Do you fathom that?"

"I do," said the servant.

"You must contact the keeper of the jail—at once. And bear in mind that the jail will be heavily guarded by the men of a certain Colonel Shu who are to be avoided like leprosy."

"Yes, Master."

"Bring the keeper to me. I do not plan to announce my presence at the mill. Come quietly, therefore."

"Yes, Master."

Old Koo thought a moment. Then he spoke the names of three other servants whom he also trusted. "Have them called," he said. "Have them come here. They will go with me. Together we will arrange some signals between us, so that when you arrive with the keeper, all will be in secret and pre-arranged."

"Yes, Master."

"Send me the steward, too. Immediately. There are considerable arrangements to be made."

"I will."

Old Koo said, "And above all, above everything, Madame Koo is to know nothing about this night's activities. Nothing until afterwards. Is that clear?"

"Yes, Old Master," the servant said. "Madame, Our Mistress is overburdened, just at present, with household duties, with the duties of arrival."

"Good," Old Koo said. "She should continue to be overburdened. I will see to that. . . . Now, go. And if all goes well, this night, you shall be rewarded."

The servant took a step backwards.

"Hasten," Old Koo said. "Time is what we are short of."

"Yes, Old Master."

The servant glided out.

Old Koo smiled. Now that his plan was going forward, there was no going back. His smile changed into a knitting of his brows. Well, well. He reached out his hand for the tea—which was stone cold—and took a great swallow. There. Fate had better be on his side tonight.

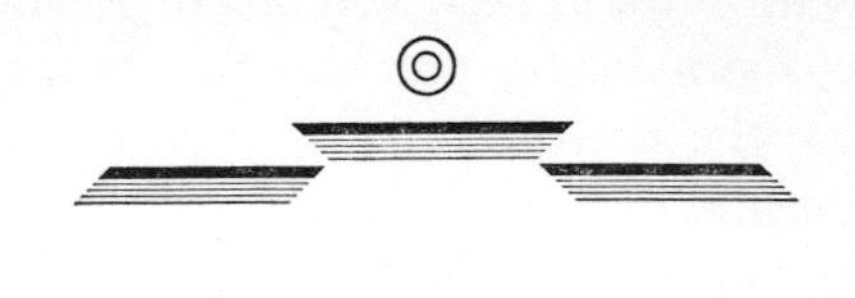

2

I

TWO A.M. Outside the jail the guards stood shoulder to shoulder, with bayonets fixed. Kerosene lanterns flanked the entrance, but the darkness was very deep—of the sort that is constantly encroaching and in which the stars seem lost. There was no wind. Repeatedly the guards stamped their feet. People—in two's and three's—entered the street at what seemed to the guards to be almost regular intervals—walking slowly.

"Move on," the guards would say.

They moved on, silently, slowly.

"A little trouble would be a relief," one guard said to another.

The other stamped his feet and did not answer.

Inside the jail, twenty-one revolutionaries, considered radical, were together in the common room which was hardly large enough to contain them. They were in chains and chained one to the other, for extra precaution. A light that was burning in the corridor kept the room from being in total darkness, since the end that faced the corridor was grilled. Huan-li must urinate—he must rid himself of his water. Their silence was most often punctuated by the sounds of swallowing (they had been given nothing to drink and no food during the fourteen hours since their arrest) and by the noises the chains made when someone shifted his position even slightly.

She was sitting, leaning back against the wall which was filthy and bug-spattered. She thought, I am a Vassar graduate. But that thought immediately departed. She thought of her "milk name"—Leila—by which no one called her any more, since her comrades called her Koo Three or simply "Girl."

Yang Koh was looking at her. She sensed this more than she saw it.

"Who was the courier to come out of your room directly after the Colonel entered it?"

Since no one had spoken for over an hour and since no one was sleeping, the voice, even while it was low, cut through each individual consciousness.

She hesitated. "I do not know who sent him," she said.

"Not your father." Yang Koh's voice twitched.

"He said he did not come from my father."

"He offered you—what?"

Again, she hesitated. "He explained to me that all was lost. . . . What he offered me was a quicker death. Cyanide."

It was as if the chains could have convulsions.

"And nothing else?" Yang Koh said.

"That was all," she said.

For a moment it seemed as if Yang Koh could retire into himself and allow the others to do the same—that he might allow them all to sink back into silence. But he was not able to. He picked her face out of the semi-darkness and said, "You are democratic—to *choose* to die with us."

"Leave off," Huan-li said roughly. "She has served us well. She is here—that is the point."

Yang Koh laughed. "The point is that she could have died for us all. She would have been enough. Huan-li, we should have thought of that. We should have pulled out, escaped, when we knew so well the way the wind was blowing. It is too costly—this. Better we should live, don't you think, to tell the story? We could have left her behind—to propitiate and expiate—the sacrificial offering. . . . The peasants will build a shrine for her out of their hearts—not for us. Our bodies are going to be unholy temples."

A rat skittered across the floor. She was proud and remote. She might die, she supposed, without a thought in her head, since her mind was apparently deciding to depart ahead of schedule.

Someone said, "You speak as though there were this great element of choice—as if we could have left!"

Another, "And how were we to know that she was not planning to return with wet and broken wings to the spun-silk womb that bore her?"

Yang Koh had begun to explore his body with his hands and had nothing more to say.

Huan-li was very angry. "In our last hours," he said, "we might be above this pettiness. . . . You taunt her when she has behaved with courage—when her courage is her own. You remind me of dogs rolling in your defilement. Now, have done."

They found that they listened to the silence that followed. They listened intently. All but Yang Koh who continued to feel himself.

"They will storm the jail and be shot," one of them announced.

"They will not," Huan-li said.

"And why not? Feeling as they do about her, will they

not make some final and desperate attempt to save their Girl?"

"No," Yang Koh said, looking up. "They expect some magic feat, some sign from heaven. They only half-believe what they have heard. They have built up the myth—now they expect the myth to behave like a myth. . . . They will wait for confirmation until they see, in the light of this new dawn, until they *see* her fall."

One of them, staring in her direction, said, "She can be proud, then. She can hold her head high, then. And what then?"

Huan-li was so angry that he was shaking. "You blame her in this hour because she is not a god and cannot produce some miracle! What would you have? You wish to obscure the tragedy, so that you need not face it. When the sun rises, none of us can be very proud, for what have we accomplished? What is it we have to bequeath to them? What shall we have gained by losing our lives? All they will know—and *it* is the tragedy—is that it could be so important when it is so little. . . . All they are going to know is that neither she nor ourselves were the ones who sold them out—that is all. For they will know, then, for sure, for absolute certainty, that they have been sold out."

"It is only memories men rally around," Yang Koh said in an unsteady voice.

The silence returned. But they could not really forgive her for embodying the bodies that they—separately and individually—must lose. They could not be reconciled to the truth: that they were to be remembered in the Third Koo Girl. She knew this, as remote as she was. She knew that each—in receding into himself—encountered the loneliness that was so nearly insupportable; better to taunt, better to cultivate some common bond of bitterness.

It was the chains that bound them, one to the other, like beads. Death skittered through—in the shape of the rat—and ran over Yang Koh's legs. He cried out. He stared at her and continued to stare at her. He thought he was going to rave. But he said, "Communist!" And said it as tenderly as though he were her lover bestowing upon her some special caress. He felt that she smiled.

"Do you smile?" he said.

"Yes."

"You die a Communist's death, anyhow," he said in the same tender voice. Forgiveness, therefore, could assume a shape more removed from itself than the rat was from death. The smile died on her face.

Death, as she perfectly well knew, was her solution. It was nothing—a matter of darkness meeting and merging with darkness. "Upon a platform," Huan-li had said once, "you stand well." She saw faces when she tried to sleep. They were not formless, but arranged in tiers, yet dream-like, and all looking up, with the mouths slightly parted. She had not slept in too long to think about. She was more apart from them than they knew—she welcomed death.

Huan-li, who was sitting next to her, muttered, "I believe I am breaking out in a rash."

"Did you finish your letter?" she asked him.

Until sundown he had spent his time with the stub of a pencil and scraps of paper which he had asked of the others, writing to his friend, the half-caste, Christopher Blair.

"I finished it," Huan-li said. "But the guard would not take it."

"Give it to me," she said. "The next time one comes, I will try."

With much rattling of chains and twisting about, Huan-li got the letter out of his girdle and handed it to her.

"Here . . . But will he take it from you?"

"If he is one of Colonel Shu's men, he probably won't. If he is one of the jail regulars, he might. But you do not know how to offer a bribe."

"I have no bribe to offer," he said.

"No," she said, "neither do I. But I do know, better than you, how to suggest that your friend, Dr. Blair, will bethink himself of a most handsome reward for the trouble of delivering it."

Huan-li grunted. Whole minutes passed.

"Sit closer," she said. "Where is this rash you think you have? Shall I rub it for you?"

"Ah, thanks," Huan-li said. "My arms and wrists. My neck, my back . . . I wondered whether the night would be long or short."

Four A.M. Outside, the guards stood as if paralyzed. Inside, the silence was deeper. Yang Koh broke it. He said, "I would give half my remaining life for a cigarette."

"You might not have time to smoke it," someone replied.

Four-forty-five A.M. They heard the heavy footsteps heading down the hall. There was the progress of lantern light, a great disturbance of shadows, thrown against the iron grill and coming through the bars to play upon them.

"There!" Yang Koh said.

"No, no," Huan-li said. "The time cannot be yet. The hour is six. The sun will rise well before six and we shall be able to see it through that hole in the wall. Be calm."

But Yang Koh—all of them—were rigid.

The key grated in the lock, turned, the door was flung open. The keeper of the jail and one of the regular guards entered.

"What is this?" Yang Koh said.

The keeper leered. He drew his lips back from his teeth,

so that they found themselves concentrating upon his teeth which were small and pointed, in his domelike head.

He said, "So you supposed you were simply to be shot, cleanly, like that"—he snapped his fingers—"at six?"

"Well?"

". . . without some previous preparation?"

"Torture," Yang Koh said, under his breath.

"Of course, torture," the keeper said. "And we shall select the most *august*—the most important of you—first."

Involuntarily their eyes turned in the same direction. But then the prisoners, to a man, dropped their eyes to the floor.

"Take me," Yang Koh said, "and let us put an end to this cheap performance, damn your dirty hides."

"But you flatter yourself," the keeper said. "First, we will, of course, take the Third Koo Girl. Indeed, we may concentrate upon her."

The guard came forward. He set down his lantern and examined his keys. Then he made his way—stepping on their feet and legs—to the Third Koo Girl and went about the task of disentangling the chains and separating hers from the rest. They watched him, satisfied for the moment, that he could be having such trouble.

"Clumsy ox," the keeper said. "Try using your head along with your hands."

When at last he had freed her, he jerked her to her feet.

"Bow to your comrades," he said.

She reeled. He caught her up and slapped her across the mouth.

"Bastard!" Yang Koh said, straining and struggling senselessly against his chains.

"Bring her along," the keeper said. "She can bow to them later. She can bow to them at six."

"Whoresons!" Yang Koh said.

"Do not be so jealous," the guard said. "Your turn may come."

Huan-li was sobbing.

"Walk!" the guard commanded the girl.

She took a step, stumbled, half-turned around. Her eyes searched their faces and they could see that she was trembling.

"Do not be proud any more," Yang Koh said, very gently.

"Heart of our heart," Huan-li said, the tears running down his cheeks, "we give you our permission to forget who you are."

They laid their hands on her and dragged her out.

II

They led her to the end of the corridor and pushed her into a dark room. There, it seemed to her that she was immediately surrounded by she could not tell how many men, but several things began to happen at once: she was gagged, lowered to the floor, and bound with rope—both her wrists and ankles—very expertly and speedily—but with care. It was the care she particularly remarked. Not a word was exchanged. Next, she was being rolled into something thick and soft that felt like a quilt. Again they were careful, making sure that her head was very nearly even with the top, so that she should have enough air. Then they bent her as near double as possible—wrapped more rope around what now might pass as a bedding roll, she supposed, two coils of it, one at the level of her knees, the other at that of her chest, and tied the ends of the rope together. She was lifted up and placed over a man's shoulder.

Her blood ran down into her head and black spots that were blacker than the darkness inside the quilt danced furiously in front of her eyes.

"Ready?"

"Ai, she is lighter than the other."

She heard the keeper's voice: "Hasten. The way is clear."

The man who was carrying her began to move.

The dark room that the keeper of the jail and the guard had pushed her into was at the end of the corridor. The four servants of Old Koo (the one with his burden, the other three with lanterns that they had not lit) had only to cross the corridor and make a sharp left turn in order to reach a narrow passage that connected the jail proper with the keeper's quarters. This passage was not one that Colonel Shu's men were familiar with, since it was not the one that was generally used. At the far end of the passage there were two gates, set at right angles, one opening into the keeper's court, the other into an alley. It was the one into the alley that the servants took, having sent one of their number ahead to make sure that the way was clear. They did not light their lanterns or pause or trade off their burden until they were three streets distant from the jail.

Back in the room, lighted, now, by a single bean-oil lamp, the keeper and the guard were conferring. They were counting out money. They were quiet about it. The keeper took two-thirds, gave the guard the rest and the guard nodded. He was grateful.

The keeper said, "Her," and pointed to a figure that was laid out on a bench in one corner. The figure was dressed in blue cotton and there was a thick blue-cotton cloth tied about her mouth. "Set to work on her," the keeper said, "and remember it is her *face* that you must mutilate beyond recognition."

"And will the Colonel approve of that?" asked the guard.

"Idiot! We already know that the Colonel does not *dis*approve of torture. How else should we have dared to get into this?"

The guard grunted. He went over to the figure on the bench and raised up an eyelid. "She will do," he said. "Old Koo has doped her well. And see her height? I swear there is not an iota's difference. She will do very well."

"Be that as it may!" said the keeper. "Remember this: neither the Colonel nor any other is to be given the opportunity for getting close enough to her to say 'yes' or 'no' about that!" Again, he pointed to the figure on the bench. "May Buddha be our helper, do you hear?"

"Yes," said the guard, "of course."

"You are not to take her out to the yard until after the others are blindfolded and kneeling in front of the firing squad. Not until the very last minute. And that is to be her 'entrance,' do you comprehend?"

"We have been through all of this."

"Yes, and you pat that money that is in your girdle. . . . Listen to me. Everything will depend on your manner of dragging her. She must appear to be gone with exhaustion and fear, you know. She must 'appear' with as little appearing as is conceivable, you know. You know how you are—in bending over her—to get that blindfold over her face—keeping her, all the while—as much of her as is absolutely possible—hidden."

"Yes," said the guard.

The keeper shivered. "The crumpled heap she makes

will pass for kneeling with the one who is so gone with fear. But after the firing, *that body is not to be examined by the idle and the curious.* Well . . . Colonel Shu and I are to pronounce death. I will handle that part of it. But you, too, must be watchful. You must distract his attention to some other corpse, should that become essential."

"I will," said the guard.

"It will only be a matter of minutes," said the keeper. "But minutes can be longer than years. The Koo servants will appear, almost immediately, to claim the body in the name of the Koo family. Nothing should go wrong there. The disposal of the corpse is their concern. What remains our concern is that it shall get out of this jail as the undisputed corpse of the Third Koo Girl!"

"There will be no trouble," the guard said. "It will all be over before you know it."

"Perhaps! But greed has led us to this. Would that such temptation had never been cast our way. If anything goes wrong, we are the ones who play the game of forfeits—we are the ones who die. It is heaven and hell we play with. And I can tell you, I shrink!"

The guard looked over at the blue-clothed figure. "I will get busy on her," he said.

"Very well," said the keeper. "I will go after Yang Koh and one or two others. This torture business should not seem too exclusive."

"Do not bring them in here," the guard said.

"And do you not mistake me for the fool I know you to be," the keeper said.

He went out.

III

Old Koo was waiting in the entrance court. In the early morning light, he appeared very pale and bloated. For half an hour he had been waiting in the court and the servants had not arrived with her yet. By his side was an enormous covered basket, with carrying poles affixed. Off and on, Old Koo would look at it meditatively. He did not speak to Lao Liang, the ancient gatekeeper, who, every few minutes, belched—who had never before seen Old Koo sitting upon a common bench and waiting and who was disturbed by the sight and who, therefore, belched. Old Koo thought it was with stealthy fingers that the dawn was stroking the sky. Neither superstitious nor religious by nature, he nevertheless did not like the looks of the sky. He was clammy, cold.

They were coming. There was the knock which they had agreed upon. Old Koo felt his heart turn over. He rose to his feet with an alacrity that no one would have dreamed him capable of. He swore at Lao Liang who was fumbling with the bolts of the Small Gate, pushed him aside, and drew the bolts himself.

The servants entered with their burden. Lao Liang was the one to close the gate.

"It is past time!" Old Koo said in a low voice, as he watched them carefully lower their burden. "Were you followed? Did you meet with some mishap?"

"No, Old Master." They were at work on the ropes. "But we thought it was wise to take a devious route."

"With the burden, our progress was hampered."

"We exercised caution."

"Good," Old Koo said. He took out his great gold watch and looked at it. He looked at his watch rather than at what the servants were doing. He did not wish to see his daughter gagged and bound. "There," he heard them say. But he turned away. He said, "You know where you are supposed to be and what you are to do, next. Take the basket and be off. It would not be advisable for you to be late."

"We will get there," one of them answered.

"Ai, never fear."

"Then, go," Old Koo said. "And may this share of our scheme . . ." (They were to return to the jail and claim the body.) He cleared his throat. "My everlasting thanks," he added.

Lao Liang let the servants out. Old Koo waved him away and waited until he had disappeared inside the gatehouse. For some reason he still did not look at his daughter but walked once around the court, looking up at the sky. When he did look, she was sitting on the quilt, with the pieces of rope around her. She was sitting with her arms clasped around her knees and her head bowed—resting on her knees. He saw the detail of her peasant's clothes; he saw she was as thin as a shadow.

He went close to her. "Get up," he said.

She neither moved nor raised her head. Had he expected ceremony? Had he expected her to prostrate herself before him?

"You must get up," he said, thinking that she was perhaps dazed from her journey. He leaned over, took her shoulder—the bones of her shoulder cutting sharply into his fat old man's hand—and shook her. She rose, then. She backed up to the wall, feeling with her hands, and leaned against it. Their eyes met.

"So it was you," she said. "I might have known."

He was so overwhelmed with pity at this first sight of her face and a sense of strangeness that he could not find his tongue.

Her eyes swept the court. "And they were afraid," she said, "that I would return with wet and broken wings to this womb." She studied the sky. She brought her eyes down from the sky to look straight at him.

Ah, she was so radically altered! He would not—*never*—have known that ravaged face or those sick and burning eyes.

"Come," he said.

"As a prisoner of this House?" Her underlip was curling.

It was his cue—("Ungrateful female wretch!" he might have yelled)—but he did not take it up. "As you like," he said, so gently that he saw how she started and how the tears came to stand in her eyes—against her will—since she must wipe so hard at them with the back of her hand.

They went through the courts—he ahead—he kept turning back, to be sure she followed. He was conscious that the dawn light touched the courts, played through the leaves of the camphor tree and the pomegranate trees and the bamboos and the cassias and became, instead of rose and gold, black lace on the courts and light-blue haze in the farthest corners. He was conscious that birds were singing. . . . There was no one about. He had given his orders to the servants and, as for the members of the family, they were still asleep in their apartments—all but the probable exception, Old Koo demurred, Madame Koo, his First Wife. It was said of her that she never slept. And Old Koo suspected that, somewhere near, and even though she was supposed to know nothing, she would be already fully dressed and waiting.

To her—to Leila (for that name which was her "milk name" seemed to fall upon her, like a cloak)—the courts were like the component parts, the sections, of some dream that she had been skirting for months and years. Now she walked in the dream, through the sections of the dream, a nightmare which was a nightmare because it was hauntingly, inescapably beautiful—compelling—how the courts were laid out, which tree was where, and where the cobblestones were smooth or rough. The courts had not changed. . . . She could wake up, screaming.

Old Koo had led her to her apartment, which was one of the best of the House, facing south, and with three large rooms and a bath that had been more recently added.

"It is early," he said, pausing at the threshold of the bedroom. "You will sleep for an hour."

He saw that she barely heard him but, again, groped with her hands for the nearest wall and, again, leaned against it.

"I will have your slave called," he said.

She shook her head. She was staring at the wide bed with its silken curtains drawn.

He did not know what to do. He did not know what he had expected but he had not expected this. What now? It was not among the questions he had asked. He had built his elaborate plan around her without its having seriously occurred to him that *she* might not fit. Things had come to a pass when her face was so decomposed with pain that he dared not even scold her. A nice pass when she stood so long in a single place, without either speaking or moving, that the question became—would she ever speak or move again? What had they done to her? His memory of the time when he had thrown his best Tang vase at her—by comparison—seemed blessed. What now?

Then it was that he became aware that someone had silently approached and was standing silently by his side. A voice said, "My lord." It was, of course, his First Wife, Madame Koo.

Old Koo turned. For a moment the silence positively churned between them. She did not need to use words, to say, "What is this monstrous deed that you have done?"

Old Koo drew himself to his full height; he seemed to inflate, like a balloon.

"Good," he said. "You have come. . . ." He had, after all, many little matters to which he needed to attend. "You have come," he said, as if he had been waiting for nothing else. "And none too soon for that, let me tell you." He indicated the Third Daughter. "Take care of her," he said, deciding he would say no more.

"Yes, my lord."

"And as for you," he said to his daughter, turning on her with sudden roughness. "There shall be no more of your nonsense. You . . . You are to report to meals with extreme regularity, do you understand? And you are to sit on my left hand. And if you do not eat one whole ham and three chickens and twelve bowls of rice each day . . . Well, I will make a present of you to the first beggar that stops at our gates—there!"

With that, he left.

Madame Koo stood as still as Leila was standing and looked at her. It would have been impossible to say what thoughts, if any, went through her head. At first Leila did not seem to know she was there. It was slowly that the expression about her eyes and mouth changed.

"Mother!" she cried. "Mother, you must save me!"

But although Madame Koo's lips twitched, she went no closer, nor did she seem to notice the arms that were held out to her.

"Take off those clothes," she said, in the same flat way she had said, "My lord."

Leila hesitated. Had it been her father, she would have defied him. But with her mother she was powerless. It was almost as if she had confused obedience, in her mind, with the next step toward salvation. She saw, as if from a great, great distance, her hands that began to fumble with buttons. . . . Her hands were clumsy. Under the unwavering eyes of her mother they became worse than clumsy—disorganized beyond belief. Her clothes became as if infested with vermin, filthy and ruinous. . . .

At last Madame Koo moved to her side and, calmly and efficiently, finished undressing her.

"I want to know the time," Leila muttered brokenly. "I *have* to know the time. Please, Mother. What time is it?"

Madame Koo went to make the bathroom ready. She came back. She said, "I should say it was almost exactly six o'clock, if that makes any difference."

They stared at each other.

"It does," Leila said.

"Now that you have come home?" It was Madame Koo's underlip that curled.

IV

". . . FIRE!"

The volley of shots echoed and re-echoed. A cry went up. There was a second volley and a third. Then—silence. The people were solidly massed in the streets. They were pressed so close to the two sides of the prison yard that were fenced in with the barbed wire, which had been electrically charged for this occasion, that the guards were prodding desperately with their bayonets.

"Stand back or we open fire," they said.

Where had the people come from when, all night, they had passed only in two's and three's and disappeared again? In every direction—for streets and streets around—they were standing now.

"She fell."

"I saw her fall."

"They had tortured her, as any fool could tell."

"Ah, Old Koo is back!"

It was a kind of protracted wail that Christopher Blair heard. "The Third Koo Girl is dead." Carried from mouth to mouth. He had not been able to get anywhere near the jail.

The West Gate was thrown open, the Old North Gate, the South Gate—all were thrown open simultaneously, with the troops of General Ma coming in across the barren fields, raising the dust, but with bayonets gleaming, entering the gates. The butt ends of commands began to sound over the roofs, the sound of marching feet began to fill the narrow streets. . . . In Sin-ss-ka Square (the principal square) there were platforms and whipping posts that had sprouted like mushrooms during the night.

Somewhere, in some alley, some minstrel was singing. He was improvising:

Third Koo Girl, Third Koo Girl,
Tall Girl, Tall Girl,
Dead in the prison yard is she,
Shot by the lovers of luxury.

The soldiers had not yet broken ranks. The odd part was that the people were standing their ground instead of fleeing.

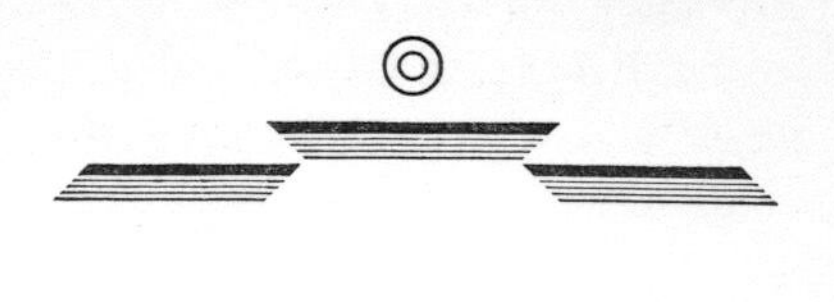

3

I

SHE opened her eyes and saw the silk canopy above her: dreaming. Birds sang and the sky looked like silk. Six o'clock would never, never, never come again. Oh, Huan-li, Yang Koh. The faces of the people are arranged in tiers, with their mouths a little open, and the troops are marching. She tried to sit up but was pushed down by a firm hand.

"Sleep."

She slept.

The servant was panting. His garments were torn, his face was encrusted with dirt, and there was an ugly cut near his left temple, Old Koo saw. But he could curb his impatience no longer.

"You have had time enough to manufacture breath," he said. "Speak, man!"

"Ai, Old Master," the servant said, standing up straighter and swiping at his face with his sleeve. "Ai! We left here, arriving in the vicinity of the jail in ample time, but having great difficulty getting through to the jail itself."

"How was that?"

"The people—they were everywhere—adhering to one another. But we finally get through, just in time. We claim the body. We put it in the basket and are let out. But the people are so close that we can make no headway. We try to turn back but the gate has been closed behind us. Someone shouts, 'Those are Koo servants!' Someone else, 'What is it they carry in that basket that is as large as a dwelling?' And before the guards can move to protect us, before any of us know what is happening, the people have fallen upon us."

"So," Old Koo said, much more calmly than the servant had expected. "What then?"

Old Koo's plan had called for the servants to carry the corpse to a coffin-storage house, stopping by the way at Dji, the coffinmaker's, to order the best blackwood coffin that he should have on hand. (Coffin-storage houses were where coffins were kept until "the lucky day for burial," set by the geomancer, should come around, sometimes a day that would be months in the future.) The Koo servants were to have waited at the coffin-storage house for Dji to deliver the coffin—then they themselves were to have transferred the corpse, throwing in quantities of lime to hasten decomposition, and nailing the lid down. Beyond that, Old Koo's plan was to have been flexible. As to whether or not there should be a funeral, and when, and what kind, in the name of the Koo Family, was to have depended on how events shaped up, on the mood of the family in relation to so macabre a joke (not that he would have expected the members of the family to attend; paid mourners could achieve the desired effect), and on whether Shanghai needed any little additional convincing. The most pressing problem had been to get the corpse clear of the jail.

The servant was continuing. "The guards could not even get their guns into position," he said. "The people were on us. I was knocked to the ground and the next I knew, there were the people, standing as before, massed and impassive and silent, except that the basket and what it contained were gone."

Old Koo looked at him.

"Ai!" the servant said, much excited. "Like black magic, it was. With the people opening a way for the basket and its new bearers and closing in behind it. We made the attempt to follow but it was hopeless—and dangerous. And the guards made great pretenses and gestures but they would not follow, either. Why, they would not even fire!"

"And where were the troops of General Ma, this while?" Old Koo wanted to know.

"At that time we could only observe that they were nowhere about. But it was early then, only a few minutes past six, so that they must have been just entering the city gates. Later, on our return here, we could see them marching, in street after street, but without breaking ranks. The people who were around the jail must have begun to disperse, because in every street there were people, lining the streets like the extra walls of houses, and when the troops entered, we saw them stand back and give the troops the room they needed to pass, but without fleeing or showing any signs of panic! The troops march and do not break ranks—the people watch and do not flee . . ." The servant shuddered. "The day is bewitched," he said.

"The day has not begun!" Old Koo said angrily. "The troops march to give the proper show of force, that is all—for the effect. Wait until they do cut loose. They will rape and burn and loot and empty hot lead into these louts. Ha! They will skitter away fast enough. They will fall all over each other in their haste to return to factories and land—*they* will be subdued! I am displeased with you."

The servant bowed his head. "Ai, Old Master. We should slap our own cheeks over our failure, but . . ."

"*But!*" Old Koo said. "The point is that you have missed the central point. You inflict upon me this long and dull recitation. . . . Buddha! As if I care what some stupid peasants should think or do about that corpse. (In a way, it is good riddance.) The point is, did the execution go off without a hitch? Did you observe it, as you were supposed to? So long as it was officially valid—the death—that is what counts. But not a word have you told me about *that!* You burden me with trivialities and superstitious drivel. Come!"

The servant said, "The execution went off without the smallest mishap, Old Master. We saw it all, from beginning to end, or, at least, Wei-sun and I did. The other two could not manage to get a good vantage point. First, the prisoners were led out into the yard and blindfolded and ordered to kneel. Then the firing squad marched out—very smartly. But still there were two missing—the fellow, Yang Koh, and *her*. We heard them call out the name of this Yang Koh and a guard dragged him out—he was gone with fear and could not stand up, yet would not kneel. The guard forced him to his knees and bent over him, adjusting the blindfold. . . . Then *her* name was called and the people strained so close that one was thrown into the electrified wires. . . . The same thing—she was dragged out. Seeing how they were both dragged, the people muttered that they must have been tortured or drugged. She was nothing but a crumpled heap when the guard had finished with the blindfold. And I swear if I had not *known* . . ."

"Yes?" Old Koo said.

"Well, so they fired. We got in. And there was the keeper and Colonel Shu himself. Together they had pronounced death—with Colonel Shu, I daresay, having gotten a less close look at her than he realized, thanks to the keeper. At all events, it was the Colonel who gestured the wide gesture to us, granting us the permission to take her off. Hence, all was perfect until . . ."

"Good," Old Koo said. "Excellent. Now . . ." He stood up. "Suppose you change your clothes. You and the other three. Dress as peasants, if you please. Let us have no more of these Koo servant incidents. Today you will be my eyes and ears, for I shall find it most convenient to be kept constantly informed on developments. For instance, the peasants must have done something with that corpse—carried it somewhere—to some purpose. And while it is a triviality—uh—you might just make it your business to find out about its disposition. What they plan to do with it, in other words, and whether they have any questions to raise about its authenticity."

The servant interrupted. "I think they are not apt to, Old Master—that corpse had been so well worked on!"

"Hmmm. Nevertheless, it is just as well to keep informed. Bring me all the news you can. But stay wide of trouble, this time. Stay wide of the troops, too. And carry ample identification in case you are stopped."

"Ai, Old Master."

Old Koo looked with affection on his servant. "You have the right to say you would rather not perform this service, since it is a day of hostilities, and I cannot require you to go out."

"Nay, Old Master. . . . To serve you is my purpose in this life and I hope it will be the same in the next."

He bowed and withdrew.

"Take care of that cut on your head, then," Old Koo called after him.

He walked slowly across the court. He knew it was no

longer postponable, as much as he dreaded it—that he must have the business out with his First Wife. He called to a passing slave and instructed her to go to Madame and announce his coming. Ah, yes. It was as well to get it over with. Old Koo considered that the House of Koo, with its high thick walls, was a fortress—invulnerable, as long as the troops of General Ma were around and the people were not armed and there was no opposing army. The House of Koo was detached, magnificently isolated on this day of "theatricals." Of what concern was a little trouble in the streets to the great House of Koo, so long as the gates remained locked and the family remained inside and was forbidden to go out? The family, indeed, could be expected to remain virtually oblivious. All but Madame who put her nose, habitually, where it did not belong. The House of Koo was a world of its own; it was a world unto itself.

Upon such a predication had Old Koo acted in the first place. The family would not care, so long as it did not feel itself threatened. Old Koo did not intend that it should feel threatened. The family was used to catering to Old Koo's whims—one of his chief whims being his Third Daughter. The family could be instructed, informally, that there was an official secret to be kept—let a few rumors fly where they would. The family code was strict and strong enough officially to preserve an official secret. It was only Madame Koo who might . . . Old Koo sighed. She was always calling a pig a pig and wanting to eat it, besides!

II

In another room of the House Madame Koo sat motionless upon a redwood chair, waiting. . . . And although there was some embroidery in her lap, even her hands were idle.

Madame Koo was neither tall nor short nor fat nor thin.

She was very average and plain in appearance except that her face had a quality of martialed serenity about it that was not seen often. Her clothes were simple—more simple than some of the servants'—and she had developed the faculty for melting into the background and seldom making her presence felt; at least that was the way she affected strangers and acquaintances. It was not the way she affected her family. Her family rather regarded her as the omnipotent, the giver and denier of all things. They said she loomed like a mountain over them but, unlike a mountain, she had the power to move. The ways in which she chose to move were, furthermore, often mysterious and always quiet.

Now, in failing to advise with her when making his plans, Old Koo had not exactly broken a precedent—he was not in the habit of advising with her over everything—far from it—but ordinarily (except in the choice of concubines) he left all the matters of family to her, considering them her province and beneath his notice.

Madame was not angry in any ordinary, sudden sense. That would have been against her nature. Who knew better than she did how her lord doted upon the Third Daughter? Had the girl asked him for the moon, he would have carved it out of the winter's sky and made her the present. Madame was not ignorant, politically. She had only herself to blame that she had been so preoccupied with the household duties connected with moving. She might have known, might have foretold, that any plan her lord made would be, in this case, beyond consultation. But that he should conceive of a plan that was beyond conception . . . That he should conceive of *any* plan—that was it! She had supposed the affair settled upon their departure from Shanghai, had supposed that her lord was resigned to the inevitable, for once. It could strike Madame now as the sort of wishful supposing that led to blind catastrophe. But not yesterday. Was it, then, she alone who had kept in constant touch with the girl's rise to fame and its implications—having long ago concluded she was irrevocably doomed, whether or not the family should ever find its way back to House and lands!

"Tah-tah," a servant said, interrupting her thoughts. "Old Master is here."

Madame Koo nodded. "Show him in," she said. "And do you go after some tea."

Old Koo entered. Madame Koo rose and bowed.

"Good morning," Old Koo said, as if the morning were virgin.

"Will my lord sit down?"

"I daresay there is nothing your lord can do better," Old Koo said, heaving himself into the nearest chair. Making himself excessively, elaborately comfortable. "And how is she?" he asked when he was entirely settled.

"Is it the Third Daughter to whom you refer?"

"It is," Old Koo said.

"Most soundly asleep, I believe," Madame Koo said.

Old Koo looked at his wife out of the slits of his eyes, trying to gauge what she knew and did not know. He decided, wisely, that she knew everything.

As for Madame Koo, she looked down at her strangely idle hands and recollected that never in all their years as man and wife had she openly defied Old Koo, her way being to obey his every order. Then, deviously and quietly, to puncture those orders that were detrimental to the family interests so full of holes that they would not hold water. Old Koo's nature was too large to bother with trying to block up small holes and usually he went grandly on, giving new orders. Madame had always known that the day would come when time or circumstance would prevent her following her method. And now that she knew that the day was here, she reacted very much as some night animal might that is forced out of its natural haunts and caught in a beam of light.

"My lord," she said. "You have ever been known for your generosity and your wisdom. You are a god among men. As Head of the House of Koo you have increased its fortunes. You have worked unceasingly toward the welfare of the family whose very existence rests with you. You have taken your obligations most seriously. With unselfish fortitude you have ever put the family's interests higher than your own, when there was conflict. For these reasons you are held in high esteem—you are honored."

"Ah, yes," Old Koo said. "Yes, yes, yes, yes."

But Madame Koo went on. "It is said that love is sometimes blind. While yours is a nobler kind, I am sure, it is nevertheless no secret how you have always held the Third Girl in your central heart. . . . Now you have brought her back. Now you have substituted some other—a factory girl, is that it?—to die in her place. What noble devotion to your own! Is it your thought that her presence in this House can remain a secret as dark as night?"

"And why not?" Old Koo said. "At least for the next few days and nights when no one is to be allowed out—or in. After that, old dear, a few rumors and whispered teahouse tales will not matter a whit."

"Meaning? You must forgive my stupidity."

"Meaning," Old Koo said, "that by that time Colonel Shu will have left town, the C.E.C. and Shanghai will have other things to think about, and that General Ma and the other local authorities are subordinate to me. . . . They *belong* to me, old dear."

"You make it so clear," Madame Koo murmured.

"Thank you," Old Koo said, getting up. Beginning to pace slowly back and forth. Beginning to waddle and roll back and forth. "As a technicality," he said, "since the

Second Daughter died in infancy, she can henceforward be known as the Second Daughter instead of the Third. Since there are so many daughters floating around, all with the Koo look and bearing, who outside these walls is going to dare to make it his business to discern the difference, particularly when we get some meat on her? At best, females are insignificant and easily confused, one for the other. An official death is not going to be disputed."

"Not even by the life, breathing and walking around," Madame Koo suggested.

Old Koo shrugged and closed his eyes, but kept right on waddling about, not minding that his hugeness had set the objects in the room to quivering or that he might, at any moment, flatten out some furniture.

Madame said politely, "There is no danger of blackmail. No danger, at all, that the peasants, upon hearing the rumors, will scale our walls in the night—to reap revenge."

Old Koo shrugged a second time.

"And you assume," Madame continued in the polite manner that was calculated to freeze the marrow, "that the Third Girl herself will be completely compliant and docile. She has always been—so compliant and docile."

Old Koo came to a full stop and opened his eyes. "What has been done is done," he said. (And where did you find so many words, silent one? I swear, you paste the very sky with all these raw and windy words.) "Curiously, I have weighed everything already. Equally curiously, I have kept the family's welfare within my orbit."

"Would anyone dare to suggest anything to the contrary?" Madame Koo asked. "In my stupidity, I seem to have forgot the hour you have named for the meeting of the family council."

"What council?" Old Koo said. "There is not going to be any council."

"You are not going to call the family together, in council, over this?" Madame Koo asked, as if in great surprise.

"Certainly not!" Old Koo said. "Is there any point in it? Since the Third Girl has never left this family, as far as the family is concerned—she has never been turned out, do not forget—it must follow that there can be no question about taking back—about her return."

"But since," Madame said, "she is now officially dead, there may be some question about her being so alive."

A maid entered, at that moment, with tea.

"You may go," Madame Koo said and watched until she saw her cross the court and disappear through the gate. Silently Madame Koo poured the tea; silently Old Koo took it.

He said, "The girl is here—she is going to stay here."

"The family will not allow it," Madame Koo said, very quietly. "You are the head of the family but in this case it is necessary for the feet to refuse to follow the head."

Madame Koo expected a rage—she expected, at the very least, to hear the teacup slammed down, since this was surely the climax to this open quarrel that they had never before had.

But Old Koo was smiling, as if, for the world, he thought she had played into his hands. His voice lost its edge, became mocking and soft, as if he assumed their contest over and done with.

"There," he said. "There. It is because you were born of country stock and reared on so hardy and frugal a standard that you cannot seem to understand how alone you are in naming the Third Girl major threat and traitor. In underestimating, at the same time, my political influence and power—in failing to absorb how all the necessary precautions have already been taken. Do you not realize, at last, how—even though I *were* to call a family council—

there would yet be no dissenting vote—unless from you, old dear?"

It was not really perceptible—Madame Koo's lowering of the eyes.

He said, "It should have occurred to you that I know the mood and temper of this family much better than you—since I was brought up in it, when you were only transplanted. No man flies higher than his family's will. I am no exception to the rule. Is that such a surprise to you? It should not be. You name the girl traitor. But you have never understood wealth—you have never understood the luxurious point of view. And when you see a pig you name it a pig and can think of nothing except its conversion into pork. The rich can keep the pig for a pet, if they please, and feed it instead of feeding on it. My dear, the rich can afford what the poor never can. . . . You name the girl traitor. They? The others? Why, they will merely name her courageous—romantic—an adventure—a welcome diversion to the drab routine of their days which they feel settling in upon them. . . . In this, the family is with me."

Madame Koo (and it was as if, in the act, the night animal, having turned this way and that in the unnatural beam of light, broke for the woods)—Madame Koo cast down her eyes. She felt Old Koo's teacup. Finding it cool, she emptied it out and poured more.

Old Koo sat down and drank it off. He sighed. "So," he said, "I will take care of the males. Will you be wanting to tell the females, informally, that in the future there is this little secret about the Third Daughter to be kept?"

"My lord," Madame Koo said. "Now that you have made it abundantly clear to me, a thick-skinned woman of country stock, that our Third Daughter's return does not at the same time endanger the family's welfare, how should I refuse? Have I not ever done your bidding? Am I not the girl's own mother? I hope I may prove my contrition. What with the cares of moving, I may plead that mine was a case of sheer stupidity and nerves. Forgive me."

"There is nothing to forgive," Old Koo said a trifle stiffly.

It was Madame's turn to rise and begin walking around the room. But how differently from Old Koo. She went from table to curio stand to window and this agitated behavior was so very unlike her that Old Koo said, with concern, "What is it now?"

"What are we to *do* with her?" Madame Koo asked.

Old Koo frowned. Again the thought returned to him: all this planning and placating around her whom he could not seem to get through to and did not—in truth—know what to do about. He said, "Well, we shall feed her."

"Of course," Madame said. "But . . ."

"She has suffered," Old Koo said. "Damn those bastards for making her suffer."

"Yes," Madame said, "she has suffered. . . . I ask myself whether she has not suffered beyond human powers of repair."

Old Koo stared blankly ahead of him. Watching him closely, Madame Koo said, "How she stands so long in a single place, neither seeing nor speaking. How sick and vacant her eyes. How . . ."

"Stop it!" Old Koo said. "Don't wrench my heart out. I know. I saw."

"Then," Madame Koo said, "you will understand my feeling when I came out from the bathroom this morning (I was drawing her bath) to discover her with a pair of scissors in hand."

"You mean . . . !"

"My lord, I fear her mind is affected—deranged. What

can we do to protect her against this pathetic desire to have done with her life?"

Beads of sweat appeared on Old Koo's forehead. "She must be watched!" he cried.

"Ai," Madame Koo said, "watched. Yet . . ."

"Watched with the utmost vigilance," Old Koo said. "This—this is surely a temporary phase. She will outgrow it in time."

"You are right, my lord, I think. And it is therefore doubly important that she be protected against herself until that time comes. Yet I am overcome with dread when I see how almost any innocent object can be turned—a pair of scissors. Whom can we trust to do this watching for us?"

"Assign an army of servants to her," Old Koo said before he caught himself up short. "No, no, that will not do." He was on his feet. "Oh, Buddha," he said. "Who indeed?" He turned on his wife. "You should know whom to trust," he said. "Is it my business—the knowledge of women relatives? The knowledge of women, at all, except as how their thighs are adaptable? I should say not—I would be in my grave, already, from boredom. *You* choose someone—someone, mind, whom I will approve—someone whose devotion to our daughter cannot be doubted. Someone who will ease her mind of this suffering. . . . I leave it to you, because I must . . . I leave it to you."

"Very well," Madame Koo said. "I will do my utmost."

"See that you do," Old Koo said. "As for me, I will supply her with such a fund of abundant life as she cannot bear to abandon." He looked at Madame. "I will love her," he said. "I will love her instead of punishing her. . . . Have me called the moment she wakes."

"It shall be done," Madame Koo said, watching him waddle off. And, "It shall be done" echoed inside herself.

III

The big front gate of the House of Koo was bolted and sealed and locked, the back gate was bolted and sealed and locked, only the Small Gate was left unsealed, but it was locked tight enough, with Lao Liang, the ancient gatekeeper, and his son, Siau Liang, instructed to share a night-and-day watch over it.

No man and no woman and no child and no servant was to leave the House of Koo until further notice, without the express and written permission of Madame (in Old Koo's name). No man whatsoever was to be admitted from the outside in. In case of emergency Madame (in the name of Old Koo) was to be called and Madame and none other was to be the judge of what was urgent and what was not.

In the entrance court Lao Liang, that ancient gatekeeper, and Siau Liang, his son, were sitting together. Siau Liang was, of course, a grown man, though he was not one of those to hasten the process, having learned to take his pleasures as they came and to grumble, in between. He was grumbling, now. He was saying, "First Old Master issues his orders —now, Madame issues her orders. We are in agitation and flux that this day will not see the end of."

"Hush," Lao Liang said. Lao Liang had spent a portion of his life hushing Siau Liang. "If there was ever a time for you to keep that mouth-inherited-from-your-mother closed, it is now."

"Well, what is it all about?" Siau Liang asked.

"Never mind what it is all about," Lao Liang said. "You know the order—there is to be no speculation and no idle talk—that is enough."

"Humph!" from Siau Liang.

The four trusted men servants, dressed in peasants'

clothes, came into the court. They had not escaped individual interviews with Madame. Their faces were grim and they greeted Lao Liang and Siau Liang grimly.

"Well, well," Lao Liang said. "Where are your permits? Each must have one, you know, and each must be stamped with the Koo Family seal."

"Rape your mother's mother," the servant with the cut on his head said, "here."

"And what are you four to do this happy day?" Siau Liang inquired, examining their costumes with interest. Lao Liang was examining the permits and could not do two things at once. Therefore, he was not listening.

"Wouldn't you like to know?" one of the servants said.

And another: "We are just to trot back and forth and back and forth. With each back and forth requiring a new permit, you understand. We are to trot back and forth and back and forth."

"Meaning," Siau Liang said, "that you are all four simultaneously afflicted with the diarrhea. Very interesting."

Lao Liang was drawing the bolts. "You know how to signal us when you get back," he said.

The four went out.

"What do you suppose they are up to," Siau Liang said, "that they must go out, dressed like that, to mix with troops and trouble?"

"You!" Lao Liang said, turning on his son. "You are begging to break your old father's and your own rice bowls, aren't you? Have you forgot that they are the four whom Old Master selected to do his errand? Should there be a leak—should a certain secret get out—should the least little rumor trickle forth—their heads shall be the first to fall and ours the next! The lesson from history and the Emperors—the value of picking a few and making them responsible for the good behavior of the rest—has not been lost on Madame. Fool, that you could have supposed their grumbling genuine! Now, enough."

"Oh, very well," Siau Liang said, sitting down upon the bench and yawning.

The steward came next. He came walking quickly, a serious and methodical man, very efficient and very dull. He wore a black-silk gown that was spotted down the front from the droppings of many meals and leather shoes which he had gotten, once, when he was in Shanghai but which he did not know the custom of polishing. The night before he had been sent forth by Old Koo; today he was being sent forth by Madame—to hire a cordon of guards. It seemed that Madame did not place the trust that Old Koo did in the troops of General Ma. Either that, or she feared and mistrusted the peasants more than Old Koo. The cordon of guards, to be hand-picked, was to be thrown around the House of Koo this night and each succeeding night—until further notice.

The steward presented his permit and was let out.

"Ill omen of an ill omen, he is," Siau Liang said, emitting a fearful yawn.

Lao Liang said, "Always needing to work your gums or sleep, I swear! Had you not been so fond of your bed, this early morning, you might have seen *her*, too!"

"I know," Siau Liang said. "And believe me, I regret it. What did she look like?"

"Well." Lao Liang scratched his head. "I only saw her sitting down upon the quilt. Only for a moment. But let me put it this way. If she is a ghost, then I should say she looks too real to be one. But if indeed she is a person, then I should contend she looks too ghostly."

"Hmm," said Siau Liang, thinking that one over, for it was a bit too balanced and too profound to suit his nature. When he looked up, he said, "The Old Crone comes. And it will be a murky business that Madame sends her forth on."

Old Koo had made the four servants his eyes and ears for the day—Madame had made the Old Crone hers. She had gold in her teeth (the ones that were left) but was not otherwise ornamental. She was shrewd and shrunken and evil, people said, though her loyalty to Madame no one contested. Had the troops already been running wild, looting and burning and killing and raping, the Old Crone would have been safe. And if—to Siau Liang—the steward was the ill omen of an ill omen, she was a witch.

Siau Liang rose to let her out. After that he stood, for awhile, listening. "And still," he said, "all is quiet. I hear no firing yet."

IV

In the wide bed, with silk curtains drawn, the Third Koo Girl, the Third Daughter of Koo, Leila, slept. There was no one else in the room except a little bondmaid who had been assigned to serve her. The maid was not busy at anything. She was looking dreamily out of a casement window, watching an oriole flitting from branch to branch of a bamboo tree.

"Pretty mite," she said under her breath. But then she turned to make sure she had not waked her Third Young Mistress. She tiptoed across the room and drew the covers more closely around her.

"When you wake," she whispered, "I will bring you chicken broth. It will nourish you, I promise."

Lightly she stroked the covers. She would have liked to stroke the half-opened hand on the pillow but she was afraid to.

Just then, there was a noise in the outer room of something being dropped. A voice was raised in a curse. The little maid fairly flew around the screen that hid the connecting door.

"If you please!" she whispered. "Be quiet."

"Listen to who's ordering who around," laughed a former slave girl who was known as Tear Drop. She had a great number of clothes over her arm and she was leaning down to pick up a toilet case which she had dropped. "I'm the one in charge around here," she added. "Haven't you heard?"

"Shhh," the little maid said. "I am the one assigned to serve her and I cannot have her disturbed."

"Oh?" Tear Drop said, still in her natural voice, which was loud by contrast. "You are out of date, my queen. I am now the one who will serve her."

"You!" the little maid said. "Why, you are the concubine to Fourth Young Master, Andrew." (Old Koo, after his return from the United States, had attached to his children such heathenish names as "Andrew" and "George Washington.") "Everyone knows that. How shall you serve her, then?"

"Well," Tear Drop said, "it seems that I am indispensable in an emergency. Poor Andrew must give me up for awhile." She dropped her voice. "You see, Third Young Mistress is very ill—she is temporarily deranged."

The little maid stared. "Why, she is not any such thing!"

"Have you seen her awake?"

"No. But neither have you."

This, Tear Drop ignored. "And is it for you to say, dear, what she is or is not? I do not quote myself. It is according to Madame that she is requiring of expert care. Since I was her slave two years ago, before she left this house, and since my devotion to her has been proved beyond a doubt . . ."

"How do you define devotion?" the little maid said, who was ordinarily too shy to say such things even when she thought them.

"Madame has asked me," Tear Drop went on, as if without interruption, "as a favor, you understand, to take charge once more. . . . It seems there is no one else who is good enough."

The little maid flushed.

"Don't take it too hard," Tear Drop smiled. "You are to be allowed to assist me in the lesser matters, if I choose. . . . And I choose, at this moment, to let you help me with these clothes. They are to be folded and put in her chests. . . . Here!"

The little maid took as few of the clothes as possible. Tear Drop was such a toad, she thought, though a toad with almond eyes and heart-shaped face. Always flaunting herself over everyone who was unfortunate enough to be beneath her. Humble enough to her superiors, of course. With her status raised to concubine, there was no living in the same house with her. Slowly, she followed Tear Drop back into the bedroom.

"She is *very* sick," the little maid whispered with her eyes on the bed. "Oh, I know that."

Tear Drop laid her clothes down on a square, redwood table and looked around her. "It *is* curious," she said. "These rooms are exactly as they were two years ago. It is almost as if time itself were turned back."

For the custom at the House of Koo was that when one of its sons or daughters left (for school or job or any reason other than marriage or a formal breaking of ties) his or her rooms were kept in waiting, whether for a month or a dozen years. Only clothes and personal effects and valuables that needed to be stored were ever removed.

"I am confused," the little maid announced.

"Oh, bother," Tear Drop said, disgusted. Tear Drop was like the willow, slender and lovely, and she could not remember when in all her life she had ever been confused about anything. "That is not your job. Just fold up some of those clothes there, will you?"

"I wish you would think about speaking more softly," the little maid said.

"She hasn't stirred, has she?"

"No, but . . ."

Tear Drop paused by the bedside. "Look!" she said. "I wish you would. *She* is our mistress. Do we laugh?"

The little maid did not answer. Instead, she laid a robe, which she had extracted from the clothes, across the bed's foot. She placed a pair of slippers, which she had also found, side by side, on the floor.

Tear Drop went to a chest and threw it open. "Good fairies, us!" she said. "Before she opens her eyes, these chests will be running over with satins and silks." Reaching for the clothes she had brought she refolded them and laid them in. She turned around.

"Souls!" she said. "What are those?"

She hurried over to the blue-cotton clothes that were lying on a chair and held up the jacket gingerly. "Stiff with age and dirt," she said, dropping it. Her deft hands went straight for the pockets, went through them. "A bit of a comb," she said, clucking her tongue. "A pencil. Not one copper cash does she have. What did she live on—air? Ah, a packet." She tore it open, perhaps expecting to find money in it. There was none. There were only scraps of paper scribbled over with characters. She read a few. Tear Drop could read well. In years past she had been allowed to attend the family school along with her little mistress.

"Nothing but hollow sentiments," she said, crumpling

the papers into a wad and dropping the wad on top of the clothes. "Take these out and burn them, eh?"

"I will in a while," the little maid said, folding again a garment she had folded twice already. "I wonder what her life has been like?"

"Quite taken with her, aren't you?"

"I wonder . . ." the little maid mused. "Did she have a lover? The song does not say."

"In those clothes? A bug for a lover, maybe. But come. You had better debase your mooning nature somewhat by a little work."

"She will be well again," the little maid said. "I feel it inside."

"Oh, well!" Tear Drop said. "There can be no doubt if you feel it inside."

She took the clothes out from under the little maid's hands, gave them a pat or two and put them away.

"That's that," she said. "Now, let us see . . ." She opened the toilet case she had brought. "What's needed here?"

The maid was not paying much attention. She wandered over to the chair where the blue-cotton clothes were and looked down at them. She put out her hand and picked up the wad of crumpled papers and smoothed them out. She had started to say, "Tear Drop, you *are* unfeeling!" when she looked up and saw that Madame Koo was just coming around the screen. Hastily, she stuffed the papers into her pocket, coughed loudly, and made herself exceedingly busy picking the clothes up.

Madame Koo went straight to the chests and examined them. Wang-ma, an old servant, came in behind her, carrying a second case in her hands.

Tear Drop said, "Ah, Madame." And her voice was ten

shades softer. "I was just checking this toilet case. There is practically nothing in it. Shall I go after perfumes and rouges?"

"She did not use perfumes and rouges," the little maid said.

Tear Drop shot her a withering look. Madame also looked at her but not so much witheringly as quizzically.

"Who was her maid in those days?" Tear Drop wanted to know. "You or myself?"

The little maid was so overcome with embarrassment (she could have cut her tongue out!) that she simply did not have it in her to answer.

"Wang-ma," Madame Koo said to the old servant. "Place that jewel case in its accustomed place and give the key to the trustworthy Tear Drop. Let the toilet case be as it was—without perfumes and rouges."

Thus Madame Koo restored harmony in the way for which she was famous: by giving each—in the same breath—reward and rebuke. But she had done this almost absent-mindedly, while her eyes surveyed the room.

"Who," she said, "put that robe across the foot of her bed and those slippers of hers on the floor?"

"I—I did," the little maid said. "I found them among these clothes and they were the ones she used to wear."

Madame Koo nodded. "Good," she said. Then, to Tear Drop, "Please, my dear. I wish you would go out to the court and see to the offerings of food that Old Master is having sent from the kitchens. See to keeping the dishes hot that your Third Young Mistress may be tempted to eat well when she wakes."

"Ai," Tear Drop said, sighing sweetly. "Anything I am able to do to add to her comfort is my most urgent wish." But as she was passing, she gave the little maid a secret look that made her quake.

"And please," Madame said, "just take those"—she indicated the cotton clothes the little maid was still holding—"and tell Quei-ling to burn them."

"Yes, Madame."

When she had gone, Madame asked Wang-ma to stay with the girl for a short while. She was solicitous about seeing her comfortably seated and told her she would be at hand should she need anything. Then she said to the little maid, "Come with me."

She led her into the living room which was furnished in a semi-foreign style, with a green carpet on the floor and a sofa upholstered in a rather startling shade of blue, an easy chair, table lamps and shelves of books. There were no pennants or Scottie dogs around, nothing collegiate to put the finger on. The luminous, white porcelain figurine on the bookcase was anything but collegiate. Yet the room had strained a point. It was *too* blue and *too* green and was post-Vassar, somehow, and in spite of a certain squared-off simplicity that was hardly Western in influence. It was the pompous and deadly serious offering of someone very young and not pompous or serious at all.

Madame Koo did not sit down in this room. She almost never had. "Do not tremble, my child," she was saying to the maid, "or send your blood chasing so quickly to and from your face. Are you convinced I am such an ogre?"

"No," the little maid said, staring down at the floor and trembling worse than ever.

A feeling of tiredness came over Madame. Ruling a family of over sixty mouths was no simple business, no more than the affairs of a state are simple. It meant the constant adjusting of quarrels, the righting of wrongs, the setting up of compromises, the divining of tensions, and the playing of one force against the other and both against the middle. And the necessity of promoting the nicest of balances in the only attitude toward herself that was workable—the balance between respect and fear.

Sometimes she longed to throw it all up, to retire, and spend the rest of her days with herself—to discover, for instance, whether she was cruel or kind, hard or soft, serene or violent or as diabolically clever as they said she was. How would it be to meet a person, to offer him tea and idly chat without the immediate prospect of having to work him toward some secret goal? It would be very strange ground, indeed. *They*—family and servants—would be shocked speechless to realize that she knew so well what they said of her. That "Madame has eyes in the back of her head" or, "Madame can smell out the smallest mess before it is hatched" or, "Madame makes up her mind and the gods make way."

"My dear," she said to the little maid, "your memory seems to be your treasure. I should like your Third Young Mistress's waking to be an act of welcome. These rooms have been held in waiting for her return, as you see. But I am hoping that you may be able to help in supplying some more intimate touches that may be missing. For example, was there anything other than that Goddess of Mercy on that bookcase?"

"No, Madame."

"Can you think of anything to add anywhere? Look around you, now, and do not be afraid."

The maid made the pretense of looking around but it was obvious she had already thought of something.

"It is her painting things," she said.

Madame Koo said, "I hoped you would mention those. There they are in that corner, do you see?" She indicated an easel and a wooden box that were partially hidden by the sofa. "But I had no idea where to place them. Where were they, do you recall?"

"There!" the little maid said, forgetting her shyness. "Beneath that casement window."

"Excellent," Madame said. "Will you arrange them, then?"

"Yes, Madame," the little maid said, stumbling over her feet in her eagerness. She placed the easel at a very particular angle to the midday light and then she went and got the wooden box and put it on the nearest table.

"There!" she said.

"You are a wonder," Madame said. She went to the table and opened the box and took out a tray that held tubes of paints. Under the tray was a stack of water colors which she began to turn through.

The little maid said, "Let me take that—is it called a palette?—and a few of those tubes and strew them around a bit."

"By all means," Madame said, slowly turning the pictures over. She noticed two characteristics about them—that they were all of flowers and that they were all done in pastel shades. Strange, she thought, that a girl who had once spent her idle moments painting flowers had turned so dangerous. She came upon one of a pale yellow la-mei blossom, one of a cassia bough, and then she stopped on one of a lotus blossom that was not finished but only outlined and a few petals filled in. Madame took this and set it up on the easel and stood back to look at it.

"Do you think," she said, "if you were to go to the lotus ponds, you might perhaps stumble across an early blossom that is exactly this faintest shade of pink?"

"What shade is that?" the little maid said. "Let me see . . . Oh, but doesn't Lao Tah-tah have a spool of thread exactly the color of that?"

"I expect she has," Madame said. "If you should happen to find one, then bring it back and put it in a shallow bowl of water—just here—on the table where your Third Young Mistress will be sure to see it when she wakes. I think the sight would be soothing to her."

"Oh, I will," the little maid said. "I will hunt most industriously. May I go now?"

"If you will be so kind," Madame said. She turned and went to the sofa and pushed at one of the pillows with her hand. She was very particular about it, turning it this way and that, until it appeared as if there was the indentation that someone's head had recently left. When she had finished, she went to the bookcase and studied the books there. But recognizing that hers was not the power to make an intelligent choice, she selected one at random, making sure only that it was written in Chinese instead of English. She took this and opened it and laid it face down on the sofa.

"Oh!" the little maid said. "Lovely. Why, it is as though she had just stepped out for a moment instead of two years."

Madame Koo looked at her. "You are not on your way?"

"I . . ." The little maid flushed furiously. "I am now!"

But Madame Koo stopped her. "Why did you linger? Have you thought of something further?"

"No, Madame."

"Nothing at all?"

"Well," the little maid said, all in a rush, "she used to eat peanuts when she read. She used to keep a bowlful around. The bowl was supposed to be on that table over there. But mostly, she lay flat on the sofa to do her reading and kept her peanut bowl upon the floor!" Whereupon the little maid burst into tears.

Madame Koo smiled one of her rare smiles. "Dry your eyes, my child," she said. "From this time on, I name you my memory's keeper. . . . Do you not feel my pleasure?

There. Go hunt the lotus and when you return, be sure to bring some peanuts with you."

"I go!" the little maid cried. She turned and ran.

Madame Koo clapped her hands. Wang-ma appeared from the inner room.

"I will stay with the girl for awhile," Madame Koo said. "Would you be so good as to fetch my eldest daughter for me? Tell her I should be pleased to see her here at her *immediate* convenience."

V

While Madame Koo was waiting for her oldest daughter who had been given the heathenish name of Helen by her father, she pondered. Let Old Koo continue to think she had given in to him. It was only love, surely, that could make him so blind. Madame Koo also had her plan. She entered the bedroom, ostensibly to be sure the girl was still sleeping soundly, but continued there, looking down at her. And what was it that the rich could afford and the poor could not? Treason? Destruction? But until the present day, until this year, when the attempt to scramble four thousand years was being made, the family was considered supreme. It was higher than any individual. Indeed, in a large sense, there were no individuals, there were only families. The family was the most sacred entity under heaven. Tsung-tse, the disciple of Confucius, had said, "Filial piety is the basis of virtue and the origin of culture." The family, what with its ancestor worship and its kitchen gods amounted, furthermore, to a religion.

There were many stories of heroic deeds performed by sons and daughters for their families. There was the one of the beautiful maid who threw herself into a melting pot in order that her father should be able to create a temple bell, commissioned by the Emperor, with a golden tone. The annals of history abounded with similar stories. But those of the other kind? Of a daughter who worked for her family's destruction? The crime against the family was a heinous crime—worse, by far, than high treason against the state. Yet here was a girl who had managed both—crime against family, high treason against the state. Historically, the punishment for the crime against the family was vested in the family and not in a court of law. Therefore, it was squarely up to the families, what they wished to define as crimes and what security measures they wished to take. There were those families that were watchful and vigorous, and there were others that had been too long with wealth and power and had gone soft with decay. . . .

Looking down at the sleeping girl, examining in detail the ravaged face, Madame thought that she had had no right to her appeal— "Mother, you must save me." For her, what sort of salvation was there?

Madame did not think, "What I am going to do to you is, in fact, a mercy." What she was going to do was hideous and nothing else. She was not given to slippery thinking. Her thinking was straight. It was her actions that were often slippery and almost always many-faceted. Take the touches she had added to the outer room: they would substantiate the opinion that the girl was mad, since she would almost certainly react to them madly. Who, indeed, would not be startled? She could depend on that and the ravaged face and empty eyes would do the rest. Also, however, the intimate touches served a different purpose: they constituted a form of revenge. They indicated that the passage of time had not been recognized, that the girl's large revolutionary activities were as nothing in this House. Oh, the girl would get the implication.

Take the choice of the slave, Tear Drop. Old Koo would

be pleased when he learned that she had broken a precedent and solicited the very one who had been with the girl all her childhood. Who could be a more likely choice? But Tear Drop, with never a yea nor nay from Madame, was also exactly the one who would *not* watch carefully. Therefore, what seemed to be would not be . . . But Madame turned abruptly away from the bed. What had to be done was not accomplished yet! The secret of her presence in this House had to be kept. Around that everything else would revolve. Well, the House was made into a virtual prison and she had taken pains to strike terror into the hearts of the few servants who had to be depended upon. The greatest enemy was time. Not she or any other could stop the flying of rumors for longer than two or three days. Therefore, what must be accomplished had to be accomplished within that trifling span. Very well. Preferably this night, then.

"Mother!" called a gay voice.

Madame gave the sleeping girl an appraising look, then softly closed the connecting door and came out from behind the screen.

"Mother, are *you* in here? Wang-ma prodded me out of bed with a stick that was six feet long. She absolutely would not allow me even to wash my face. I am a fright. But never mind, Wang-ma said, never mind. With fifteen dragons she has dragged me over here. And *what* for, I meekly, sweetly ask. What for?"

Half of this speech had come floating in from the court. Helen's voice was a floating, airy kind of voice. The other half came while she was standing framed in the door. Helen was twenty-four. Her body was deliciously distributed, with warm curves, not too plump anywhere. Her complexion had a fairness and a radiance about it that marked her as a beauty. She was wearing a pale-blue silk dress, the color of the sky, and earrings that were inlaid with blue kingfisher feathers and the high-heeled foreign slippers that Madame considered so despicable. Madame knew surely that someone had already told her that she was lovely enough to have ushered in the day. She could easily afford to call herself a terrible fright.

"Good morning," Madame said.

Helen, who was looking about the room, said, "Dearest, you leave me speechless."

"Doubtless," Madame said. "Come in and sit down."

"Shall I?" Helen said. "Do I dare when I can so plainly see that you are up to no good?"

Which was the way with Helen, Madame thought. She was as direct and open as Madame was secretive and devious but often to the same ends, which was what few people guessed.

Madame sat down on the only straight chair. Helen nestled into the overstuffed one, while she murmured, "I don't know, I don't know."

Madame Koo said, "You are aware, are you not, that your Third Sister has returned?"

"I certainly am," Helen said. "Some nasty military oafs had ordered her killed, or something—is that it? And we are not to refer to her otherwise, or something . . . Dji-bo woke me at a most unfortunate hour to tell me about it."

"After which you went back to sleep?"

"After which I lay in bed thinking."

"So?" Madame Koo said. She felt her old uneasiness around Helen who was, in a sense, her most successful accomplishment—her masterpiece. It was not simply that she was strained or shy, as some artists are, when confronted by her own best work. It was more that the masterpiece itself knew too much about the tricks that had gone into the making.

"I trust your food for thought was sweet?" Madame Koo said.

"It was starvation stuff," Helen said. "I am looking to you to provide me with a more adequate diet." Her eyes were busy while she was talking. Nor had they overlooked the picture that was on the easel.

"Thank you," Madame said. "I wish, in that case, that it could be more sweet than bitter. . . . When you see your sister, you will be both grieved and shocked."

"Aren't you afraid . . . ?" Helen glanced toward the screen. "Won't she . . . ?"

"No," Madame Koo said. "I gave her a sleeping powder early this morning. She sleeps soundly. If we keep our voices low, we will not disturb her." She paused. "You will find that your sister is deranged."

"Now, Mother," Helen smiled, pulling at one of her earrings. "I shan't believe a word you say—on principle, you know."

"I trust that you will be able to believe your own eyes?"

Helen raised one of her perfectly arched eyebrows which had the effect of making her seem only mysterious and unassailable.

Madame Koo did not have the time to waste upon niceties. She said, "Your sister is insane."

Helen said, still smiling, "You have never forgiven her, have you, for running off? But if she would not marry Mr. Sze then, I doubt whether she will consent to marry him now. Mother, dear, why do we not give up gracefully?"

"For your sister," Madame Koo said, "there is unfortunately no longer any question of marriage—to anyone. Nor can so petty a question as my forgiveness enter in.

It seems to be hard for you to absorb but your sister is mad."

Helen looked hard at Madame Koo. Madame met her look.

"You shall see for yourself," Madame said, "very shortly."

"I shall have to see!"

And Madame said with a bitterness that caught Helen's attention, "Yes, you shall see—as if through a pane of glass—those things that you are never to know—hunger and terror and suffering. You shall see, I promise you that."

Helen was silent.

"I believe," Madame said, "that you have ever been fond of your sister. In her present condition she must be humored. That is why this room—with half-finished picture and opened book—appears as it does—to assist her in blotting out a past that is too painful for present remembrance. She should not on any account be allowed to dwell on it or speak about it with anyone. She should not be excited. That is why I am soliciting your help."

"Is it?" Helen said. She had been listening intently but as a person might who was expected to hear two things at once.

Madame knew that Helen was very well aware that she had no intentions of divulging the true purpose that lurked behind the request Madame was about to make. That is, assuming there was a "true purpose" which Helen most definitely and unfortunately had assumed there was. The question remaining was, could Helen scent it out? She was very busy trying and Madame was equally busy throwing out small whiffs of the wrong scents for her to follow.

"It is necessary," Madame said, "and in this, as in all other matters concerning her, your father and I agree . . . It is necessary that she be constantly watched. I have accordingly selected the best possible maid to assist . . ."

"Whom have you picked?" Helen wanted to know at once.

But Madame said, "Time enough to discuss that later. . . . A maid cannot be made entirely responsible. The major responsibility, indeed, should fall to one who understands the pathetic condition she is in and cares deeply for her recovery. I have selected you."

"You do me such honor," Helen murmured.

"I am glad you do not name it an imposition," Madame Koo said. "It will not be easy, you see, for your sister has an obsession—she is intent upon taking her own life."

Abruptly, Helen left off playing with her earring. She did not stare at her mother. Though her talk was free and even impudent when abstracted from her manner, it was her manner that always qualified her speech and labeled it charming and a compliment to the person so addressed, that placed the person within the inner circle that only a beauty, at least in the Chinese society, is allowed to cast about her. Helen was too well bred to stare. But she sat, now, as immobile as Madame Koo was sitting. For some moments a charged silence vibrated between them.

Then, Madame Koo said quietly, "It will be your duty to protect her against her own violence. It is the days I fear most—the nights can be managed. You must guard against her turning against herself in every way, you must question even her simplest acts. Above all, see that she is never alone in her bathroom. And remember that even such a lame object as a silk sash may be thought of, when the mind is tired and sick, as a means toward hanging oneself from the rafters. . . . Oh, you must be vigilant but also gentle. Encourage her to forget and to be happy with us."

Madame Koo rose, which was the sign of dismissal. "You will be aided by the excellent maid we spoke of.

But understand that it is you who will bear the brunt of the responsibility for her welfare. I will so instruct your father."

Helen had also risen. But instead of leaving, she dallied about the room, playing with the switches of the electric lamps, running an idle finger along the books in the bookcases, ending up with studying the picture that was on the easel.

Watching her, Madame knew she was preparing to name her price—to strike a bargain. Bargaining was an instinct with Helen and nothing in itself to become alarmed about. She had started, when she was no higher than a bamboo shoot, for candy. But in this case the price she fixed would be interesting. Even with following wrong scents, she would not have failed to take into account an urgency in her mother which, because she knew her so well, Madame was unable to hide completely. Yet, Madame felt, if she had hit on the *right* scent, she would now refuse to bargain at all. In all fairness to her, she would turn her mother down flat.

Helen sighed. "What if she should swallow a knife or tear up a bed sheet? It would be better, would it not, if I were male and weighed two hundred and sixty-five pounds? How long would this have to go on?"

"We hope it is temporary," Madame said. "And she is dangerous only to herself—otherwise, of course, you would not be asked. I think it will not last long. It will depend largely on you—on your skill and kindness."

"Insane people throw a monstrous scare into me," Helen said. "Let's put our heads together, you and I, and think of someone else."

Madame Koo said nothing. She waited.

"Oh, oh!" Helen said, as if she had that moment dropped something that was breakable. "Oh, dear. I was at the very point of telling you I was your obedient servant when I thought of Little Dog."

Little Dog was Helen's nephew. His father was dead (he had been murdered by the half-caste, Blair, or so the family claimed) and his mother had remarried and left the House of Koo and Little Dog had somewhat embarrassingly appropriated his aunt to be his mother instead.

"Oh," Helen said, "Little Dog would die if I did not let him spend the nights with me. . . . Isn't it too bad that I cannot help you after all?"

Madame Koo had been waiting for this. She said, "Naturally, I do not expect you to disappoint Little Dog and I have, therefore, made due allowance. Indeed, that is partly why I have given the choice of a dependable maid such careful consideration. The nights, as I said before, can be managed. And whether or not Little Dog entered into the picture, I am not so inhuman as to expect you to assume a twenty-four-hour duty. How could you? Each night, you may give to your sister one of the sleeping powders that I shall give to you. Then, you must sit with her until she soundly sleeps. The powder, you see, will invoke the deepest kind of slumber. Yet, so as we do not place our faith too singly, there is the maid who will be on constant nightly duty and whose business it will be to instantly know should she, by some strange chance, wake up. Under these circumstances, I can see no reason why you should not carry on both duties, can you?"

Helen again sighed. "Do you know what I dreamed last night, Mother?" she asked. "I dreamed that I was surrounded by a great many trunks and servants. It seemed I was on my way back to Shanghai. And you were lighting firecrackers and tossing them up in the air—seeing me off, I suppose."

"Indeed?"

"A crazy dream," Helen said, "isn't it? But then I had another that was even crazier." She dropped her eyes. "In it your Old Crone came to me and said in the most pontifical voice, 'Young lady, your marriage has been long delayed. I and my mistress wash our hands of you, altogether. Go out, therefore, and choose your own husband.' " Helen laughed. "The effrontery!" she said. "Can you imagine that dirty old thing intruding herself into my dreams?"

So, Madame thought, the price was named and it was even steeper than she had foreseen. She was not in any position to haggle, though.

She said, "Should you, my daughter, faithfully discharge your duties, I can see no reason why you should not be allowed—afterwards—a short vacation in Shanghai."

"Really, Mother?" Helen said. "At the Park Hotel or the Majestic?"

"I have never been near those foreign places," Madame said, "but it is possible that one of those might be arranged."

"Oh, heaven and earth!" Helen said. "Six months at the Majestic. What a lark!"

Madame Koo let that pass. "I have meant to inform you," she went on, "that for some time your father and I have been thinking it over and it seems to us in view of the times and your modern education, you might be allowed some choice concerning your future husband. Of course, he would have to be acceptable to us."

"Of course!" Helen said.

The charged silence vibrated again between them. Helen was the one to break it. With her eyes on the picture of the lotus flower she said, "You have now told me quite all that I am to do? There is nothing more expected of me?"

"Nothing," Madame Koo said. "Positively nothing more."

Helen shook her head.

"I am willing," Madame said, "to make—uh—certain concessions because I can afford no lip service and no careless watching. Your father's favorite daughter is involved and your father handed to me the trust that I must now hand you. Were I not the mistress of the house and overburdened with duties, I myself would do the watching. But since I cannot, I must know that when you say you will watch that you *will* watch and not fall asleep over too much food. Is that clear?"

"Mother dear, nothing is clear except the great unclearness. But I obey . . . I watch till my eyeballs roll out on the floor like marbles. And that is enough?"

"Yes," Madame said. "You need not tell the others about the girl's obsession as it would only create a hurting strangeness between her and them. Everything must be made as easy for her as possible. Say only that she is ill to the point of being deranged—since that is obvious. Say she is not to be excited."

"And is that all?" Helen said.

"Yes," Madame said. "Perhaps you have a few arrangements that you would like to make at your own court. You should be back here in half an hour."

"Half an hour," Helen mused, turning toward the door.

"Half an hour," Madame said.

VI

Madame Koo thought: all was now arranged, all was in readiness. It was to appear to be suicide—to Old Koo and to Helen. Since the body would have to be immediately disposed of, the others could whittle away at rumors however they would. What was stamped across Madame's heart was murder.

"Mother, you must save me." And then? Yes, this. It would haunt. She might not again take up a child in her arms or know a peaceful hour. A price! (For with Madame revenge and murder were separate. Revenge she fully intended the girl who had tried to undo her family to feel. But murder was the safety measure that was not related to revenge but to Madame's consciousness—to her conviction that the family was endangered by harboring this too-famous enemy.) It fell to Madame to pay this price—to make this sacrifice to the family who would never offer thanks, but only blame, should they ever learn of it. . . . It would not occur to them that the time had come when they could no longer afford to forgive or take in a beloved enemy. Old Koo was right. Ah, the rich were a soft and spoiled lot.

Against her will and better judgment, Madame returned to the inner room and to the bed where the girl lay. Staring down at the sleeping, haggard face, she thought it strange that she who was destined to destroy her should yet be the only one who understood her.

Outside, the troops marched to subdue the peasants; the lesson was being taught. When the lesson was considered learned, in two days, or three, when the House of Koo would have returned to normal—well, then, as Madame calculated, the stories and the rumors that would get out would be so garbled, so mixed with madness (it was well, always, to mix rumors with madness) that the family would have no trouble; the family would easily survive them.

"The Third Koo Girl came back, you see, on the very day she was supposed to have been killed. She was quite mad. I tell you this in utter confidence but she is—I mean—she was at our place for an entire day (or two or three). Then she disappeared. Some say . . . No, I tell you, she was with us but she is no longer. What happened? But I told you once! She disappeared."

Madame would also send out her own version to further confuse the others. Hers would please the simple peasant mind: that upon the same day the Third Koo Girl was shot to death in the prison yard; at, in fact, the self-same moment and hour, the demented ghost of the Third Koo Girl returned to haunt the Koo Mansion. Indeed, it did assume so lifelike a shape that there were those who became confounded—who swore that she was not a ghost, at all, but as quick with life as the next one. Had she not quite disappeared again these same would have sworn that she had risen from the dead.

Which, Madame thought with a restlessness that was utterly foreign to her nature, depended upon the concrete and indisputable proof of her death—which was—her death. And by this death Madame Koo was damned—for the sake of the family the girl had damned herself in attempting to destroy. ("Mother, you must save me.") Very well. Madame, looking down at the sleeping face, must breathe, "But I am more alone than you."

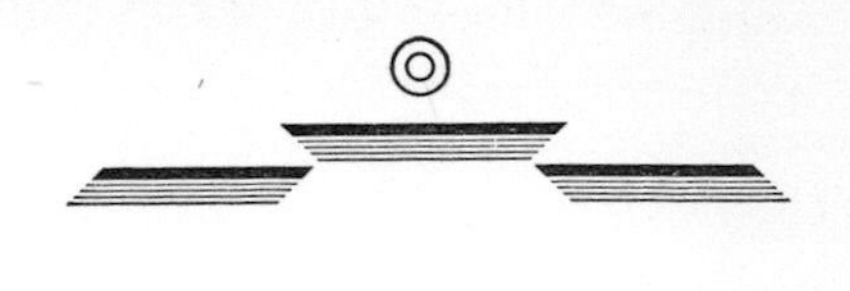

4

I

THERE were no sounds of rickshaw bells—all vehicles, rickshaws and wheelbarrows and carts, had disappeared—no sounds of venders hawking their wares, of women washing at the canals and quarreling. There was not the ordinary hustle and bustle, no ordinary press. Shops had put up night boards and the alleys were as clean of people as old bones are of meat, but the streets continued to be lined with them: standing close together, bunching, forming small tight clusters, moving their mouths and breaking off their gestures. Christopher Blair heard one name circulating among them—the Third Koo Girl's.

An oppressive and curious pall of silence hung over the city—curious, since it could not possibly be defined as silence, what with the gross sounds of tramping feet bearing in from every direction, with the tail ends of orders resounding over the roofs. Yet it was a silence—indisputably.

In the Street of the Seven Brothers (where Christopher Blair was) the troops entered, marching six abreast. The people stood back, stood flat to the walls to give them the room they needed. Their faces were closed and masklike. The soldiers were watching these faces, as the faces were watching the soldiers' faces. Trading look for look. It was obvious that the people had disobeyed a natural law when they had failed to flee before these troops, and it was therefore the soldiers who were afraid, with their knuckles showing white beneath the stretched skin of the hands that held the guns. . . . They were afraid. But who is not afraid of stones falling up instead of down? Blair thought it was like the third act of a bad melodrama that could not get started, with the closed and secretive faces jamming the works, with the curtain jerking up and down and the orchestra coming in on the down beat, over and over. But *something* would have to happen.

It was said that (after the troops had entered) all the city gates had had to be closed—to keep the peasants out. Troops stood three deep along the walls. It was said that the new sections of the city, which were outside the city walls, were thick with peasants, coming in from their farms and villages and steadily coming.

General Ma had bought the two companies of troops that had garrisoned the city. The people understood that; they understood that there was not even a remnant of an army left to represent them. The Third Koo Girl was dead and their army had died with her.

In a few streets the soldiers had thrown up sand bags and tangled barbed-wire barricades. And perhaps their officers were waiting for the commands of their superior officers.

The people had been sold out and they knew it at last. They knew General Ma and the reputation that the troops of General Ma had; they had had experience with these troops of General Ma before. Old Koo was back and the Third Koo Girl was dead—they knew all of that.

In Sin-ss-ka Square (the principal square), where the whipping posts and the platforms were, the public floggings and the major speeches and the executions of "little Communists" and radicals were to have taken place. The scene of "the lesson." Which was to have been combined with the raping and the burning and the looting—in retaliation for the time when these people had dared too much. Here in the square was where wild feelings were to have been whipped up and shaped—with scapegoats offered—and the new deliverance. At the north end of the square a lone agitator was standing upon an overturned fishtub (instead of on one of the platforms). The square was not deserted—shoulder to shoulder the people stood around him.

"My good people," he cried. "My good friends! Hear the truth. Communists have ruled this city for these two months. . . . They are criminals! Liars! They have perpetrated a monstrous fraud. They promised to give you work. Have they done it? No—they have only polluted our great revolutionary party—they have only helped you to starve. They promised to make you rich. Have they done that? We can agree they have not. Now, those who are your friends are back. To save you from a bitter fate." Seductively: "Return to the land, my friends—it is time, it is past time. Old Koo, in his generosity, will take you back—the gentry will have you back. Yes, and the rents are to be reduced! Workers, return to the factories—it is time, it is past time—you have starved long enough. Old Koo, in his generosity, will take you back and pay you, too. Ah, poor deluded ones, what is the task before us? *To eliminate Communists!* These Communists who have fed you nothing but treachery and lies, these Communists who are the sore to our city's body, who have polluted everything. We rid ourselves of villains and thieves. We pay respect to our fathers and to our fathers' fathers and to the time-honored ways. Today we eliminate and exterminate, we *kill* these thieves who came in the night. We *kill* these whoresons and troublemakers. We *kill* to rid ourselves of evil. We *kill!*"

He pointed, at random, to one of the people and cried, "There is a Communist—let us kill him! Let us . . ."

The people stood, neither turning away nor leaving, neither listening nor not listening. Poor agitator, with his voice getting thinner . . . It was not even his own image in a mirror he was haranguing.

Christopher Blair turned and started off. The voice had stopped altogether. He looked back. The people were still there, as immobile and impassive as ever. It was only that the agitator was no longer there and neither was his fishtub.

It could not go on, Christopher Blair thought, as he continued to hear that name that was passed from mouth to mouth. The tension would mount and mount and mount and then? It was now almost ten o'clock. He passed three houses of prostitution—all closed. Had one been open, he would have taken his time in it with the oldest, ugliest, most sluttish. That was his mood and disposition.

He must press as they pressed, stand as they stood, to let the soldiers pass. But he kept on walking. He would have snatched the name from them and spread out his hands, priest-like, to pronounce the benediction: "Lord have mercy on you."

At last he made a turn toward Pu-tang Street and the blacksmith shop, dimly aware that he was hoping he would never reach it. . . . He thought of his mother, that cultivated and beautiful Chinese woman who could trace her ancestors back for twenty-seven generations and who had the heart of a slave, and who would not approve of him now. His father, a Virginian, gentle and scholarly, would not have understood. His mother would have understood intuitively and fully and disapproved. ("You mourn, my son. Go home." And he, "Mother, make my bed.") A man can tie a can to a dog's tail in order to accomplish mourning.

He understood that. What he was not sure of was whether, at the moment, he wanted to kill or be killed. Neither. The people stood with their backs to the walls and passed the name back and forth. He insisted that he walked alone—he walked conspicuously—he passed some of his former patients, "walking miracles," who testified to his medical skill, who recognized him and turned and stared after him. Never mind. Fear did not have a voice. Nor sorrow either. The people had no voice. And if he could not find the most sluttish slut to lose himself in, he would at least have none of them. Miserable people. Fools, expecting their miracle. He heard it, he had to hear it, the name, again and again and again, passing like chain lightning, repeated, over and over, with the tension solidifying like poured cement. Chain lightning and poured cement. (*But the soldiers would not march, in ranks, forever.*) He had to hear it, her name, casting its spell, and to know that she had never belonged to him. Could it matter? Unless he recalled that in front of the firing squad, they had been made to kneel?

Nobody spoke to him; he spoke to nobody. Time was not going to stand still.

At eleven o'clock there was a great concentrated burst of firing. Inside the West Gate a detachment of nerve-ridden troops fell upon each other, firing their guns at such close range that they were blowing off each other's faces, fighting as close as wrestlers, except with guns and bayonets and grenades. Such close-packed slaughter, it was said, had never before been witnessed. The West Gate guards, in a panic, threw open the gates in order to escape, and the peasants then came in quietly, picking up the guns of the dead and piling the bodies into a heap. The news of this incident traveled fast. The peasants, it was said, held the West Gate behind their barricade of dead soldier flesh.

The oppressive and curious pall of silence (that could not possibly be defined as silence) returned.

II

"Hello," Andrew said. His shadow had come in ahead of him and was wavering on the sunny floor.

"Andrew," Helen said, more to the shadow than to the man, "you aren't supposed to be in other people's bedrooms. Go away, dear."

"I have a perfectly legitimate excuse," Andrew said, advancing a step. "Doesn't that make a difference?"

"No," Helen said. She was waiting for her sister to wake up, and knitting furiously on a pink sweater with six steel needles which she seemed to be using all at a time and which were going fast enough to be throwing out sparks. "I am sure it is very ingenious and convincing," she added. "But take your excuses and your uninvited self some other place today."

"I could be looking for Tear Drop," Andrew said.

"In here?" Helen said.

He was now altogether in the room. Helen glanced at him, but it was the wrong thing for her to do insofar as her firmness about him went. Nobody had ever had the heart to be very firm with Andrew. He was so wraithlike, slim, and his features were so sensitive—although, Helen noticed, they were beginning to be overlaid with a puffiness, especially around his eyes. Andrew had used to say that people violated his sense of form. But Helen thought it was he who failed to come through according to the laws. Nothing could ever have made him sporting or cosmopolitan or at his ease. Yet he was wearing flannel slacks and a tweed jacket, which made him seem simply ridiculous and lost.

"Darling," Helen said to him, "you could have thought up a better excuse than that!"

"No, I couldn't," Andrew said. "And I tried hard."

He was looking all around the room, taking it in. "People of action," he said, "have it all over us—me, that is. (Did you hear the firing?) I would like to be resting in that bed."

"Why?" Helen said, though she had not meant to let Andrew get started.

"Can you really ask?" Andrew said. "To have *done*, to have accomplished—it doesn't matter what. Even to have lost. Have you heard the soldiers marching? Think of the hard, good feeling inside." Then, "I hope her passion and her sense of humor didn't get too crossed up with the rest of her. . . . (It's an odd little secret we are to keep, isn't it?) But what use does Leila have for my beautiful bitch, do you suppose?"

"What do you mean?"

"I mean," Andrew said, going closer to the bed, "that they have borrowed Tear Drop from me and given her to . . ."

"No!" Helen said, her fingers and needles suddenly tangling.

"It's not that I begrudge the loan," Andrew said. "But it certainly provokes my curiosity. Does Leila want Tear Drop?"

"The perfect choice," Helen said. "The perfect maid!"

"Oh, no," Andrew said, sighing a little. "The perfect bitch. Now, I appreciate perfection even as it relates to bitches, but . . ."

"You," Helen said, frowning, "operate in reverse."

"Exactly," Andrew said. "If it's done with finesse, I quite enjoy being lied to and cheated and done out of everything I have. But I don't go around imposing my standards on unsuspecting relatives, you know. Ah, but that's it—doesn't Leila suspect? Didn't she learn a thing or two when

Tear Drop was serving her? Intriguing, I must say. I want to find out . . ."

"I am just beginning to find out," Helen said, cutting him off. "Andy, won't you please leave? I have to think."

Andrew hesitated. "No," he said gently and apologetically. "I don't think I can." He took another step toward the bed.

"Don't!" Helen said.

"What is it?" Andrew said slowly. "Is she scarred or deformed or something?"

"Never mind," Helen said. "But just don't look at her. I don't want you to do it. Really!"

"But . . ."

"I haven't yet," Helen said. "It isn't fair, that's all. Come back later and look at her when she can look at you."

This caught Andrew up. "Yes," he said, nodding. "You're absolutely right. It isn't fair, is it? But, you know, Helen, I am the kind of miserable goof who always reads other people's mail and goes through their pocketbooks and drawers—that's the devil of it. I have to look."

"All right," Helen said. "Go ahead. I give up."

But Andrew wavered. He looked at Helen out of his eyes that were always intense—even over the smallest matters. He put his hand in his pocket and took out a cigarette and lighted it. This act gave him strength or weakness. He turned, all carelessness and worldly ease, and went to the bed.

"Oh!" he said.

When he turned again he raised his cigarette jerkily to his mouth and blew out a great cloud of smoke to float between himself and Helen.

Helen continued knitting. "Poor Andy," she said, under her breath. (Andy who was sensitive to all things at once.) "Poor Andy," Helen repeated.

He was on his way out.

"Where are you going, dear Andrew?"

"To take some bicarbonate of soda," said Andrew.

The dream was not a dream, no more than the sky was silk. Perhaps, if you could only find it, there was some other way out. . . .

Beauty was not truth—that was what she knew in the moment before she awoke.

She sat up and opened her eyes.

Without looking up from her knitting, Helen said, "Will you have your tea?" She put down her knitting and rose. "I will have to call your slave," she said.

"My slave?"

It was then Helen looked at her sister—simply because it was no longer postponable.

"Leila!" she said. "You fool."

She crossed the room, sat down on the edge of the bed and took her into her arms.

"Why do you hold me, Helen?"

"Because you need to be held," Helen said. "What did you do—just give up food and live on principles?"

"Why am I here?" Leila asked.

"Because this is your home," Helen said. "Don't ask another stupid question. Lie still. I will bring a basin and wash your face. Do you need to go to the bathroom?"

"Have you gotten bossy, Helen?"

Helen laughed. The sound of the laughter seemed to startle Leila who—until now—had been more asleep than awake. She drew back sharply.

"Please," she said. She swung her legs over the side of the bed. Her feet touched the slippers that the little maid had placed for her and recoiled. Watching her, Helen saw her shake her head as if to clear it. Then her feet found the slippers, for the second time. She stood up. Automatically she reached for the robe and her fingers strayed over the soft, warm material.

"The spun-silk womb," she said. She went toward the bathroom.

"Leave the door open," Helen said.

Leila went in and turned around slowly. She drank two glasses of water, one after the other. She retched—but in the way that led Helen (who had jumped up) to believe she was used to it and not surprised. She let the water run for awhile, looking down at it, putting her wrists in and out of the flow.

She came back into the bedroom and walked about lightly, almost without balance. Once she tapped upon a table as if she would sound the wood. She passed around the screen and into the living room. Helen followed, her own head reeling with uncertainty and unanswered questions. Was Leila insane? She had thought to be able to tell, somehow, the first time she looked at her. And it was that, if the whole truth must come out, which had filled her with such dread, which had combined itself with the other more delicate reason—that it was not fair. Why had Mother selected Tear Drop? For what, if Leila was not insane, had she bargained?

Leila was not walking about the second room. She was standing still in front of the easel.

"The shade," she said, "is delicate, isn't it, Helen?"

"Yes."

"Exquisite, don't you think? I started it this morning before my nap. And before that, when the dew was still in the cups of flowers, I paid a visit to the lotus ponds."

"Of course, dear."

Leila, at last, looked away from the easel. She looked

down and saw the bowl of peanuts that was on the floor. She started so violently that Helen also started.

"They are only peanuts!" Helen said.

But Leila smiled a strange, half-smile that Helen had never seen before.

"You are sick," Helen said. "I wish you would go back to bed."

Leila held out her hands to the room. She said, "I thank her for this."

Helen shivered. "Come back to bed."

"Do you know what, Helen? Revenge can be as real as peanuts. It can be something to get your bearings by. It can be kindness itself."

"Hush," Helen said. "You mustn't talk like that."

There was a cough behind them.

"Oh, merciful Buddha!" Helen cried. Her heart had nearly failed her. . . . But it was only Tear Drop, she saw, standing in the door with a tray in her hands.

"Good day," Tear Drop said in an off-hand manner. She bowed first to Helen, then to Leila.

"Tear Drop," Helen said. "You ought to be ashamed of yourself, sneaking up on us that way. Why don't you learn to wait until you're called? Or at least learn to announce yourself?"

Tear Drop merely smiled. She set down her tray and began to remove the lids from the bowls. It was nothing she did or did not do but her manner was negligent and insulting.

Leila went close to her and began to look her up and down. "You, too," she said.

"Sit down," Helen said hurriedly to Leila. "Wouldn't you like a bite to eat?"

"No," Leila said to Helen. "Get out," she said to Tear Drop.

Completely ignoring Leila, Tear Drop addressed Helen. "Our Old Lady, the Grandmother, bids me inform you both that you are invited to come to her court this afternoon for a game of mah-jongg."

"How lovely," Helen said. "There is nothing I want more to do, this day, than to play at mah-jongg."

"Nor I," Leila said.

But it came to Helen that she was overlooking the perfect excuse for getting Tear Drop out. She said, "Tear Drop, go to our Old Lady and tell her we shall be happy to attend. After your return, why do you not prepare some of that delicious almond soup that is your specialty and that she is so fond of? We will just carry it to her."

Tear Drop did not want to go. "If . . ." she began.

Leila was walking slowly around Tear Drop—for the world, Helen thought, like an animal closing in for the kill.

"You had better go," Leila said with peculiar, spaced emphasis on every word.

With what Helen thought was sublime indifference, Tear Drop said, "I will make the soup in this court. When Third Young Mistress is ready to dress . . ."

". . . we will shout to the very housetops for you," Helen promised. "Now, go."

Tear Drop bowed herself out.

"Have a cup of tea," Helen said. She took out her handkerchief and patted her forehead with it. "Eat."

"No," Leila said.

"A little," Helen said. "You do have to start in again, sometime, you know . . . Anyway, do sit down."

"It is not my place to sit down," Leila said.

"Oh," Helen said. "Everything is becoming complicated. Now, Leila, why can't you sit down? I cannot think of a single reason on earth why the plain act of sitting should present a problem."

But Leila did not smile as Helen had hoped she might. She continued stalking—what? An imaginary Tear Drop? Walking around and around, she reminded Helen of some emaciated tiger, except that her eyes were more empty and more sick than any tiger's. Suddenly she raised her head, listening, it would seem, intently. "What time is it, Helen?"

"It—it's"—Helen looked at her watch—"noon—twelve o'clock."

"Six hours," Leila said musingly.

"Yes, dear." Helen could not help it—she looked over her shoulder.

"Helen."

"Yes, dear."

"Helen, I have been working for the dissolution of the lands that belong to this family—for the dissolution of the family itself. I . . ."

"Oh, that," Helen said. "If that's what you're worrying about! You know, dear, I don't pretend to be an intellectual and when I get near intellectual topics, I sound so shallow I annoy even myself. . . . But I do know where you got those funny ideas—in college. And since it was Father who sent you there, in the first place, with the whole family's approval, they can hardly be held against you, can they?"

Leila said nothing.

"Nobody does hold them against you," Helen said. "All any of us want is for you to get fat and happy again, don't you see?"

"No," Leila said, "I don't see." She took another step toward Helen. "But I lied when I said I did not want that food. I want it, you know, Helen."

"But, Leila! Darling, for goodness' sake, eat it! I simply don't understand."

"Today," Leila said, "doesn't belong to me. I should be in a coffin with the lid nailed down. . . . Well, and so there are prisons and prisons, aren't there? And, do you know, Helen, that this prison is going to make me remember the other one as a sort of paradise? Well, I will eat. I will eat until I'm sick."

In a violent, uncontrolled motion, she fell on the food.

"Oh, Leila, slowly!" Helen said. "Slowly, dear."

But Leila either would not or did not hear her.

III

In the early afternoon, various women members of the Koo Family began to drop past the Third Girl's court on one pretext or another. Helen had to greet them, for Leila had returned to the bed, after she had eaten, and was again sleeping—a black and absolute sleep, this time. The women came bringing little presents which they covertly offered. "Not a real present," each would say. Helen thanked them and since they were so loath to leave, she asked them to stay awhile in the outer room, which they did. Tear Drop and the little maid served them tea.

When the hour of the Old Lady's mah-jongg game arrived, Helen sent Tear Drop to her court with humble apologies (the Third Girl, after all, was too ill to come and Helen therefore could not get away) and the almond soup. Madame Koo had not come. She sent inquiries and a dozen fresh eggs but she was (according to her maids) very busy and would be over later.

Helen had the reputation for being a perfect and original hostess, always keeping the conversation on a gay keel, and often serving combinations of delicacies that no one else thought of, or else remembering—from five years back—that a certain person liked a certain dish a certain way.

Since, this afternoon, Helen was hostess by proxy, it was an occasion for her to scintillate. She tried, but because fear was sifting into her thoughts like grains of sand into the bottom half of an hour glass that has just been turned upside down, this was not proving to be one of her more outstanding achievements. Fear, the nameless, trickling kind, was a new experience to Helen. Was Leila insane or not? What was insanity? Helen had supposed it was something as obvious as rain. Leila was not insane. Leila was sick and tired and maybe a little delirious but she was not insane. Each trip that Helen made from the living room to the bed, in order to make sure that Leila slept and was contemplating no harm to herself, made her feel more certain. This growing certainty was the center of Helen's panic which, as the hour passed, seemed to trickle faster and faster because time was running out.

For years, ever since Helen had finished her schooling in Shanghai, she had been begging in every way she knew (and she knew a number of ways) to be allowed to have some say-so concerning the choice of her future husband. But although, by a deal of wangling, she had managed to forestall several her family had considered for her, she had not gotten any further than that and meanwhile she was getting no younger. Now, in the space of a single day, she had been granted that wish and a vacation in Shanghai, to boot. Why? If she would take good care of Leila, who was insane, and keep her from committing suicide. . . . Helen looked into a mirror that was on the toilet table to see if her hair was really standing up on end or only felt like it.

Helen knew nothing about the stakes that had been involved in the revolution. She had no real notion as to what was going on outside today. . . . What she did know with unerring certainty was that shot through the situation were shafts of urgency and desperation. Leila was urgent and desperate; her mother was urgent and desperate. And her mother had been willing to pay a dear price for Helen's help which, Helen had been astute enough to discover, she had urgently and desperately needed. There it was, then. But if the reasons Mother had given were not the real ones? They weren't; Helen knew they weren't. All other matters, like Tear Drop, aside, why should Mother, at this late date, begin to be open and straightforward? If Leila really were insane, Mother would have said she had the smallpox!

But if Helen was in the dark about the nature of the desperation, she knew very well what was expected of her, what she was being paid so well for. Whatever it was she thought or might come to think, she was to corroborate, in every interested quarter, the official version—which was to say, Madame's version: that Leila was insane and had the obsession of wanting to commit suicide.

There was only one small ray of hope which Helen cherished—it was an inkling she had always had. It was just an inkling, she admitted, and would probably be vigorously denied by almost everyone else. This inkling was that Leila was her mother's as well as her father's favorite daughter. This, in spite of the fact that Madame had always been hard on Leila, had punished her more severely than her other daughters. But—or so Helen thought—she had been hard on her in almost exactly the same way she was hard on herself, as if in disciplining one sturdy and passionate nature she alone knew the value of imposing that discipline on another.

If Helen was right in thinking that Leila was greatly loved by Mother, then whatever it was her mother was considering, it could not be harm to the loved one, could it?

A ray of hope could not compete with the sands of fear. Oh, no, Helen decided miserably. If Helen had been able to sit down and think the situation through for ten consecutive minutes in a row, she might have arrived at some plan of action of her own. As it was, she was back and forth, looking at Leila, welcoming more aunts and cousins, saying the things to each that each wanted to hear, murmuring that Leila was deranged and not to be excited, seeing about the tea and—oh, bother! If only Leila would stay asleep until she could get rid of them.

Out in the court Little Dog was chasing a yellow butterfly. Little Dog was seven years old and by the laws of inheritance the future lord and master of the House of Koo. He was full of the sense of his own importance. His father, Lincoln, the oldest son of Koo, was that one who had been butchered by that half-caste doctor, Blair. His mother had disgraced herself by marrying some other—in the very face of the fact that the family had planned for her to be a "virtuous widow." Therefore, Little Dog was everyone's responsibility—not just Helen's. In him was vested an entire family's future security.

Nobody else could so much as catch a glimpse of the yellow butterfly which Little Dog insisted was in this court and no other court. He said it was hiding in the cassia bush into which he immediately peered when he gathered that his aunt or anyone else was watching. The balance of the time Little Dog marched back and forth, like a guard. He took out his sword from its sheath, every so often, and poked it at the darkest courtyard corners and made faces at them. To them he also announced periodically that he was Koo, the Great Revolutionist. (He certainly wished his Aunt Leila would hurry and wake up!)

"Little Dog," said a giggling maid who came mincing along with a basket over her arm, "whom do you wave your sword at?"

Little Dog glared at her. "Stupid silly," he said. "I do

not suppose you have ever even heard of the Dragon's Butterfly!"

The maid's eyes grew wide. "Why, no, Little Dog," she said. "I must be incurably ignorant— I have not!"

"Then, beware!" Little Dog said. "And don't be walking along and swinging a basket. For this is exactly the very day that the Dragon of the Western Hills opens his mouth and spits out the yellow butterfly that has horns on his head and a tail behind. And if he is not pierced to the bone in flight he will kill everybody in whatever place he lights. . . . Now, will you ask me what I am doing?" He drew his sword. "Be gone."

The maid shrank. She crept toward the doors, looking constantly over her shoulder and letting out little screams.

"What's the password?" Little Dog asked her after she had disappeared inside. He returned to his marching.

The women who had come to see the Third Girl, on one pretext or another, stayed on and on. They chatted in low voices with each other and kept their hands busy (lest Madame or the Old Lady show their faces) with knitting or embroidery. For while the House of Koo had been decreed modern by Old Koo after his return from the United States of America (with bathrooms and electricity installed), it was actually strict and old-fashioned since it was ruled—as everyone well knew—not by Old Koo at all but by the Old Lady and Madame. Therefore it behooved any women of the House who were educated to shuffle off their educations quickly when they returned to it and to mind their manners. . . . The routine of their days was settling in upon them. They were never allowed out of the House. They kept to the women's courts and for recreation —they were remembering—there was mah-jongg and there was gossip. For them, therefore, the Third Girl's coming was a great event which they were not going to pass up without a struggle. It was the adventure (Old Koo was so right) that they must squeeze dry. It would be their topic of conversation for weeks on end. There was not one there who was not determined to see her in the flesh before the sun had set. It was a wonder the Old Lady herself (as frail and brittle with age as she was) had not come, for her curiosity was not as withered as the rest of her—not by any means.

George's wife was present. George Washington Koo was the second-son-by-the-First-Wife of Koo. All of Helen's and Leila's half-sisters who were not away at school or married were there. They had the same father but different mothers from Helen and Leila. The others were aunts and cousins and concubines of varying generations and ranks and ages, and their maids. Old Koo's newest "Shanghai Concubine" (the one who had the snakelike walk) was present, but since she should not have been and since she did not have the breeding to know it, she was being made the butt of the ladies' sallies—to pass the time.

"I have heard that the Shanghai Nah-nah is so clever that she will take over all of Madame's duties. Is that true, Nah-nah?"

"No," the Shanghai concubine said with a toss of her head. "The Shanghai one is too busy with other duties."

The ladies did not raise their eyebrows or cover their mouths with their hands, although they got the inference well enough and would covertly examine the hussy for pregnancy later.

They speculated about the troops, which they had heard marching.

"Lao-yeh says they belong to General Ma."

"Indeed? What are they doing?"
"Impressing the peasants."
"They make a vulgar noise."
"Do they not!"
"But the General is extremely elegant. They call him 'the Gentleman General,' I think."
"Well, well."
"No one is to go out."
"And is there anything new about that?"
"Is it they who were rude to the Third Girl?"
"Shhh."
"We are to sew up our lips about that. It was all a mistake, eh?"

And so on. Everyone, at one time or another, studied the half-finished lotus flower that was on the easel.

Helen was everywhere, at once. ("Tse-yuen, my sweet mouse, you have not touched your tea! It is a hideous variety. You must let me change it.") But Helen, the ladies were quick to notice, was far from being herself. She seemed to have forgot that her function in life was to please. Nor did she even notice the fascinated and envious glances that were cast in the direction of her high heels. Helen was the only woman in the house who dared to wear them—more specifically, who dared to defy Madame's displeasure enough to appear in them. Helen, this afternoon, was very close to performing like an automaton.

By three o'clock, when the women had still not departed and showed no signs of doing so, when Helen had received no orders from Madame, she had to conclude that Madame approved their being where they were—otherwise she would have sent them packing—and that she wanted Leila to come out and meet them. When the aunt-of-the-highest-rank-in-kin, therefore, asked the time, Helen formally excused herself and went into the bedroom. A hush feel over the ladies. Some rearranged their dresses, others put aside their embroidery.

"We must remember that she is deranged," said an aunt.

"We are not to be disturbing," said an older cousin.

In the bedroom Helen woke Leila by taking both her hands in her own.

"You cannot sleep longer," she whispered. "Little Dog has chased his butterfly for eternities, waiting for a sight of you, and he is such a child that he cannot stand eternities."

Tear Drop had followed Helen in. She was among the shadows, which suited her well, and whether or not she was in a more gentle mood, the shadows made her seem so.

Leila stood up. Tear Drop began to lay out her clothes. The voices in the other room rose suddenly, then fell just as suddenly.

"That is not Little Dog!" Leila said.

"No," Helen said. "Those are your kinfolks, remember? Cousins and sisters and such?"

Leila looked wildly about her. "I must . . . Oh God, Helen, I don't have to face them!"

"Now, dear, it isn't a matter of facing them. Relax. Tear Drop and I will just dress you."

Leila permitted them to take off her nightclothes. When she was naked she seemed to try to huddle into herself, to burrow down, to be overcome with shame. And that was so unlike her and she was somehow so thin and so exposed that Helen felt she could not bear it. She swallowed a lump in her throat that was the size of an egg. Leila was silent and docile while they dressed her. She neither helped nor hindered. When they put the lavender silk gown on her and buttoned it down, she followed their hands with her eyes.

"Sit down," Tear Drop said, when they were through. "I must have some light to comb your hair by." She switched on the electric lamp and together they half-pushed, half-led Leila to the chair that was in front of the toilet table. Tear Drop took down her hair.

"You must have combed it occasionally," she said, running her fingers through it. "It is the only part of you that I recognize." She went to work, combing straight through the tangles, jerking Leila's head back as she did.

"Gently!" Helen said. "My goodness, Tear Drop, if you would rather plow a field, I will go at once and arrange it." But Helen did not say more—it was no use, for the war that was between them was too old and not the kind that could be arbitrated.

Tear Drop had finished. She had done it up in a loose knot on the nape of Leila's neck. Surprisingly, the blue-black hair shone in the light and gave the face a frame. Helen plucked Leila's eyebrows and her hands were as gentle as Tear Drop's had been cruel.

"Hand me the rouge," she said.

"There is no rouge," Tear Drop said. "Third Young Mistress does not use rouges."

"Well, then, hand me my purse." Carrying purses was a custom Helen had picked up in Shanghai. She found her compact and rubbed the barest bit of rouge into each of Leila's cheeks. Then she touched her lips with the lipstick and stood back.

"Merciful Buddha," she said. "Leila, you are an advertisement for Coty's!"

The lipstick and rouge had accomplished a miracle—along with the hair. She had to give Tear Drop credit for that. Leila appeared beautiful. It was a beauty of a special kind—the kind of beauty that was curiously enhanced by hollow cheeks and haunted eyes.

"Oh, dear," Helen said. "I ought to suffer a little. I look too well tended." Maybe, Helen thought, it was Nature's way of reimbursing Leila for what she had been through.

Tear Drop was manicuring her nails. Helen got the key from her and opened the jewel case.

"Let's see," she said. "Nothing lavish . . ."

"There," Tear Drop said, "that will do for the present."

"If you are through," Helen said to Tear Drop, "why not go after a bowl of noodles for your mistress . . . ? To give you strength," she added to Leila.

"I cannot eat now," Leila said.

"All right, all right," Helen said. "You don't have to eat." She studied the jewels. "Would you rather wear the diamond clasp or the amethyst earrings?"

Leila made a sound that caused Helen to turn abruptly. Leila was backed up against the wall; her shoulders were shaking and her knees were buckling under her.

"Why, Leila!"

"Don't make me do it, Helen. I am more afraid of those women than I was of whole armies."

Helen smiled. "Now, *siau-mei*," she said, using the old form of endearment, "they are not going to swallow you up. It will not be too hard for you—just a few minutes. Won't you believe me when I tell you that you have no reason to be afraid?"

"But you don't know, Helen."

"Yes, I know."

"You don't know me!"

"Maybe," Helen said. "But I do know them, *siau-mei*, very well. And they are not ogres. They are as anxious to please you as you must be to please them."

"Oh, Helen, don't you see? If I want that, my heart is twice a traitor."

Helen shook her head. That, she freely confessed, she did not see, at all. She said, "You will find only Little Dog with fierce eyes and a sword. Come!"

IV

Christopher Blair lay face down upon his bed, where he had thrown himself when he had finally reached his room behind the blacksmith shop.

Vaguely, dimly, the sounds of marching feet were borne in to him. He could imagine that having marched from one end of the city to the other, his uncle's soldiers about-faced and marched back again. Again and again. Wooden soldiers in a musical comedy rather than in a bad melodrama. What they needed were teapots and umbrellas. . . . The latest of miracles: never before had the people stood waiting so patiently to be killed. Blair kept his eyes closed but he did not sleep. Not a muscle in his body moved. He heard the footsteps in the court—the door opening.

His servant. Who had been in the Blair Family before Christopher Blair was born; who, therefore, had all the rights of "Old Servant."

"Master? I have been looking for you *everywhere!* I combed the streets."

"Did you?" Blair turned over.

"The day is bewitched," the servant said, shaking his head, going about the room, emptying ash trays. Blair watched him. He watched him gather up the dirty cups and pick up the old newspapers and fold them and place them one on top of the other, on the table.

"There."

"And what is going to happen?" Blair said, putting his hands under his head and staring up at the ceiling.

"There will have to be a great letting of blood. After dark," said the servant, "if not before."

"You are informed?"

"They plan a funeral."

"A funeral."

"A funeral . . . It seems the peasants have acquired the corpse of the Third Koo Girl. Tonight they will make a funeral."

"So that the dead may bury their dead."

"That remains to be seen."

"But I do not want to see it," Blair said.

The servant gave him an odd look. "The day must culminate somehow," he said. "The day must end."

"True," Christopher Blair said, closing his eyes.

At headquarters there was much confusion, much going in and out on the part of couriers and runners. In the main room (the room where Yang Koh and Huan-li had been talking) all the chairs that were ranged around the walls were occupied and other men were standing and walking about. The brass spittoons were in constant use. It was Colonel Shu at the wall telephone, now.

One old man with a sparse beard would stroke his beard and say, "Never was such a blunder made." Each time he said it a respectful silence would fall over the room.

Someone, sooner or later, must break it. "It is not quite as we expected."

Or: "When do we get started?"

"What about the West Gate?"

"Yes, what about the West Gate?"

And looks were exchanged.

In a smaller connecting room General Ma was in conference with several members of the Board of Gentry. Old

Koo was not present but those who were present could be considered, in a large sense, Old Koo's representatives. General Ma was trim and elegant in a British tailored uniform—he was in character—sitting a little apart from the others, very languid in his chair. A map of the city was spread out on the table around which the gentlemen were seated.

A sad-faced gentleman was saying, "So the people stand about like blocks of wood and stone. Why is that so frightening? Why do the troops behave as they do? That is the question. They have their guns. Why, they are armed to the hilt. Frankly, General . . ."

All turned toward General Ma, whose fault they considered it was, and who was engaged in building an exquisite temple out of his exquisite hands.

"General, if you please."

"General, your opinion."

The General sat up a little. "Hirelings and bought troops are always afraid of their shadows," he said. "And their shadows, today, would seem to be the people. They feel so unpopular." He sighed. "I do hope," he added, "that might makes right, eh?"

Some of the gentlemen coughed.

"We can be reasonably sure," said the General, "that everything is Shanghai's fault."

The gentlemen cast down their eyes.

"Such a mistake to have killed her," the sad-faced one said. "Such a blunder, I swear!"

"It is awkward," said General Ma. "To have first named her Communist and then killed her—well, it would seem that we have succeeded admirably in making them all Communists today."

"Ai, and when we needed scapegoats so badly."

"True."

"Well, the order never emanated from us. Would we have thought of touching Old Koo's daughter?"

"Why do you not call in Colonel Shu?" said General Ma. "Perhaps he can give us some suggestions on how Shanghai would like us to proceed."

The gentlemen were silent. General Ma was quite well aware of what this silence was meant to communicate: the queer mood and temper of this day is what none of us foresaw. But the troops are your troops, dear General, you are the one from whom all orders emanate, and so how do you propose to get us out of this awkward position? And is it that your troops and your officers have refused to carry out your orders? Is it you who are slipping? What is at the root of this? Action is what we must have—and at once!

"Gentlemen," the General said, considering his hands, "as far as the populace is concerned, the wrong leaders seem to have been executed, thus making for the complete failure of the theatricals which were to have ushered us in. We have our lesson from the Emperors, for not even the Emperors remained when the populace was united against them. (My troops do not fire because the populace is united against *them*—they make a solid and too silent front, when what my roughnecks are used to is terror and dissension and flight. Perhaps they feel that they would be firing into themselves—I would almost be afraid to probe, lest I discover such a mystical identification.) To retrieve our major mistake (this execution which we did not initiate)—to operate successfully on the canker, now, it seems to me necessary that we resort to a drastic step."

"And what is that?" asked the sad face.

"Gentlemen, the peasants are planning a funeral for tonight."

"What!"

"A funeral?"

"You mean . . ."

The General nodded. "We have already had one little incident—one little affair," he said, "the affair of the West Gate."

"Yes, we have been waiting to hear about that."

"Suppose we come back to that in a moment," the General said. "If we should allow a major incident, do you see, if we should allow *them* to start something—mass together—demonstrate . . ."

The gentlemen were askance.

"Except for that handful at the West Gate, they are not armed," the General said as pointedly as Old Koo had said it the day before. "Why not allow them to whip up their own feelings since they will not allow us to do it for them? Why not? Why shouldn't they be allowed to work themsleves into a frenzy over this funeral? Let them run the gamut of their grief and anger, bring everything to a head, work into wild hysteria—which is so easy to handle? Ah, gentlemen. A quick stroke of the knife, then, and all will be over. Indeed, I would be willing to guarantee that, by morning, they will be in different mood—subdued—ready to return to factories and land—deeply impressed with us and our reforms. I can personally guarantee all of that."

The gentlemen were dubious—they demurred. What about the West Gate? Well—nerves. But let them hold the West Gate for awhile—that was the point—let it give them false feelings of security and power. Had they not snatched a certain corpse right out from under the noses of prison guards? The point was that since there was no suitable site for burial inside the city itself, the peasants would have to build their funeral plans around a way to get in and out of the city—the West Gate. . . . And? *All* plans could therefore revolve around the West Gate—from a military standpoint, it would prove most convenient.

"Let us hold off," the General said, "until they get the funeral under way and have reached a climax of their own. Let the troops—for all practical purposes—cease their marching—their display of force. Let them appear intimidated." The general paused. "And it might be good policy," he went on, "to reach into our coffers and to issue a week's good pay to these soldiers, that they may not be induced, for the sake of gain, to overcome their present reluctance to rob and rape. . . . It is, in other words, necessary to our plan that by tomorrow, after our quick stroke of the knife, business should seem as usual."

Armies of warlords were seldom paid. Traditionally, pay day was the permission to loot and rape. But the gentlemen understood that a general bargains best when there is trouble; it was not for them to quibble over—how much of this pay would be going into the soldiers' pockets and how much would stay in the General's. Indeed, it was becoming increasingly apparent to these gentlemen that this plan that General Ma was so courteously presenting to them was already well under way—no doubt! One or two, including the sad face, and he was—next to Old Koo—the largest landowner thereabouts, took advantage of the silence that had fallen over them to listen intently for the sounds of outside activity—for marching troops—and they heard none. They regarded General Ma meditatively.

As for the General, he seemed entirely composed. . . . He fitted a cigarette into his holder and raised the holder to his thin, faintly smiling lips.

"Well, gentlemen?"

"The General knows best," murmured the sad face. "We will issue the pay," said the sad face, "and rely upon the General's stroke of the knife."

There remained the delicate little matter of Old Koo to think about. Would he approve? Would the funeral add to his embarrassment, provoke his displeasure, give him reason to become miffed with them rather than with the C.E.C. and Shanghai? But watching the General's face, they decided to let the matter rest. General Ma had never yet been known to command his troops without first ascertaining Old Koo's desires. They could place their faith in him there. If there was any blame to be unloaded, he would see to it that it fell on Shanghai, as far as Old Koo was concerned, instead of them.

"Let us consider it settled," said the sad face.

"*Hao.*"

"*Hao.*"

Or, "Good, good," said the others.

"We seem to be in full and happy agreement," said the General, with his smile.

V

Meanwhile, at the House of Koo, Helen was facing her sister.

"Remember," she said. "You are not to greet them as a Daughter Returned. All you need to do is to bow to them generally, in the easy spirit of a lazy afternoon when your women relatives have come from another court to yours. Neither Grandmother nor Mother is there. So—bow. Then take the lowest chair. I will do the rest. Are you all right?"

Helen did not wait for an answer. She drew Leila around the screen and pushed her forward. "Bow," she whispered.

To Leila, the women were a continuous, rainbow blur of silk—of shell and pink and blue and rose and palest green. They melted into each other and she could find no beginning and no end to them. They were serene. They were wave upon wave of serenity. They were beautiful. She did not know what she did. She did not think she bowed. When she was steadier, she tried to find a vacant chair. But a soft sound—as soft a sound as the blurred colors were soft—a sighing, gentle, crooning sound—rose from the women.

"Ai-ah."

"A ghost."

"Oh, what have they done to her?"

The women of Koo closed around the girl. They touched her with their hands. They sighed. They stroked her hair. They dabbled at their eyes with dainty handkerchiefs.

"Ai-ah."

They pushed her toward a chair and made her sit.

"Ai-ah."

"She must be built up," said an aunt. "I shall bring her my special prescription of ging-sing."

"And I," a half-sister said, "shall offer her my tiger-bone wine."

There was a bustle at the doors. Maids scattered. They fell back and fell over each other. A cracked old voice was heard.

"And what is the meaning of this?"

"Lao Tah-tah lei-tse," a maid had the presence of mind to announce. "The Old Lady comes."

"Take your places," Helen whispered. "At your embroidery. Hurry!"

The Old Lady entered like a dry wisp of wind. She was so exceedingly shriveled and ancient and little that there were those who could not imagine how Old Koo had ever come out of her.

"So!" she said, peering intently all around her. "No one could spare the time to come to me for a little mah-jongg this afternoon."

All rose and bowed. Helen went forward to lead her to the highest chair.

"Do I hear correctly?" Helen said. "Does the Grandmother accuse her daughters of forsaking her? What injustice! When the truth of it is that the Old Ancestor has picked us clean!"

"Impudent hoof!" the Old Lady said to Helen. "Be quiet."

But Helen, as she was settling her in the seat of honor, went right on. "Lately," she said, "and let everyone here be my witness—lately, in Shanghai, the Grandmother beat us all so badly that she has filled up all her money boxes to the brim and is reduced to throwing her earnings out to the street dogs because she has no more place to store them. This, while we—poor, innocent lambs that we are—have not so much as a copper cent left among us and must sit here and wait for our allowances to be issued to us before we can go and lay ourselves open again."

Everyone laughed. They could not stop for sheer relief. It was well known how the Old Lady loved to win, but who except Helen . . . There was no doubt about it—Helen had saved the day. They promptly forgave her all her earlier inattentiveness. Indeed, they would have forgiven her anything! Already the Old Lady was cackling, tapping Helen on the shoulder, and offering to make her the formal loan of a copper since she was such a pauper.

Tea was brought. Helen said it was not good enough and ordered *Lung-shing*. She would not let the Old Lady touch any of the sweetmeats either. She said they were for the consumption of the present society of paupers and sent Tear Drop off for better.

"See that what you bring pleases our Old Dearest," she said. "Or we shall serve you up instead."

The ladies were so ready to laugh over even the silliest trifle that the Old Lady's temporary pleasure seemed suddenly to give way to darkest suspicion and remembrance. She sat up very straight and took the gold stickpin out of her hair knot and with it, scratched the top of her head which was bald except for a few stray strands. This was a bad omen. The Old Lady was so old that she had come to rule by whims. She thought it was rather gratifying that she had become so unpredictable—even to herself. She often sighed and said, "I wonder what I shall do next." That was funny. What gratified her was that everyone else found it most expedient to wonder, too.

"Hmmmm," she said, waiting for the flickering light of remembrance to assist her; noting, with approval, the terror her "Hmmmm" had provoked. What was it that had happened this morning? Something out of the way, something she had meant to do a thing or two about. . . . Ah! "All of this fuss over a mere nothing of an errant daughter," she said. "I think I should order her heart cut out and presented to me on a stick. Where is the toad?" Then seeing what happened to the faces around her, she laughed. "Well?"

"Well," Helen said, "what kind of stick should we get? A pointed long one or a short thick one? I would not dare go out and just pick up any ordinary stick for . . ."

"*You* cut out your tongue!" the Old Lady said.

"It is done," Helen said. "Shouldn't we play a game of mah-jongg here—providing the Grandmother stakes us?"

The Old Lady waved her down. "Do I punish you all?" she said. "Or do you produce her?"

Helen said, "In all seriousness, Grandmother dear, the worthless thing is sick and deranged—she would not amuse you."

"Piffle and tosh!" the Old Lady cried. "Who asked to be amused? Where is she? Go fetch her at once."

"We have no need to do that," Helen said, "since she is in our midst and only waiting for her chance to pay obeisance to the Ancient One."

"Where?" the Old Lady cried, half standing up. "Here? Then what, pray, is she waiting for—the moon to hatch little moons? Come forward!"

Helen literally pulled Leila out of her chair. "Leila," she frantically whispered, "you will have to do it. I know I told you there wouldn't be any ceremony but I didn't know . . . Here comes a maid with a cushion. Leila, if it's the last thing you do . . . !"

Leila stood stunned and wavering.

"Come closer," the Old Lady said, shading her eyes with her hand and peering out from under. "My eyes are dim and I must see clearly the one for whom my daughters have neglected me." She cocked her head to one side. "Ai, let me prod my failing senses. . . . *This* is the daughter who ran away and broke the sacred contract with the man of her family's choice. Ai, indeed! Hmmmmmmm. And have I been consulted upon the punishment to be meted out to her?"

"Leila!" It was Helen from behind her. Helen gestured to the maid who then went forward and, bowing very low, placed the cushion on the floor.

Leila took a step. Her eyes swept the room. She took another. Then she knelt—down in front of the shriveled little morsel of a woman.

For a moment the room was deadly quiet.

The Old Lady said, "You may rise and come to me."

She rose and went. The Old Lady craned forward and opened her eyes as wide as she could.

"Heaven and earth!" she said. "Who has starved her? Who has abused her? Wretches! Fiends! Did they not understand that she was a daughter of Koo? Shame, thrice shame. Whom do I punish? Who here is responsible?"

A wailing rose. The Old Lady's sobs were higher than any other's. Leila inclined her head and listened: the sound was made for her. When she raised her head, she saw Little Dog, with his sword, standing in the threshold, glaring at her.

"Limb of our limb," the Old Lady was crooning, "flesh of our flesh . . ."

"What's the password?" Little Dog said.

The wailing ceased. The wailing changed into laughter.

"Is that my Little Dog?" the Old Lady wanted to know. "Bring him to me that I may smell his sweet flesh."

"What's the password?" Little Dog said.

"Buckets of tears," Helen said, giving him a push. "That's what the password is. Go to your great-grandmother, meat dumpling!"

Little Dog went reluctantly. When he passed his Aunt Leila, he said, "The dragon's butterfly is out in the court. Where is your sword?"

He was helped onto the Old Lady's lap and sat stiffly while she stroked him and blew little puffs of wind down his neck.

"My little sweetmeat," the Old Lady said. "Tell us what you have been doing."

"I am a revolutionist," Little Dog said.

"Ha-ha," the Old Lady cackled. "Where did you learn that?"

"I didn't learn it," Little Dog said. "That's just what I am." He looked at Leila. "Wherever she goes, I'm going. I'm going to follow her all over the earth."

"Buddha help us, then," the Old Lady said. "We must persuade her to stay at home."

Little Dog stared at Leila; Leila stared at Little Dog. The ladies were between laughing and crying. The Old Lady looked on them all with love. Madame Koo was in the door.

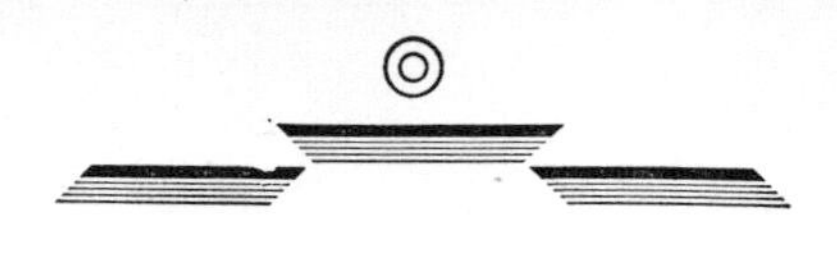

5

I

MADAME KOO'S plan for murder was one that was simple in design. She had, as she had promised, given Helen the sleeping medicine—three powders—"to begin with," she said. Each was wrapped separately in rice paper and folded only as the Chinese know how to fold packets. All of these powders, if examined by the naked eye, would have appeared the same—in color yellow, in texture fine. Two of the packets contained sleeping pow, ders; one contained raw opium of excellent, most potent-grade.

Little Dog ceased to be a great revolutionist and a dragon chaser when the sun went down. He became, instead, a fat and rather fussy little boy who needed his Aunt Helen to ease him over his twilight sense of lostness and into the land of dreams where dragons and revolutionists bow to each other. Sometimes, furthermore, Little Dog waked up from his dreams and cried for his mother. Nobody knew beforehand, of course, when Little Dog was going to wake up and discover that he had turned into a tight little ball of loneliness. But they did know that when he did, it was Helen and only Helen who knew the special kind of nonsense to murmur in his ear; who knew how to make her arms into the softest, safest circle. No one, so far, had ever had to make Helen stay with Little Dog. She would not have forsaken him for the world.

Madame Koo had said, "The nights can be managed . . . I am not so inhuman as to expect you to assume a twenty-four-hour duty. How could you? Each night you must give to your sister one of the sleeping powders that I shall give you. Then, you must sit with her until she soundly sleeps. . . . The powder will invoke the deepest kind of slumber. Yet, so as we do not place our faith too singly, there is the maid whose business it will be instantly to know should she by some strange chance wake. Under the circumstances, I can see no reason why you should not carry on both duties, do you?"

Helen had been chosen by Madame for many reasons—for her popularity with family and servants, for her abilities to gloss and charm, for her habit of keeping her own council, for the indisputable fondness she felt for her sister, for the sake of receiving the Old Koo's wholehearted approval of Madame's choice. However, not the least of these reasons had been Helen's necessity of dividing herself and her talents between two disparate duties.

There were several advantages to Madame's plan. First, she herself would not have to go near the scene, except as she had gone in the afternoon when everyone was there and pleased to see that she, along with the Old Lady, officially sanctioned the Third Girl's return and bade her an official welcome.

Second, there were characteristics about the drug that were decidedly advantageous. The victim, without suspicion, sank into a deep sleep. Madame had from her old-style doctor the sedative prescription which had a little opium in it. Thus the taste of all the powders was near the same. There was no immediate appearance of alarming symptoms to attract the attention of attendants—no gagging, no tearing pain, no screaming. Helen would be gone before there was anything to notice, and Tear Drop would not care enough to notice until too late. . . . Tear Drop would be the one to discover the body, Madame was almost sure. She would not wish the shock of discovery on Helen. She, Madame, would be called. Madame, in turn, would call her lord for whom this entire business was being staged. Together, they would call Helen. They would question her, they would question Tear Drop (who could be blamed for making the opium available). With Helen to corroborate, he would see and he would believe. It would hardly be necessary to point out the advisability of instantly disposing of the evidence. Let the family manufacture whatever rumors they would—a small trickle of the "truth" could only make them more confused. ("Some say she killed herself. She disappeared.")

Finally, there was the tradition that surrounded the taking of raw opium: it was the way, in that part of the land, that young women who had disgraced themselves in the eyes of their families took leave of the world. It was also, of course, the way of unhappy wives and slave girls. But since the Third Girl was neither wife nor slave, the significance of her departure—to Tear Drop and Helen and Old Koo and to whoever else should finally hear "the truth"—could not but be apparent. This, quite in spite of all the wide gestures of love and forgiveness.

The House of Koo was not without news of the impending funeral. Madame had had her informers; Old Koo had had his. They had also had reports upon the queer temper of the day and the even queerer behavior of the troops. They had been given details upon the West Gate affair. They were assured there were no rumors that the authenticity of the corpse had been disputed. Old Koo pretended to be impatient, but the truth was that reaction had set in and he was rather frightened over what he had done and over what was (or was not) happening. . . . He knew perfectly well that Ma had not been able to get those troops to fire. The comforting thought that the peasants were not armed came to him again and again. Of course, Ma would not—never—allow the funeral. And yet the thing seemed to be assuming rather ominous proportions. And frankly, the thought of the funeral gave Old Koo the quivers.

Madame seemed less perturbed, although she did check with the steward about the cordon of guards that was to be thrown about the House. She seemed, even, to view it with favor—as macabrely appropriate to her own plan—as, indeed, the crowning touch, if only the timing could be worked out. But since she had already given Helen the powders, the chances had to remain one out of three. . . . She called in two of the four servants Old Koo had used and told them that should the funeral take place, they should attend, if they would be so good, and she assigned to them a task that they were to carry out. . . .

Night came and outside the House of Koo all was yet quiet. Within, the women relatives had returned to their respective courts where they would begin their endless speculations about *her* and begin to rediscover old jealousies and half-forgotten but most revealing insights into her character. In one court a servant was prevailed upon to sing "The Song of the Third Koo Girl."

Tear Drop and her assistants were clearing away the tea things and Helen had just said they ought to begin to think about the evening meal when Old Koo appeared with six servants in his wake. The servants were bearing the most elaborate dishes of food imaginable—sweet-sour pork, cold cut abalone, pickled mushrooms, a whole roast duck, chestnut soup, and a dozen sauces.

"Father," Helen laughed, when she was examining them, "you will set up a combustion in her poor stomach!"

Old Koo fanned himself and said it was very hot. He stole anxious glances at his third daughter.

"My dear," he said two or three times but never could finish his sentences.

Leila looked at him only once—a long, tender look. She said, "Do you remember when I learned to count? I have thought of it."

He left, after that.

Leila barely noticed the food. Helen had no appetite, either. Because there seemed to be nothing to say and because a sense of utter desolation was getting the best of her, Helen suggested they make ready for bed. She rearranged the objects on the chest a dozen times while Tear Drop was in the bathroom with Leila. She heard the water running for the bath, heard the almost steady splash-splash of it, heard the water running out, but did not hear a single word pass between the two. She turned down the bed.

When they came out, Helen told Tear Drop that she might find something that needed doing in the outer room. Tear Drop bowed and left.

"Get in bed," she said to Leila. "You will have to sleep for a hundred years, you know, to catch up."

But Leila was more preoccupied than docile. There was a fixed stare about her eyes, a jerkiness about her movements, and she would ask the time repeatedly.

Helen's fear became a fear of the night and an in-turned passion—a fear that the sleeping powder was not potent enough. She patted the bed. "Come, sweet," she said. "Do you think you can sleep?"

"No," Leila said.

"Come on," Helen said.

Leila lay down but could not seem to keep her legs still.

"Even revenge can lose its meaning," Leila said. "I do not ask why *she* came this afternoon and pretended to forgive me and welcome me back to the family's bosom. I do not care."

"Good," Helen said. "For awhile, you must not care about anything."

Leila sat up.

"Lie back down," Helen said. "Your talk about revenge, *siau-mei* . . . This morning you said you thought that the way Mother had arranged the outer room—with the peanuts and the picture—was a form of revenge. It may be merely her way of expressing her terms of forgiveness. Have you thought of that? Without using words—she very seldom uses words—she may be saying that you will only be truly forgiven and taken back if you will agree to conform to the family's rules and ideals in the way you did before you ran away. In that case, she is leaving the choice open to you and it isn't revenge at all."

Helen was surprised and pleased with her analysis. She had meant it—invented it, really—only because she felt such a need for calming Leila. But the more she thought about it, the more plausible it seemed. It might even explain Tear Drop. But there! She had been wasting her breath— Leila had not been listening.

Helen felt her own helplessness; admitted, now, the strangeness that was between them. . . . There was nothing she could do. She could not, under any circumstances, invent a make-believe world for Leila as she did for Little Dog.

She said, "Your duty tonight is to sleep. And I have a sleeping powder here that will help to start you off."

Leila said, "Tell Little Dog . . ."

"Tell him?"

"Tell him there isn't any password."

For a moment they stared at each other. Then Helen took one of the packets out of her purse and reached for the tumbler of water that she had earlier placed on the table. "Take this," she said. "Sit up a little. . . . Tomorrow we can decide whatever needs deciding."

"Tomorrow?" Leila said, sitting up. She held out her hand for the packet that Helen had opened, creased it once down the middle, raised it to her mouth and shook the powder into it. She took the tumbler from Helen and drank. "Ugh!" she said, shuddering. "That's bitter enough." She lay back.

"I will just sit with you for awhile," Helen said, going about the room and turning off the lights.

"You're sweet," Leila said in a more normal voice, "but you don't need to do that."

Helen found her chair and sat down. "I am not sweet," she said. "I really don't know what I am."

II

The moon had not yet risen. The silence was intense. It was very dark. She could make out the shadow forms of furniture but nothing more. She recrossed the room, slipped around the screen into her bedroom, cautiously approached a chest, and opened it. Her hands—working fast—hunted through the contents but came upon only silks. She tried the second chest with no better luck. She thought, this will not do, I must take the chance, I must get hold of some of Tear Drop's.

Again she crossed the room and passed around the screen. In the second room she paused. She went to the easel and groped for the picture of the lotus blossom. Finding it she tore it, once, from top to bottom and dropped the two pieces to the floor. She went to the door, then, that led to the court. Tear Drop's room was adjoining—she might have entered it from within but she preferred the outside entrance. Tear Drop, if she remembered correctly, was a light sleeper and if she woke her, it would be as well to be able to run.

She took her time about opening the door which would surely squeak. At last she had it enough ajar to slip through it. She looked briefly up at the stars which seemed small and cold and stepped forward. Immediately she sensed someone was there and froze.

"Who is it?" she said, dropping her right hand to her hip, backing up.

"Do not be angry," the person whispered. "It is only I."

"Come here," she said, swinging around. The voice was close and to her right.

"Please . . . It is only a maid."

"Then what are you doing here like the midnight thief?" she said in a tone that was lower than a whisper. "Do you want Madame to catch you? Be off."

"I was merely . . . That is . . ."

"Come. Out with it."

"I— I am merely taking Tear Drop's place and keeping watch."

"Where is Tear Drop?" she said more gently, for she was now able to make out the small shadowy form.

"She—she is asleep. We take turns, you see."

Something, some hesitation, made her persist. If Tear Drop were not around, it would be the greatest blessing. "Do not be afraid," she said. "I am sorry I spoke so roughly. Tell me. Is Tear Drop not in her bed over there?"

"No," the little maid said softly. "That is, she will fry me in oil if she hears I told, but the fact of it is that she has been sleeping with your fourth brother for quite some time. Tonight he was in a depressed state and insisted she come to his bed. She asked whether I would see to your wants for awhile and I said that I would . . . But I hope . . . That is, I solemnly promised I would not tell."

Leila smiled. "Never fear, little maid, that I would betray your secret. Do I remember you? How long have you been in this house?"

"For five years I have served here, though they still call me 'Sin le-ke' ('Newly Come'). You would not remember anyone so lowly as I, oh Third Young Mistress, but I used to sweep your court. And I—I have followed your career." Then when she added, as though it explained everything, "It was I who remembered about the peanuts," Leila reached a decision.

She said, "I remember you—how you used to pause after each stroke of your broom and consider the clouds that were drifting into heaps or the birds that were singing. . . . I wondered if you were a poet. And I thought I would sometime paint you in a dreamy stance you had."

"A poet!" The little maid laughed. "A lazy, lazy maid, the others say."

"Shhh," Leila said. "If I were in trouble, would you be willing to help me?"

"I would die for you," the little maid answered at once.

"It is nothing so poetic as that," Leila said. "But it is necessary that I secretly leave this place and I cannot go out into the streets, at night, in silks. Do you think you could find the clothes that I came in? Would you help me in that?"

"But, Mistress, those clothes were burned. And as for your leaving, how can you do that? All the gates are triple locked and bolted. No one can bribe Lao Liang. Why, as of today, no one of us is even allowed in the front courts. How can you leave?"

"In the work I was in," the girl said, "there was the opportunity to learn many things. Do not fret yourself over what is my concern. Only help me to locate some clothes that are made of coarse blue-cotton cloth—of the kind that were burned. Can you do that?"

"Oh dear," the little maid said. "I think that dying for you would be easier, after all. Where *should* I find them? In this house even the lowest amah wears a better grade. . . . But, wait! I still have the suit of clothes I came here in—five years ago. My family are country people and the stuff of that suit is hand loomed and rough enough. The trousers would be too short, though."

"Never mind," she said. She had been thinking ahead in leaps and bounds. "Go after them. Do not forget some cloth shoes. And bring me a small knife—the smallest you can find, with a narrow, pointed blade. A clasp knife would be the best. Also, if you find it possible, a long stout rope. Do not bother with one that is less than twenty feet in length and do not waste your time hunting for it—I can get along without."

"The clothes—a knife—a rope," the little maid said, much baffled. "Anything else?"

"As if they were not enough," she said. "But yes, there is still something more, if you can carry it. Do not make two trips. I have taken a sleeping powder and I may be more groggy than I realize. If you can get it without attracting attention, I should like a pot of very strong tea."

"I will try," the little maid said.

"Then, go," Leila said. Using the old proverb, she added, " 'Be as swift as the wind and as silent as the tomb.' If any should see you passing and question you, what will you say?"

"That I am carrying clothes and tea to my sister-maid, Ching-mei, who is sick. She is, in fact. The rope, if I get it, I will conceal."

"Good," Leila said. "The only thing better would be if you were not seen."

"I understand," the little maid said. She glided across the court and was gone.

Leila went back to the bedroom. She stood for a moment, thinking. What had she forgotten? And what if the trick with the knife did not work? She went in the bathroom, turned on the light, then pulled the connecting door closed except for a crack that made enough light for her to see by but not enough, she hoped, to be seen from the court. She took off her robe and nightdress. She had forgot about underclothes. There were no cotton ones in the chests, she knew. It did not matter—no one would be undressing her. She found some that were silk and put them on. What else should she do? She sat down on the edge of the bed and took her head in her hands. She did not know how long she had sat, in a semi-stupor, before she heard the maid stumble over something in the outer room. She went to meet her.

"I was not seen," the little maid said breathlessly. "Not by anyone, I think. I spilled a part of the tea, though."

"Good for you," she said, taking the pot from her and setting it on top of the chest. "Spilled tea is certainly the least of our worries."

The maid dropped the clothes on a chair. "I found a rope," she said, "in the storage room. Will it do, do you suppose? Shall I help you dress? I wonder if the trousers will fit? Let me pour the tea."

"The rope is excellent, I am sure," Leila said. "Now, we shall see about these clothes." She picked up the trousers and put them on. The maid was feeling around for something that would do for a cup. She found the tumbler and filled it.

"Will you drink?" she said.

"Thank you," Leila said. "I need something to hold these up." She indicated the trousers which were indeed very short and tight in the crotch but otherwise falling off.

"Oh," the little maid said, "I brought you a girdle. . . . Here it is." She handed it to her.

Leila secured it around her waist.

"Why are you leaving?" the little maid asked.

"Because I want too much to stay," Leila said, "perhaps."

"But I do not understand. I am confused. And you are sick, too, are you not? Somewhat deranged? Perhaps . . ." She caught herself up short. "Oh, I wonder . . ."

"You wonder whether you *ought* to help me if my going is a part of my derangement? Hand me the jacket, will you?"

The maid held it out. "I cannot see well," she said. "But it is too big, isn't it? Oh, I know why. Because you are so thin."

"It will do," Leila said.

"Please, allow me to button it while you drink your tea."

"All right," Leila said. She drank the tea in quick, hard swallows.

The little maid said, "It was rude of me to speak of—of your . . . I did not mean— If you are mad, I could only wish . . ."

"Of course."

Then, shyly, the maid said, "Wherever it is you are going, will you—that is, could you have any use for a lazy maid?"

"No," Leila said. "Where I am going there are no masters and no servants, little one. But on this night you have already done me enough service to last my lifetime."

"But . . ."

Leila put down the tumbler. "Did you happen to think about socks?"

"No!"

"Never mind. I can do without. The shoes, now."

She put them on. "These fit," she said.

"That means our feet match!" the little maid said, much delighted.

Leila looked sternly at her. She said, "When I am gone, they will question you. Have you thought about that?"

"Y-yes and no," the little maid stammered.

"Has it occurred to you that Tear Drop will pin the blame for my escape on you? And—in that case—that the absence of these clothes of yours would most surely be discovered?"

"W-e-l-l," the little maid said.

"Or have you once considered what then would happen—that you would be disgraced and dismissed? Hand me that knife I asked you for."

The little maid fumbled through her pockets. "This is the best I could find," she said.

Leila took it. She went over to the toilet table and dropped to her knees in front of it and pulled the jewel box toward her. "Open that bathroom door just a crack more," she said. The maid did so. The lock would have been easy enough to break but Leila did not wish to break it. She inserted the tip of the blade of the knife into the lock and gave a short, quick twist to the right. The lock snapped open. She raised the lid.

The little maid was dumbfounded. "Only thieves can do that!" she said.

"I am a thief," Leila said, staring down at the jewels that were dully glittering. "The sapphire and diamond earrings should do. She has always coveted those." She lifted them out. Then she closed the box and snapped the lock shut. "There," she said. There was no evidence that it had been tampered with. There was only one set of keys and they were in Tear Drop's possession. She stood up. "Go out to the court and make sure that no one comes," she said.

When the maid had gone, Leila put the small knife in her pocket. She emptied the rest of the tea into the tumbler and drank it off. Tear Drop could have brought her the tea. She left the pot where it was. She looked carefully around the room, picked up the rope from the chair, turned off the bathroom light, waited for her eyes to adjust to the dark, and slipped out.

In the court the little maid signaled to her that all was well.

"I still have a piece of business to attend to," Leila said. "You keep watch at the moongate. Should someone come, meow like Tear Drop's cat. Wait for me there."

She went to Tear Drop's room and opened the door. She felt about until she came upon a pigskin trunk and opened that. Thank God she had already moved it from Andrew's court. In the trunk she found a padded winter garment. She ran her fingers along the seams until she came to a corner. This she split the smallest fraction with her knife and stuffed the two earrings in. She pushed them into the opposite corner and refolded the garment. Her hands, then, continued to explore until they touched a particular grade of cotton that was far finer than the clothes she was wearing but yet the coarsest she had felt of those in the trunk. Being careful not to muss the arrangement of the rest of the garments, Leila took out jacket and trousers and made them into a bundle, which she took under her arm with the rope. She went out to the court again. At the moongate, she stopped.

"Where are you?" she whispered.

"In front of your nose."

"I have never seen such darkness," she said. "My nose must be the size of a signpost."

The maid giggled—a half-hysterical sound.

"You must be quiet," Leila said. "I am going, now, to the library court where the old gingko tree grows close to the wall. You must not follow me. . . . Indeed, this is what you must do. Return to your quarters. If Tear Drop stays with my brother, my absence may not be noticed until morning. You will say that after my sister left and after Tear Drop left, you sat about for an hour. Then, since it was growing chilly and since I seemed to be fast asleep and since Tear Drop neither offered you her bed nor left you with any very definite instructions, you returned to your place. Tear Drop is the first in authority and my father will not be pleased that she took her duties so lightly. I have also made very sure that suspicion will be cast her way."

"But—but why?" the little maid said. "She did give me all kinds of instructions. Besides, I would be most happy to take the blame. I . . ."

"I am sure you would," she said. "But I will not allow it. . . . I have bribed Tear Drop to look the other way, do you see, and to procure me a rope and a suit of her clothes to leave in."

"But why? It is not fair. I would much rather . . ."

"Why? We have a very old grudge to settle between us. She will understand, never fear, that it is I who have framed her. That is what I would have her finally to understand. And there is no disgrace that can undo her as it might you. She is made like the eel."

But the little maid was on the verge of tears.

Leila touched her shoulder. "Do you want to deprive me of my last word with her?"

"Oh, no," the little maid said. "You do not understand. It is only that I have always longed to suffer nobly for some great, historic cause. Why can it not be for you?"

"Because," Leila said with a smile, "I have turned out to

be only a lost and mistaken cause and think how disillusioned you would be. . . . But time passes. Should any question ever come up concerning your suit of clothes—which I think it will not, since there is a second suit that's missing—you must say that you sold them to a peddler, last New Year's, to pay a bit of a debt. Now . . ." She had started to say "Good-bye" when she realized that after all of this planning and procuring and arranging, she did not have Huan-li's letter! Of course, she didn't. The letter had been in her clothes. It was hard for her to believe that she was either that groggy or stupid or both.

"Dear God," she muttered.

"What is it?" the maid asked.

She thought wearily: to forget the point, to make the most elaborate plans around exactly what was forgotten! Obviously, she could not deliver a letter if she did not have it. All day, even in her sleep, she had heard the soldiers marching. It was important to her to deliver the letter. Like tearing the picture in two. She couldn't send the dead any messages but she could—she might have carried the message that the dead had left—left over as she was, without death as she was, caught in this house with these living ghosts whom she loved. But the letter was lost.

"Are you sure they were burned?" she said.

"What?" the little maid said. "What ails you? Have you developed a pain?"

"The clothes—my clothes. Could you swear they were burned?"

"Why, yes," the little maid said. "I told you that. Really, after we have gone to all this trouble to get you more!"

"There was a letter," she said.

"A letter?" the little maid said. "A letter?"

"Yes—a letter," Leila said, turning away.

"A letter," the little maid murmured. "Tear Drop examined the contents. There was not any . . . What did the letter look like?"

"What does it matter?"

"Well, but . . ." Suddenly the little maid was patting herself, feeling through her pockets at a rapid rate. "Was it a queer-looking letter? Was it written on various scraps of paper? Was it . . ." The little maid pulled something out. "Could this be it?"

Leila turned around. She put out her shaking hand. The little maid laid the scraps of paper on her palm. Her fingers closed around them. She said, "I . . . You will have to understand that I do not know the words with which to thank you."

"But don't thank me," the little maid said. "I don't know why you should since you will not let me take the blame."

"Well, go then," Leila said, "without my thanks but, if it is all the same to you, with a corner of my heart. Go. I will wait here until you shall have had the time to get safe to your place. Good-bye."

"You will not come back? Will I never see you again? Oh, take me with you. Please!"

"I cannot. And there is no more time. Go, little one."

The little maid went.

III

She shifted her rope and bundle from one arm to the other. She used the passages as much as she could and kept close to the walls. Twice she stumbled. Once she fell over a stone bench. Once she heard someone call out. Each time she froze and waited, knowing from experience the extreme advantage of waiting. At last, she reached the library court. She flattened herself against one side of the gate and inched around it until she had a view of the library itself. No one was there.

She crossed the court. She and Andrew had used to climb the ginkgo tree when they were children. They would drop from a particular limb onto the wall and there, flat on their stomachs, they would throw small rocks down on passers-by. It was then their father had ordered broken pieces of glass cemented into the top of the wall—not to discourage thieves, he said, but his children.

Leila knew the tree well—at least, she once had. When she reached it, she slipped the coil of rope over her left shoulder and fitted the bundle of Tear Drop's clothes under it. The tree rustled and rattled and made a gigantic noise as she climbed. It was a slow and awkward business, what with the rope catching at branches and the bundle constantly slipping down. Either her memory was not as good as she had supposed or else she was too big to fit it—she was reaching for branches that were not there and bumping head-on into others.

When she was as high as the wall, she stopped. Leaning out, and here her increased height was her advantage, she rested the bundle on the wall's top. Good. Until now she had thought of the bundle as a plain nuisance, designed to hinder her progress, but she could use it to step down on and thus save the trouble about the spears of glass. Bracing herself, she took the rope, girdled it around the tree's trunk and slid it down until it was resting in the crotch of one of the larger limbs and could slide down no further. She tied a slip knot. Then, still holding to the rope, she backed out a short way on the limb, dangled one foot below her and groped with it until she located the bundle and stepped gingerly down on it. She heard the glass tinkle and crunch and felt it flatten out beneath her weight. She listened. Fantastic that no one else was hearing all of this noise! She brought her other foot down. Fortunately, the glass did not cut through the heavy cloth soles of her shoes to her feet.

It was ink dark. Her back was to the cobblestoned alley below. She took the rope in both hands, now, and swung out. Throwing her weight to her feet and keeping them flat to the wall, she started down. She reached up for the bundle and dropped it. Then, hand over hand, foot over foot, she went on. It was almost too easy. She was down before she knew it. Once there, she had difficulty finding her bundle. She was squatting and feeling around for it when she heard voices at the south end of the alley, to which the library court was very near. At first, she could not distinguish words but then she heard someone say, "Do not show your lights. . . . These will stay here. You men! Go to the other end of this alley. Each approach of the Koo House is to be guarded. Quite, now. Proceed."

She had decided to let the bundle go. It was essential she beat the ones who were heading toward her to the north end. Just as she started out she stumbled over it. She scooped it up. She felt about frantically for a stone but could not find one. She remembered her knife. She took it out and threw it as hard as she could in the opposite direction from the one she was taking. It fell with a clack to the cobblestones. The men swung about.

"Halt!" one shouted. "Who goes there?"

She crouched and noiselessly ran. She gained the corner before they turned and started after her. They had their flashlights on and their guns in hand but she knew the terrain better than they did and by keeping to the alleys, she soon lost them.

She paused and tried to shake loose the bits of glass that were stuck in her bundle. Scooping it up, as she had, she had scratched and cut her arm and the palm of her hand.

Her pursuers were shaken off, her panting had subsided. She had encountered no soldiers—there were no soldiers about! She saw the shadowy forms of people in doorways and against the walls of houses. But no soldiers . . . What was the meaning of this? How quiet it was!

. . . She had left the House of Koo with its ghosts, which was an achievement. She would deliver the letter, next. She looked up at the far-off stars and thought it was nice that they had nothing to say to her and she nothing to say to them: so comforting.

She entered Sin-ss-ka Square and started to turn back when she saw it was filled with people. But she paused. She was, in fact, arrested by the scene before her: the square, very dimly lit, filled with the people talking in low voices or not at all and standing only as people do when they have stood for a long time in the same place, for the same purpose. For awhile, she stood still and remote. But then the unreality of the scene, its dreamlike quality, provoked her to remember the shadowy strangeness of the streets she had passed through. . . . *These people should not be here. These people should be in their homes.* . . . Perhaps she had been gone an eternity, that she no longer understood anything. What had happened to the soldiers—and what had gone wrong with the taking-over?

She took a step forward in her bewilderment. Then she heard it, the tail end of a name—". . . Koo Girl."

So. She had not died in the prison yard, as she should have, but had returned, instead, to the spun-silk womb—which news must have traveled. Nor could she hope ever to make it clear to them that she had been forcibly taken. She looked at them—at how close they stood—sensing that they were welded together by the power of the now-soiled name. In their despair revenge would be what they were after. By now they would be saying that she was the one who had invited her father's return, she who had not been true to them. And she, of course, was not to be allowed to walk alone under some indifferent stars or to deliver a letter. Looking at them, she thought she might have told them that always, always her nose had told her they smelled—an aristocrat to the end—one who, in her father's house, had been kneeling. . . . Let it be the end. It would do no good to dwell longer upon what General Ma and her father and his friends were up to—how they were turning the name to their own use, now. She remembered the courier and her own courage. . . . Strange. What was the people's wish—to find her and kill her? Was that what they stood in this huddle about? Let them plan no further; without arms, let them go no nearer to the House of Koo. She accepted—she was at their service.

A woman was looking her over, looking her up and down, looking particularly at her bundle.

"What do you have?" the woman asked. "Stones?"

She took in her breath sharply. "Yes. . . . And you?" She moved in closer to the feeble light, waiting for the act of recognition.

"No stones for me," the woman was saying. "When I have spent my whole life in a kitchen, do you think I would put my faith in stones?" She laughed shortly and drew from her sleeve a wicked-looking implement.

"What is that?"

"A meat cleaver. And do not imagine I cannot use it."

She said, "My imagination is fertile. I can see you using it."

"Ai!" said the woman. "And with pleasure, you can believe me."

"I believe you."

"But come," said the woman. "Do you have any definite

news? Have you heard when they will enter this square with her?"

"Was that the plan?" she asked.

"Why, of course," said the woman. "You do not suppose they would skirt this square, do you, with its platforms and whipping posts. Not hardly." She stood on one foot and scratched her ankle with the other. "Oh, they will be here. Have patience, that is what I say. You know how an ordinary funeral can drag itself out—there is no telling about our Third Koo Girl's."

"No telling at all," the girl said, after a pause. And then she said, "But since I have friends I promised to meet, I ought to go about finding them. Greetings, woman."

"Greetings," the woman said.

Under her eyes, the girl started off—almost without balance—drifting from group to group.

"*They will carry torches.*"

". . . *our Third Koo Girl.*"

"*We hold the West Gate, I tell you, and it is what we shall use.*"

"*We will carry her to the hills.*"

". . . *Let them try it, that is all.*"

"*I will never forget the time I saw her. Tall she was and* . . ."

". . . *the Girl.*"

She stopped in one of the doorways and leaned her head against a cool wall. Pride or shame, joy or sorrow. She put no name to her emotion, as she leaned there. . . . She submitted. Gently she closed her eyes and her bundle dangled loose from her hands. She could have slept on her feet, leaning there, for her breathing was gentle and her heart beat only in the farthest regions of her body, remote from her center. Leaning over, leaning sidewise, she retched. A man spoke to her. "Woman, are you ill?"

"It is only that I live too long," she said, speaking gently.

"Yet your voice is young," the man said. "Perhaps, instead, you have stood too long. We all stand, this day. Now, I. I do not retch but I have the piles."

"A hindrance," she murmured.

"Indeed! You are feeling better, I trust, after your riddance?"

"Ai," she said. Then, half-averting her face, "Did you ever see the Third Koo Girl?"

"Once," he said, "at a meeting."

"I hold her in my heart," she said.

"And I. And do we all."

She said, "And how have you heard she died?"

"Why, in the prison, of course."

"Is that how it is spoken?" she asked.

"How else?"

"Well, but suppose," she said, "that *they* should say she had not? Suppose that *they* should say she had left that prison for her father's house?"

"Ha!" said the man. "Let them say what they like—traitors, with their traitors' filth. Did we not see her fall? You retch and I have my piles. We bury her tonight."

"Ai," she said. "We carry her in the hour of her death. . . . Like a child in the womb, I carry her. Heavy am I, with her."

"Woman," he said. "Those are woman's feelings. A man's are loftier—they are higher up."

"May Buddha relieve you of your lofty piles," she said, smiling faintly, leaving the doorway, and moving on. The low sound of the man's laughter followed her, for a moment, sweetly.

But that bitter drug she had taken was gaining on her, she felt, as she made her way slowly to the other end of the square. . . . Stones, talk of the West Gate, the name passing from one to the next. Her mind was not too clouded to receive the people's mood. She had become expert at that. Indeed, it fastened tenaciously on her mind as she had learned to let it do, for she knew well the leader's secret that the leader must be the most sensitive and articulate of followers.

She went to stand by a different wall. Considered, somewhat tediously and laboriously, plots and counter plots. Who fostered? Who opposed? Whose lie was this and how had it been achieved? Plots and counter plots—but she had no way of knowing. Whatever was back of it, they needed her dead to cover the death of their cause. Tonight they would make this funeral and nobody had better try to stop them, she thought with a mixture of pride and grief. Tonight, the counterrevolutionists were right to leave them alone—if they were. If they were not, not even she, with her telltale body, could intervene. Oh, she might break up the funeral by some bold and dramatic gesture, but what she might start in its stead, she shuddered to think of. No power could send them home tonight.

She could lay down the name. It was time. She was no longer responsible for it. It was theirs. She gave it to them freely—it had been so much too much for her. They were the ones who had first created it. Their lie was beautiful. She thanked them for it. She was nothing, any more, and the peace of that was overwhelming. She tried the words in her mouth, "The Third Koo Girl is dead." Very moving, very beautiful.

She turned, after one last look about her, and left the square by way of a narrow street. Behind her some torches were rubbing the midnight sky but she did not look back.

IV

Christopher Blair had left the blacksmith shop, asking himself no questions, well aware that questions would have broken his decision down. He had left it at ten o'clock, with the single, overpowering feeling that he could no longer stay in it. . . . There were limits to everything and there were the limits that the blacksmith shop imposed on his spirit. Suppose he could not, after all, allow the day to culminate without him.

He had left the shop quietly, hoping that his servant would not hear him, sure that he had, sure that now he was one of these shadows not three yards from him. The street where he had chosen to wait was lined with darker and lighter and shorter and longer shadows, merging into each other and into the darkness. They had been standing so long that it was like a dream—most illogical, most unreal.

It was midnight when the procession turned into the street. And as either a funeral procession or as a popular demonstration, it was queer. No bands, no exploding firecrackers, no banner carriers, no shouting of slogans, no singing or weeping or loud wailing or yelling. The point of any Chinese funeral was to make a great and resounding noise. It was as if the people, having held themselves in check all day, found themselves still held in, fettered by the day's queer mood. The sight that met Blair's eyes was flat and in no way impressive. There was just the coffin and the people walking with their torches that were crazily bobbing. It was so quiet that Blair could hear the torches spitting.

As the procession came on, the shadows, one by one, quit the doorways and fell in. Blair saw the coffin when it passed. It was made of rough wood and appeared small. It was roped around (as only the coffins of the poor are done) with two sets of rope which were made fast to a single carrying pole. Four men, who looked like farmers, were the bearers. The coffin pitched and rocked in its ropes.

Blair roused himself as if from sleep and joined those who brought up the rear. There was no talking. He might almost believe that he—and everyone else—was sleep-walking. He did not know how long he had been walking when he became aware of the sound of their padding sandaled feet, in concert. He listened. Then he did not listen because it was so steady and so hushed that it was like the sound of the ocean that cannot be actively listened to for very long. It is just there, whether or not one listens—an insidious sound, slowly and imperceptibly swelling. There were no soldiers anywhere.

In the darkness, in the torchlight that so unevenly smeared the darkness, the faces of the people seemed to swim. Yellow faces in yellow light. They swam, floating like balloons around him, detached, with nothing between them and their padding feet. The faces were suffering. They were afflicted.

He was not at the rear of the procession any more but toward the front. How still it was, how desolate. The faces had had their tongues cut out at the roots. Even the sound of their feet was the echo of their silence. City of narrow streets. City of the dead. Phantoms walk and not even the dogs come out. A corpse led them, rocking in its ropes.

The sound of their feet became louder and slowly louder and louder until they were like the tide rolling in upon some eroded, lonely beach.

They surged through Sin-ss-ka Square, gathering up shadows. For it was necessary to suppose that the people were shadows. They took a turn and a second turn, heading west.

Christopher Blair stumbled. He was praying. "Oh God, oh Jesus Christ, oh Buddha, don't let it happen. Save us or kill us now."

They entered a long and silent street and came to a long, silent wall that was on their right. They slowed. The rushing, roaring sound of their silence fell in fearfully upon itself, as if washing and sucking at the wall. It was the Koo Family wall. Ahead, locked and barred, were the Koo Family gates.

A man near Christopher Blair said, "Hold this!"

His thin voice scraped across a giant nerve. He thrust his torch upon some other. In the torchlight they saw him reach in his garments and take out a smooth, round stone. He crouched and heaved it. It cleared the wall. There was a short and flickering scream that instantly ceased.

The man laughed. The people laughed.

"Sons of bleeding whores!" they yelled.

"Sucking pigs!" they yelled.

"Traitors!"

"Swine!"

Another stone arced through the nervous torchlight. The people screamed and pushed. The ones who were nearest beat on the wall with their fists, they knocked their own heads against the wall and struck their own cheeks with their flat hands.

"Let us kill the swine."

A man heaved his lighted torch that raced through the dark and threw out sparks but fell short of the wall. Others tried it.

"Kill, kill," they cried.

"Bash in the gates!"

They beat against the gates.

"Climb the wall!"

Ones were boosted up.

Christopher Blair was pushed to his knees. Someone pulled him up and said, "Master, it is time to leave."

"Leave me alone!" Christopher Blair replied.

And ahead a rocket, so bright it was dazzling, lifted slowly up to hang suspended in the black sky. Blair saw it. Instantly, there was gunfire in the offing. "That will be at the West Gate," he muttered, staring up at the rocket that was already fizzling. The next instant soldiers came pouring into the mouth of the street.

"There!" Blair shouted. "There!"

A shot whined over their heads. A whole splatter of shots.

"Turn back!" Blair yelled.

But there was no turning back. He heard the firing from their rear. They were trapped. It was too late and it had always been too late.

"The troops," the people all but chanted. They went to meet them. They threw stones. They produced axes and hoes and iron rakes. Those with the coffin held it protectively, now, shielding it, instead of themselves. Shots stuttered through the crazy torch-yellow dark. On all sides men were screaming and falling.

"Charge! Advance!"

Time after time the people regrouped and clumps of them with stone and torch and rake would charge the gray-coated soldiers with the guns.

"Break it up!" the soldiers yelled.

"Advance!" cried the people, rushing the soldiers.

A hand grenade was thrown. They were cut down like blades of grass in a field.

"Advance!"

Blair realized his servant was hanging around his neck, choking the breath out of him.

"Get off me!" Blair said.

"Advance!"

The people rushed past, pulling him on, while his servant pulled him back. Somebody hit him over the head with a burnt-out torch. He staggered but could not possibly have fallen. Bodies wedged him in on every side and for the moment that his mind went blank he saw the long, silent wall and heard the vomiting and grunting and panting and choking and thrashed and floundered back to consciousness where it was all around him, especially the choking which accompanied their sobs.

"I am still here," he heard his servant say.

A second grenade was thrown.

"Charge!"

"I am hit!" cried one of the coffin bearers.

Men fought to take his place. But one who got through seemed to be holding a bucket in his hands. He raised it high above the coffin and turned it upside down. Another pushed through and did the same. Blair was too dizzy, too far gone to wonder what they were doing—but he heard the people scream.

"It's kerosene!"

"Yellow dogs of traitors!"

They turned to tear the two men limb from limb but there was such a crush that there was no telling which were guilty. They seized and killed the two or three that seemed most likely before they turned and charged.

At any moment one of the flying torches would surely strike the coffin.

But it was not a torch that hit the coffin—it was a grenade. There was an explosion. Flames leapt into the air. The coffin divided into twenty pieces. Those who had held it were likewise gone. Then the silence came over the people as suddenly as it had left them. They stood there. And suddenly there were great gaps among them and there did not seem to be so many people. The soldiers held their fire.

The silence, this time, did not last long. It was broken

by the moans of the wounded. Christopher Blair's servant grasped his arm firmly and whispered, "Come away."

Blair freed himself. "Can't you leave me alone?"

He groped and picked his way in the direction of the nearest moan.

But the soldiers were moving in, jabbing with bayonets or the butt ends of their guns and waving their flashlights in tight, jerky circles.

"Be off, be off!" they said, stepping on the dead, as they came, stepping on the wounded whose moans changed to screams.

Some of the people hoisted wounded relatives to their backs before they went. Some of them who had lost track of their relatives called them in hoarse voices. But for the most part the people scuttled off, willy nilly, like rats. The wounded who were able dragged themselves or crawled but were often knocked over or walked upon.

Christopher Blair had picked up a torch that someone had dropped and was trying to prop it against a stone.

"Go!" he was saying to his servant. "Go after my bag!" A soldier came up from behind and nudged him in the ribs.

"Be off, now."

"I am a doctor," Blair said. "I am needed."

"A doctor?" the soldier said musingly. In his mind doctors were associated with the fine art of bleeding and with the prescribing of poultices and herbs—a fancy of the rich. "Then what are you doing here?"

He prodded again, questioningly, with the butt end of his gun.

"Master," Mei-kung, the servant, said. "You can see there is no use in this. Are you forgetting you have no hospital and no supplies? What do you imagine that you are doing? What good would your bag be? Come along."

Blair had the torch propped and was looking into the

singed, blank face of a woman. . . . Her arm was off directly above the elbow. He ripped the tail off his jacket, ripped it into two strips.

But the soldier's patience was wearing thin. "Do I use my bayonet?" he asked.

"*O-mi-to-va,*" said the woman. And died.

Mei-kung, the servant, took the impatient soldier aside and put a bribe in his hand and some words in his ear.

The people had scuttled away, and the moans and screams of the wounded were breaking off or ending in gurgles. That was because the soldiers were making the rounds with their flashlights and bayonets, shining their lights and thrusting their bayonets. Some were angry and directed their thrusts into bellies and groins—slowly and with a twisting motion. "You thought us afraid to shoot, did you?" But others made their thrusts not unkindly but because it was less trouble, the only thing to do if the relatives did not care for their own. One skinny runt of a soldier said, each time, "Buddha have mercy, Kang-ying have mercy."

And it was all over before Blair could prop his torch a second time.

"Now, will you come away?" said the servant. The soldier was by his side.

"Yes," Christopher Blair said, "I will."

V

She had no clear idea how long she had been walking or where. Off and on, she remembered that the rocket had risen to hang like a jewel in the sky. She remembered the firing. Later, people had come hurrying down the street where she was—some moaning, some dragging others, scuttling along, looking nowhere.

It was still later now, with the dark labyrinth of narrow streets empty even of shadows. She was feverish and confused and forgetful. Often she thought that the revolution was in the future, that she was still in Canton, dancing the foxtrot and living in a cubist flat. Freedom was whether or not to bob the hair.

If only she could stop walking! Her mind walked backwards, bright as day. She was a baby sitting in her father's lap, learning to count by counting his rolls of fat, getting shaken up by his laughter. "Father, you are funny and fat." She was stroking a cross-eyed cat. "I love you, cat." She was standing in front of a clock at Vassar. "What time is it?" Huan-li said, "I itch so terribly."

She reached her summing up: I love you, cat. . . . Mother, my feet are very big. Mother, I want to live.

"Have you seen the Third Koo Girl?" she asked loudly. Her voice echoed up and down the street.

"I am dying!" she said loudly.

"Dy-ing . . . ing," echoed up and down the street.

She changed her street. She said, "Tear Drop, *wretched* slave, it is for you I fought." Her ears began to yammer, her teeth to chatter.

She said, "I had no idea I was composed of so many noisy parts."

A voice said, "Woman, help!"

And before her, something hunched into a curious shape.

"Woman, I am hurt."

She bent over. "And I am dying," she whispered, sitting down beside it and seeing it to be a soldier.

"It is my head," the soldier said. "They threw this stone at my head and at first I was merely dizzy a bit, but now I cannot walk."

She hugged her bundle and said, "I saw the rocket go up."

"Ai," the soldier said, "that was our sign and we charged them. But they must charge us, with their rakes and stones, Buddha grant me my head. It was very crowded and the blood ran. Then the thing exploded and we held our fire."

"Hmm," she said.

"The coffin exploded," he said. "And who was to say if a ten-foot ghost might not step out of those flames? We held our fire."

"Hmm." She rocked back and forth, hugging her bundle.

"All day they had us sweating. We charged the ones who had the stones with guns. It was a lesson we taught."

"There are ten hells," she said, laying aside her bundle and putting her face close to the soldier's face. "And demons. And a ghost that will lay her long hands on you, to haunt."

"But orders are orders," said the soldier, in a good stout voice.

"Where is your gun?" she said. "I will borrow it to kill you with."

"I do not have it," the soldier said. "I lost it, trying to walk."

"A pity," she said.

"Just help me a little, instead," the soldier said. "Just help me to my place and I will put a coin in your hand."

"I told you, I die."

"So you did," the soldier said. "Shall I pray for the safe journey of your soul through the ten hells?"

"No," she said, taking up her bundle and pushing herself up with the help of a wall.

"Shall I pray for my own?"

"No," she said. "Do not pray."

"But I am lonely," he said, after her. "Do not leave me. *O-mi-to-va*. Some thief will come and pick me off."

"Do not pray," she said, walking away, "at all."

A dog howled. Her ears yammered, her teeth chattered. This was it. What happened to the howl after that?

Another street. There was no end to the tangle of them. She fell sprawling over a body. It took her a terrible time to get up.

"Oh, bother," she said. "Damnation." She locked her arms around herself and her bundle.

A watchman came walking toward her, with his lantern over his arm and beating his little gong for the second watch of the morning. He veered to one side when he saw her. But she edged up to him.

"Watchman," she said, putting her face close to his. "Do you see the Third Koo Girl?"

"The Third Koo Girl is dead!" the watchman answered. He hurried on. He looked over his shoulder and then he began to run.

"Damnation," the girl said. Her legs were folding beneath her. She was falling. She was kneeling into her death. Crumpling into a curious shape.

The letter . . . It did not matter—Huan-li's scraps of paper. She could never make it now. Never mind . . . Her bundle (that stupid, stupid bundle) slipped out of her hands. She did not care. But her head found the bundle. Well. She laid her head down on it and instantly she slept.

VI

Whether rat or dog or dream, something waked her, leaving its slimy, cold impress on her. The cobblestones beneath her were slimy and cold. She sat up. The coldness had reached into every cell of her body and brain. Standing up slowly, with her bundle, she thought that delirium and fever were better.

The late moon had risen and hung like something stillborn and deformed in the sky. She got her bearings. She was in the Ki-tsung section. Pu-tang Street was no great distance and Pu-tang Street was the street where the blacksmith shop was. She went slowly, stopping often, avoiding the alleys and walking close to the walls. There seemed to her to be an absolute silence that she did not care to break, absolute emptiness that it was not up to her to fill. She stumbled over no soldiers and no bodies. The moonlight slithered up the ancient cobblestones of the street, always ahead of her. The walls rose straight up on either side.

Before this I was not afraid, she thought. Before this, I was not alone. She was wet with icy sweat.

She reached Pu-tang Street and looked up at the signs, trying to read them. Wang the Little's was hung vertically and not difficult to find. She stopped beneath it. The shop was shuttered and boarded tight. She could not imagine knocking or calling out when a whisper would be too much. She must have waited whole minutes, hoping desperately for the return of her delirium. Finally, after several false tries, she made the contact of closed hand to wood of door.

"Those within!" she called. The echoes jammed her ears. "A—a friend is here to see the one named Bao."

No sooner has she finished than she heard a voice from the other side say, "Go away."

Her hair stiffened at the roots. She trembled. Was someone waiting on the other side of the door merely to tell her that? She looked over her shoulder. She turned and looked up and down the street. Then, as if it helped, she closed her eyes and called out, "I will not go away! I have come to deliver an important message to the one, Bao I-sung, and I will just stand here and knock and call until you have opened!"

"Go and disembowel your mother," said the person within. "No man opens his door this night. Go away."

Instead of answering she turned around and began to knock—steadily, deafeningly. But in the process she dropped her bundle and was just leaning over to pick it up when she heard a bolt shot. The door was opened a crack.

"Now, listen," said the voice. "If indeed you are woman and not devil, pass me this message that is important enough to disturb the dead about. I am the servant of Bao and no business goes to him except through me. Demented hag, hand it to me and for the love of Buddha, be gone."

But at that moment there was a different, deeper voice. "Who is it?"

The door was opened wide. She saw two men, one stocky and short, the other tall. The short one was only half-dressed but the tall one was completely so, in Western style clothes. He held a smoking lantern in his hand. He would be Christopher Blair. Perhaps it was the fault of the hour and the street and the moonlight, that he seemed to stand so still. Unable to speak, like her. The opening of the door, his final act—hers, the knocking and calling out. The servant shuffled his feet and grunted. Christopher Blair raised his lantern up. The light blinded her eyes and she drew back. He jerked the lantern higher.

"Who are you?" The words rang up and down the street.

She trembled. The lantern came down in one long motion.

"If," she said, moving her cold lips, "if you are Christopher Blair, I bring you a message from your friend."

He motioned for her to enter. She stepped over the threshold. The door was slammed.

The servant, who had slammed the door, spoke to her in

a savage whisper. "Give it to me. Can you not see he is in no condition for visitors? Give it to me and depart."

She put her hand to her pocket and touched the letter. She said, "I will give it to him."

He was already walking through the shop. She followed, picking her way. A forge loomed like a wild beast out of the shadows and what looked like broken parts of skeletons hung down from the rafters. In one corner, a boy was stretched out on a bench, asleep and snoring loudly.

"What is the trouble?" someone called timorously from the upper regions.

"No cause for alarm, good Little Wang," she heard the servant call back. "A mixing-up of street and house. It is all settled now."

"You let no stranger in?"

"Oh, no," the servant called back. "Nothing like that."

The boy on the bench kept on snoring.

She followed the way Christopher Blair had taken—out the back door and into a small court. On the other side of the court a door stood open. She could see a section of drably furnished room, with Christopher Blair standing at a table where he had set his lantern down, his back to door and court.

It must be that her nerves had played tricks on her outside: the guilty must always start at the most innocent questions. He had never seen her. As the bearer of Huan-li's letter, she could be anyone—a guard's wife. Well, it was an odd hour for a guard's wife to be calling, but her husband would beat her if he knew she did these little favors for the poor prisoners and the gentleman had said it was most important and naturally he had assured her that Blair Doctor would give her—well, a considerable reward for her not inconsiderable trouble.

She spoke impatiently to herself: "Come, hurry up. One more role. What is that, more or less? Stand with bowed shoulders, be vulgar, and keep your face away from the light."

Absently, she counted seven stars that followed tightly, one after the other, down the sky. She crossed the court, counting her steps as she had counted the stars, and reached the door. The room was very dingy and awry, and sparsely furnished. The bed, perhaps because it was made up at this hour, gave the impression of abandonment.

Christopher Blair's back was still toward her. It occurred to her that while she had been in the court, he had not moved. Leaning in the door, she looked more closely at him. One of his hands was gripping the table edge, the other was flat on the table but bent sharply back at the wrist. The servant's words fled through her mind, "Can you not see he is in no condition for visitors?" She noticed his shoes. They were very dirty and stained with dark patches. His trousers were stained in the same way, with blood.

"Are you . . . Are you wounded?" she said.

"No," he said in a low and unsteady voice. "I have been to a funeral."

She turned away. She took the letter out of her clothes and laid it on a chair. He had straightened up and was staring at her.

"You are . . ."

"Yes," she said. "I am. . . . I could have spared you this."

"I knew you outside," he said.

"I know." She had known. It was a game she had played with herself out in the court. At that moment, she feared damnation and eternity for the first time. She thought, we have to pray—in the end we have to do it. . . . She would hesitate to ask him to help her as far as some canal. She sat down on the chair where she had put the letter down. She was crying. She had not cried in years. He was watching her and his look was stern. Layer after layer of darkness was enveloping her. The room seemed to be walking around—the chairs were walking and the lantern, too. Next she knew she was lying on the bed—conscious that it was his arms that had carried her to it, his arms that had lifted her up and put her down. . . . He was feeding her soup.

"I have lost my bundle," she said.

His look was not so much stern as level.

"There was never the time for us to meet," she said.

"No," he said. "Tell me what happened."

She told him briefly: how she had been carried from the jail to the Koo House, and how she had escaped that House.

"Yet," he said, "you know you were executed. . . . You fell. A wail went up that I was near enough to hear . . . And that funeral was planned around the corpse of the Third Koo Girl."

"I don't understand." She felt impelled, almost, to insist, "I am real."

His look did not release her.

"Did anyone see you during the day?" he asked.

"Of course. Family—servants—lots of people."

"Did anyone follow you here?"

"No."

"Take this."

The spoon clattered against her teeth. She swallowed more of the soup. He was sitting beside her on the bed. . . . She felt it was no accident that she had hunted him out tonight—that the letter had seemed so important for her to deliver to him. "Huan-li's letter is on the chair," she said. It was, she decided, one of those dispensations between heaven and hell, although she was not clear as to what was the dispensation—the letter or their coming together. Her eyes were closing. In her dream love and death were standing side by side in the room. She saw clearly what she had never seen—that love and death were the same—they had the same face and body. Their look was stern.

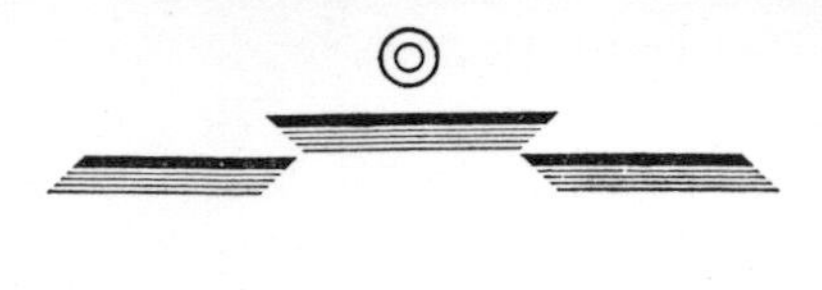

6

I

DAY dawned. And the city was quiet. General Ma moved the great share of his troops out to surrounding villages, as his peace gesture. In Sin-ss-ka Square a few "little Communists" were shot. The people understood. The workers of Wang Widow's Bridge Mill were the first to say that they would go back to work.

And so, by noon, shops were opening. Thugs and beggars (whining their age-old complaints) and venders were about, as well as the women who collected ordure from house to house out of the earthen *kangs*. By late afternoon boats were plying the canals and rickshaws were brought out of go-downs. Housewives haggled in the markets, poor children played shuttlecock in the alleys, fortunetellers and geomancers set up their stalls in temple courts, a few restaurants, teahouses and brothels (those that were assured of protection) opened their doors. . . . If there was any whispering or weeping over lost relatives it was being done in back rooms and rear courts.

The coffinmakers were sorry more bodies had not been indentified and salvaged. They said that considering everything business was exceedingly dull. The priests, too, were disappointed. They claimed that the people were so secretive about their dead that they did not want any fish-head drum beating or masses said.

The lesson was taught, the "quick stroke of the knife" had accomplished its miracle.

Christopher Blair sent Wang the Blacksmith and his family away on an extended visit to some relatives. He paid him so well that Wang the Little could not refuse. Blair explained to him that he wanted the place to himself for awhile, that he was weary of listening to the pounding that Wang did at his forge and was more than willing to pay for some peace and quiet.

It was after Christopher Blair and his servant had seen Wang and his family off. They were still in the shop, with the door to the court closed. The servant took occasion to bang things up and down—he nearly broke an incense pot that was sitting on a shelf.

"You did not serve me in my fourth year in Peking, did you?" Christopher Blair asked.

"No," the servant said, unable to contain his displeasure.

Blair was casual. He lighted a cigarette.

"It was the year I had the scarlet fever," the servant said. "Ah-loh served you."

"Yes . . . And so you wouldn't remember the woman —girl she was, then—Li Tuh-ying—the one I kept that year, in the house on Soochow Hutung."

"I remember some talk of a Li Tuh-ying," the servant said gloomily.

"Well," Blair said, "she has fallen on bad times—been mixed up in a few things. Which is why I got rid of Wang . . . And I would rather you did not mention her existence to anyone."

The servant stared at the closed door. "You will keep her again?"

"Yes," Blair said. "I will keep her again."

The servant had nothing to say to that.

"You may serve us our evening meal at six," Blair said, dropping his cigarette and stepping on it. "And since Wang is gone, let's keep the shop shuttered."

II

The second day. The House of Koo was locked in silence, its gates sealed and bolted, still. Some men were working in the street that fronted it and they could hear no sounds at all drifting over the walls. Not even the sounds of cooking or servants' quarreling or small wing of laughter. Nothing.

They worked without zest. The ones with stretchers had finished the day before. There were no more bodies or definable parts of bodies to be disposed of. They had baskets and they picked up splinters and stones and burnt-out torches and a few hopelessly broken farm implements. Scavengers had long since made off with the rest of the debris. They laughed when they found a tooth sitting up neatly in a crack. . . .

It was still very early when they had filled their baskets. They left and left the mangy yellow tramp dogs sniffing and drooling behind them.

Inside the Koo walls, those who observed the silence knew that it was about to explode. Their collective attention was fixed on one of the central living courts where Old Koo had taken to his rooms and would not come out and would not be waited upon. He had retired to his quarters and sooner or later he would explode from them. That was what all knew and what all were waiting for. Old Koo was famous for his rages. He was about to have one. The prediction was that this would be the worst of his career.

Although the door that led to Old Koo's rooms was closed, the court that commanded it was not empty. Nor was the one adjoining, which was connected to the first by a moongate. Crumpled on the far side of the moongate, in the second court, was the steward who was not sitting on stool or chair or bench but on the ground which was very unfitting for one of his status. Though the air was cool, he was dissolved in sweat. One of the four trusted servants stood near him. He stood attentive, immobile. The little maid was also in this court. She was very pale and fidgety. She had spoken to no one in some hours and no one had spoken to her. She was passing the time by getting up and sitting down.

In the other court Tear Drop was sitting on a porcelain stool. Her hair was uncombed, her clothes were rumpled, and there was a fixed expression about her eyes that was hard to define. Not far from her (but, in fact, as far as the moon is from the earth), Old Koo's Number Five Brother was installed, in a chair, in state. A maid stood ready to wait upon him. A table had been placed at his side with a pot of tea on it. Number Five, or Fifth Uncle, as Helen's generation knew him, was the only brother of Old Koo's generation who was yet living or at home. Two were "from home," managing family interests that were located in other provinces. Fifth Uncle was partially deaf and was poetic by nature. He had four concubines. He was only present because it was meet that he should be. Except for the show of courtesy, no one was paying any attention to him. As for him, he was vacillating between dread and the line of a poem he was composing in his head.

On the opposite side of the court, Madame Koo was holding an interview, in a low voice, with the officer of the guards who had been expressly hired to watch the House on the fatal night. This officer had already been interviewed by one of the trusted servants and by the steward before his collapse. But because their reports had been to the effect that "he knew nothing" and because Madame had not chosen to tell either the steward or the servant of a rope that had been found girdling the ginkgo tree, Madame had deemed the reports unsatisfactory. Customarily, she would not have picked her husband's court for such an undertaking. But it was necessary that she be on hand when his rage broke. At least, she thought so. She had been in his court for almost all of the twenty-four hours since Tear Drop had conveyed to her the news of the Third Girl's disappearance.

Helen was nowhere in sight. She had taken to her bed, much to the annoyance of Little Dog, who considered these latest developments untenable and frequently said so. His nurse, who was frightened out of her wits by everything, was dimly considering gagging him.

George Washington Koo, the oldest living son of Koo, was standing about five feet away from his mother and was periodically punctuating her words to the officer of the guards with his frowns. Sometimes he glanced in the direction of the fallen Tear Drop and sometimes he took out a small black notebook from his breast pocket and looked inside it, fluttering the pages when he did. He was well set-up, wore exceedingly well-cut Western clothes and had the habit of saying in English, "Good lord." He could not actually hear what his mother was saying, although he was making every effort. He would have liked to move in closer but he had not been invited, a strong word in Madame's vocabulary, which all her children understood.

"I need not further explain," Madame Koo was saying to the officer, "that this slave girl who has escaped, is one of the Old Master's favorites. . . . When you were so well paid, how could you have been so lax?"

"Ah, but Madame!"

She dropped her voice. "We know of the rope, you see. We found it, girdled around the ginkgo. How is this?"

"Madame, I assure you, it must have happened before . . ."

"And I assure you that it is for your own benefit that I ask of you the truth." The trace of a malevolent smile appeared on Madame's lips. "The escape of a slave girl," she said, modestly lowering her eyes, "need not be such a calamity to any other than him who names her favorite. Is that not so?"

The captain started. He leaned slightly forward. And now it was as if the smile that had been on Madame's lips were transferred to his. So! Was he to understand that Madame was jealous of this thing of a slave? Was he to gather that the slave was the old man's chosen bedmate? Was he to deduce that Madame was not so sorry to find her gone? Had he found in Madame a friend, after all?

"Ah, Madame!"

"Yes?" Madame Koo said, making a gesture with her hand that the guard seemed to understand perfectly.

The guard said, "Madame, she did scale the wall with that rope. At almost the exact same moment that I was posting my men on the east side of the compound."

"At what time was that?"

"At ten o'clock. Well before the—uh—principal disturbance."

"I see. Go on."

"Had they already been posted . . . ! But you understand. . . . I arrive with my men then. We are not yet in the alley when we hear this noise—which would have passed for a cricket's chirping with any others. But not with us. We flash on our lights, we call for whoever it is to halt. We draw arms. But she has the edge on us. She has already gained the connecting alley before we are on to her. We give chase. We pursue her hotly. We open fire. But, with the edge she has had from the beginning, how can we catch up with her? It is beyond human power. We lose her."

Madame Koo looked steadily at the officer. Her voice sank to a whisper. "Should you be able to produce—her body, let us say—it might be worth your while."

Greed showed in the officer's eyes. But he said, "Ah, Madame! My profound regrets—you are now in possession of the extent of my knowledge."

"In which direction did she go?" Madame Koo asked, after a pause. "Where did you lose track of her?"

"It is hard to say with exactness, Madame. She did a deal of doubling back. However, it was in the neighborhood of Za-kiu-li, where the beggars' village is located, you know, that we began to lose hope."

Madame Koo nodded thoughtfully. She said, "So that you and yours may not be undone by the Master's wrath, my advice to you is this: Take your men and disappear for awhile. You might find occupation at Kun-shan, let us say, for a month? This city, I believe, can get along without your presence for such a period."

The officer rose. "I understand, Madame. I am very grateful. I assure you that I shall pray for the day when I may return your favor."

"It is nothing," Madame said. "The mob that carried a certain coffin afforded us no great unpleasantness." (Madame, by no token suggesting that General Ma's troops might have had something to do with it.) "Who could have foretold this minor accident?" she added. "Farewell."

The officer bowed deeply. He bowed to Fifth Brother Koo. He bowed to George. He bowed again to Madame. The manservant (the one of the four) who had seen him rise, came and escorted him away.

"Did he know anything?" George asked, coming up to his mother.

"Nothing at all," Madame Koo said. "I should have left him to you, my son."

But when he said, "Well, then!" and started purposefully off, Madame called him back and said simply, "Stay with me here."

George said, "Of course!" He came back and took the chair that the officer had vacated. "Mother," he said, "I hate to press it, but we ought to start a search. I really do not think we can afford to wait for Father's decision in this. I will be willing to take the full responsibility for it. Don't you think I am right?"

In matters of business Madame Koo had great respect for her son—as, indeed, did the whole family. He was naturally astute and single-minded and he had learned many excellent methods at the Harvard School of Business. More and more his father had come to turn over affairs to him—particularly those concerning the factories. As young as he was, George had already made amazing gains. He had increased the number of silk mills they owned from one to three. But George's knowledge, Madame felt, was specialized. It was not the involved and paradoxical kind that bore on human nature. . . . Of all Madame's children, George was the least in her mind because he was the most obedient and dependable. Looking at him, though, she wondered why his mouth remained wistful—in contradiction to his hard, calculating eyes and to his mind which, even in dreams, must wrestle with figures. Her lord contended, she remembered, that not even George's capacity for evil was interesting since it would inevitably add up in columns. He was glad to turn over his business to him, he said, but he could not abide his company and was inclined to swear at him without provocation. . . . But the wistful mouth? Had no one thought to pat George's cheek—at any time? Madame promised herself to look into the matter of his personal life in the near future. Perhaps his wife was not affectionate.

She said to him, "We can discuss the necessity of a search later, my son. But now. I will just go in and glance at your father, who is the first responsibility of the dutiful wife and filial son."

George looked dubious. He was mortally afraid of his father. On the other hand, he took all responsibilities seriously. "Do you think you should?" he said. "That is, would you rather I did it?"

Madame Koo smiled. "No," she said. "But I wish you would be so good as to question Tear Drop again. Because you were the one with the ingenuity and the foresight to think of searching her things, I feel if there is any information to be squeezed out of her, you will be the one to do it."

George nodded. He took out a cigar from his gold case and capped it with a gold cutter which he wore on his watch chain.

"I may slap her," he said.

"That might be effective," Madame Koo said, rising. "I shall be back in a moment."

She crossed the court. When she reached her lord's door, she paused but she did not cough or knock. She opened it noiselessly and entered.

Old Koo was sitting, like a Buddha, in his chair that had been made especially to accommodate his size. His eyes were half closed, his hands were folded over his paunch, his complexion was gray, the way it was when he had his mighty attacks of indigestion. He seemed unnaturally bloated. He looked as if he might not have moved for hours.

There was everywhere evident, around him, the desolation of so large a nature. The room seemed as mute and as bloated as he was.

Madame Koo neither spoke to him nor bowed. She took the blackwood chair that was nearest the door (the lowest chair) and sat down. Moments passed. There was much to be done. One might have thought she could ill afford these moments but she would have been willing to sacrifice almost anything to them because she knew that when the dam that held back his rage gave way, he might very well throw caution and reason to the winds. He might not remember—he might not care even if forcefully reminded—that the Third Koo Girl had died in the prison yard. That would not figure in his thinking because he would not be thinking but storming, instead, over his daughter's impertinence and ingratitude. Oh, Madame could hear him. "She leaves in the night like a thief, dear Buddha! After that tempest of trouble I went to. Oh, blight of my heart, wretch, may ten thousand curses descend!" And he would call in the officer and his guards (and though he could not lay his hands on them, now, that was the smallest and coldest comfort), he might very well call in the police, or General Ma and all his staff and to them scream out a hundred orders with the Third Girl's name attached.

Madame had not been prepared for the funeral. She had never heard, in all her days, such a roar go up from a crowd, she had never marked such massed frenzy, and she had listened to the reports of the two servants who had attended from beginning to end with mounting awe and disquietude.

But if Madame shuddered upon looking backwards, that was nothing to what she felt when she turned her thoughts to the present and immediate future—to the people, if or when they should discover fraud.

And it was Madame Koo's belief that the authorities, having witnessed a day they had wished on themselves by ordering her killed, would not now be so opposed to a general (if belated) smearing of her. It would do them no harm at all, should they be able to demonstrate that the people had made fools of themselves for believing in her who, as it turned out, was as corrupt as the next. Further, this program would be rendered twice sweet, could it be carried out as Old Koo's own orders. Not only could the program go ahead, but the wrath of Shanghai and the C.E.C. against Old Koo also brought to bear.

. . . And while it was to General Ma and his efficient handling of the mob that Madame was indebted, it was nevertheless General Ma whom she most mistrusted. She did not like the news that he had removed the great balance of his troops to outlying villages. When a house controlled as much wealth as the Koo House did, there was no one left to trust; there was no one on one's own side, in truth, and even though one did "own" all the authorities. General Ma was ruthless, ambitious and clever. Like Madame, he was a psychologist. The funeral would not have failed to make its impression on him. And Madame did not feel that with all his knowledge of that curious day, he had predicted any more accurately than she had the intensity of its climax. She wondered, for instance, what might have happened had he been on the scene, had he been in personal command of his troops rather than (as was almost certain) having issued his commands in advance. Prior to that day and night, Ma would have considered Koo so powerful as only to be placated. But if her lord started screaming his orders, would not Ma be the first to see how the Koo House had become newly and disastrously vulnerable—the perfect target? Would he not be the first to take due advantage, particularly since there was not even the risk of offending?

Cloaked securely behind her lord's commands, could he not industriously search for the girl, only incidentally turning the populace as impressively against her as it had once been for her; only incidentally demonstrating that she was, after all, a genuine Koo, typical Koo filth and only incidentally rendering the search ambiguous by keeping his searchers more quiet than his agitators—only incidentally drawing Shanghai's attention to Old Koo's breach of faith—to his defiance. The agitators busy on every street corner. "Friends, she never died for you! You made your funeral in vain! And friends, she spent that day you mourned her in her father's house—that is the truth of it." Agitators were not known for their accuracy. "Where is she now? Where would you say, good friends? It is said how they search for her. Should *we* search for her, good friends, in her father's house where she has been and where she is? Shall we search for her there?"

And in the event of a second uprising, the difference could be that the troops of General Ma, being quartered at some little distance, would not be able, though they made every effort, to reach the scene in time.

With Old Koo out of the way, General Ma would stand to gain immeasurably. The tie-up between warlord and gentry was as traditional as was the propensity of each for knifing the other in the back, given the opportunity. And what a perfect opportunity this would be, Madame Koo somehow thought General Ma would not fail to see.

Never was the need for secrecy about the girl more drastic. And the only hope under heaven was if Madame, being present, could handle her lord's first great spilling-over, that time of screaming orders. If she could keep the heat of his anger within the bounds of room and house until he should have cooled off sufficiently to allow the dawn of reason. He would see, then, what he would be too blind and bloated to see before. There would be a chance, then, the only chance that Madame asked for. For as she saw it, her plan could go ahead. True, a cog had slipped; the girl had taken herself off. But she had disappeared. There was no reason why the garbled rumors that were tinged with madness could not travel—providing there remained the paucity of "too-real" details. The existence of a rope, for example, she was anxious to keep as quiet as possible—at least until she could allow a bona-fide slave to make her departure. There was not even any reason why General Ma should not hear the rumors and laugh, providing . . .

But it came to this: could she scheme against—cajole—bargain with—or persuade a thunderstorm to hush before it had run its course? Could she hold up a dam when the river was rising and the rain falling and the water was pushing? Madame was no worker of miracles. How was she to keep him from knocking her out of the way, for instance, and throwing open the door and shouting? That would be all it would take. . . . She had gone over in her mind a dozen different plans, but upon close examination, the structure of none stood up.

Madame Koo was on the brink of defeat. She would not leave Old Koo simply because the fact of her staying was her last stand. But sitting in the blackwood chair, waiting, she considered this defeat as carefully as she had once considered success. . . .

"Let her be killed," Old Koo said in a voice so quiet and final that it was more terrible than any wrathful blast.

"Yes, my lord."

"Let the slave who helped her escape be flogged to death."

"Ai, my lord."

"But let the flogging of the slave take place in a distant court. Gag her that I may not be distracted by the sounds of her screams."

"It shall be as you say, my lord."

He continued in the strange, flat voice. "Dead or alive, let the Third Girl be found and brought here. I will not leave this room or take food until she is before me. If alive—so much the better. With these hands"—he raised his white, puffy ones—"with these hands, I will throttle her. I will press with these fingers upon her pipe until the wind shall rattle and tear in its struggle. But the wind shall not get through. . . . Go! Let no man or woman enter that door again, without her."

Madame Koo rose and bowed. She said, "It shall be done, my lord."

Noiselessly she opened the door and noiselessly she left.

III

Back in the court, Madame Koo stood still for a moment, her blood turned too thick, too cold, for her relief immediately to flood her. She saw her son standing over Tear Drop. Noted the defiant look in Tear Drop's eyes and the dark-red stains upon her cheeks. Thought that George might slap her from now till sundown without . . . The chance that she had hoped for was given to her, her plan might go ahead. . . .

Silently, and while George had his back to her, she crossed the court and went through the moongate into the second. She beckoned to the manservant who had returned from escorting the officer of the guards out of the house. He came quickly to her side.

"And did you check with Lao Liang while you were at the gates?" she asked him.

"I did, Madame," the servant answered. "According to him, Wei-sun had just reported. He had been combing the district around the railway station. So far—nothing. Not a trace."

"The others?" Madame asked, referring to the other two of the trusted four.

"They have not been back, this morning, as yet."

"Very well," Madame Koo said. "Do you go out also, now. If she is not found by the time the sun has set, we may have to call in others. We may have to institute a search. I do not wish to do that, you understand."

"Yes, Madame. I understand."

"Therefore, may you all redouble your efforts. And should you find her today, I shall increase the reward to one thousand silver dollars, each, regardless of who does the finding. In addition, I shall pay five thousand dollars bonus to the one who actually locates her. Tell the others so, should you see them. Tell Lao Liang the same, that he may pass on the word when they and the Old Crone come in to report."

"At once, Madame."

"A slight change in procedure," Madame said. "You will recall that I specified that under no conditions was the girl herself, when found, to be brought to the house? That, rather, word of her condition and whereabouts and capture should serve the same purpose? That you should bring this word direct to me and then wait for my orders?"

"Quite so, Madame."

"It is now become necessary that she should be brought. If alive, then after dark. If dead, then well disguised—in a basket of the kind that charcoal is brought in. But I will speak in more detail of this to Lao Liang. . . . Meanwhile, look for a corpse. Discreetly question canal dwellers —boat migrants. Haunt the poor districts—the alleys and beggars' huts. It is my opinion that you will not find a woman walking but a corpse. Let your minds be adjusted to such a probability." Madame Koo paused.

The servant, who had been hanging onto her every word, now took the opportunity to examine her face covertly. By it he knew that he should etch her next words with black ink and a stylus into his memory; that he should allow these words a higher place than any that had gone before, regardless of seeming contradictions.

"Whatever it is you find," Madame said slowly and distinctly, "let it be a corpse that you bring."

"Ai!"

"And if there is aught to be done, any act of completion to be performed, then let it be done quickly and cleanly. I shall examine the corpse most thoroughly."

"Exactly so."

"Go, then."

The servant went speedily off.

Madame Koo turned. She stopped in front of the steward and looked down on him.

"Your master's rage is no ordinary brand," she said.

He started. He saw who was standing over him and scrambled to his feet. "Oh, ai, Madame! Ai, oh . . ."

"I said that your master's rage is no ordinary brand."

"Oh, indeed!"

"Just so," Madame Koo said, allowing her eyes to travel slowly up and down his person. "He who waits for the storm to break, waits in vain. Your master will take no food and will keep to his rooms until a certain person, alive or dead, be found."

"Oh! Should I . . . ? That is . . . ?"

"You should do what you think best," Madame Koo said ominously. She watched him put on his gold-rimmed glasses and dust off his robe; watched his efficiency returning like a lost sheep to its fold. Then she repeated, almost word for word (but with different inflections) all she had said to the servant, but concluding with: "If the corpse is not found within three days, on the outside, consider that you are at liberty to seek employment elsewhere."

"Ai!" he gasped, badly confused by the pitch and swing of his emotions. (First, the talk of huge rewards and a one-day limit. Then, the talk of cutting off his very livelihood—his all!—and a three-day limit.) "But then I must be off!" he said. "I must get to work! Will you write me a pass? That is, could you . . . ?"

"Lao Liang has his instructions," Madame Koo said. "He will let you out."

She would leave it to him, she decided, what plans he should make and what he should do. Such a vain and cowering one as he had got ahead in life by infinite and cunning ways.

She glanced in the direction of the little maid who seemed to be beside herself, who was trembling and trying to speak.

"Do you know where she went?" Madame Koo asked her suddenly.

"No! Oh, no!"

"Very well," Madame said. She smiled gently at her. Then she returned to George, through whom she intended to make it common knowledge—the order that Tear Drop was to be flogged to death.

IV

Helen heard Little Dog's voice out in her court.

"If she doesn't get up!" he was saying at the top of his lungs. "If she doesn't get up *this minute*, I will have a fit. I will fall flat on my face and hold my breath till I turn blue all over and die!"

She heard the ineffectual mutterings of Little Dog's nurse. She rose. She went quickly to the door and opened it and said, "Boo!"

Little Dog's eyes popped.

"Come here," Helen said.

He came. She rumpled his hair. She held him in the curve of her arm and pulled his ear. She knelt down and took his square chin in her hand.

"You smell like an owl, my lamb," she said.

"I smell like a lamb, my owl," Little Dog said, beginning to dance up and down.

"If a centipede has fifteen legs," Helen said, "how many legs does a centipede have?"

"Twenty-three!" Little Dog shouted, jumping higher and higher.

"Well?" Helen said. "Go away and play."

He rushed off, his nurse scrambling after him, shaking her head, tottering dangerously on the stubs of her tiny bound feet. "Little Dog," she cried. "Not so fast, Little Dog!"

Helen turned back to her room and broke a rule of the house by closing the door, once again, behind her. It was considered rude and inhospitable to close one's door in the daytime.

She sat down on the edge of the bed. She thought, a breath of life and then—silence and the sick, dizzy, empty wrechedness. *She to corroborate in every interested quarter the official version . . . !*

She had heard Dji-bo, her maid, gossiping with somebody in the passage, earlier this morning. Dji-bo had said, "The story is this—mind!—that she has disappeared! Disappeared, if you please, with the gates thrice bolted and locked and a cordon of guards surrounding all four walls of this place."

"Guards?" said the one who was less informed. And this was news to Helen, too. "What guards?"

"What!" Dji-bo cried. "You mean you did not know of the guards? Well! My lad, you know, stands in with Siau Liang, the gatekeeper's son. There were guards on every side of the house, believe me. And all that commotion out front—that mob—that firing—and . . ."

"Yes," said the other. "We have all heard mutterings about that." And a nervous giggle. "The Third Koo Girl's funeral. But, pray, what do you make of it? I say it is downright eery. What are we to believe?"

"What indeed?" Dji-bo said. "That she disappeared? A very likely story, is it not, what with the locked gates and the guards. Unless we are to presume that she was, after all, a spirit or a fox paying us a visit, while all the time, her earthly self remained outside in a box. Buddha!"

Because Dji-bo did not know of the rope. Very few, it seemed, knew of the rope. Helen wondered whether she and her father were the only ones who did.

"I am not superstitious. My own opinion of what happened is this," Dji-bo had said to her companion. But at that point Dji-bo had lowered her voice and Helen had no longer been able to follow her. Not that she needed to. She knew, without hearing, what Dji-bo's opinion was—what some of the servants' (those who were not superstitious) and all of the family's opinion was and was meant to be: "What else, if not that she did away with her life? Both Madame and First Young Mistress were afraid of it. They both say she was quite mad. She must have hung herself from the rafters or cut her veins with a pair of scissors. Her body must have been discovered in the very early morning and carted off—to avoid complications, don't you see, in lieu of the silly, mistaken funeral that the peasants staged. It is as plain as mud."

Exactly as plain. How many times, these twenty-four hours, had she been back and forth over it—from the time Dji-bo had first told her Leila was back, through, "I am not sweet—I don't know what I am," until her mother had called her to her father's court. She lay down.

She remembered: "*Nothing is clear except the great unclearness.*" This was no longer descriptive, since Helen was aware that the truth was all around her, trying to break through. *She to corroborate* . . . But if she was to corroborate the official version on every hand, and if the official version was what she had understood it (that Leila was insane and obsessed with suicide), what had gone wrong? Why had her mother confused this version by planting the rope around the ginkgo tree and by bribing Tear Drop to seem to be the seemingly fleeing Leila's accomplice? Were these last-minute improvisations? For her mother had not mentioned suicide to either Old Koo or Helen. She had said, "The girl has left."

Could it have been the funeral that had made her decide to play her hand sooner than she had intended? In that case, had a suicide not been as satisfactorily suicidal in appearance as the original plan had called for? What about that strangely timed and terrible funeral? It *was* eery. Was there a connection?

This was the part of the great unclearness that remained unclear, that Helen wandered back and forth in, losing her way.

Well, Leila had not scaled the wall. That was clear. She had not climbed over it and into her own coffin. . . . Had Leila known? What had Leila known? Had Leila known and let Helen leave? Had she lain there waiting for the stealthy sound of steps, for the opening door? Had she already accepted her fate?

"*Tell Little Dog there isn't any password,*" Leila had said.

Ordinarily Helen did not let her left hand know her right hand's business. Ordinarily Helen kept as wide of trouble as if it were a communicable disease requiring quarantine. As for ugliness, Helen was apt to call it beauty or to pretend it did not exist or to circle around and around it waiting for an opening to slip over or under it. Helen had carried the game of deception two steps further than her mother—first, she tended to play it with herself as well as others; second, since she was so ornamental and decorative, she was expected "to prettify," as Andrew put it, to brighten things up as she went along, which was a responsibility. Helen had been fashioned to please. It was understood that she should give forth a glow that others might warm themselves in passing.

Now, this same Helen turned over on her back and opened her eyes and said it: "Leila is dead. Leila was murdered. Mother murdered Leila."

Then, as if one piece of straight dealing necessarily led to another, she added, "Mother bargained for and received my help, without which she apparently believed she could not have done it." There! Fear was given a name.

She heard the footsteps in her court. She heard the door that opened. She kept her eyes on the ceiling.

"Get up," Madame Koo said.

"She was insane," Helen said. "She was obsessed with the desire to end her own life. I was to take good care of her."

"Get up."

Helen laughed. She laughed up an ascending scale. "I was to encourage her to be happy with us."

"Get up."

Helen stood up and faced her mother.

"You are overwrought," Madame said gently. "Your mind has been too busy weaving its tale of suspicion . . .

I should have come to you sooner, *pau-pei*, but I could not get away."

Her mother had no right to be gentle, Helen thought with a final shudder. And she had no right to be soothed. She raised her eyes. She looked into her mother's eyes and thought she had never before remarked their depths—their tenderness. Oh, it was strange. Terrible and strange. And her mother had just called her *pau-pei*, which she had not called her even when she had been a child, and which meant "precious.". . . Strange. And these undemonstrative people could move you, could mean with their words (since they so seldom used them) what others could not.

"This is all I would have you believe," Madame Koo said slowly. "For your sake, as well as mine, I hope that you will believe it."

Helen waited. She knew—knew surely—that she would be able to tell if her mother spoke the truth or not. No liar, no matter how skilled, and her mother was exceedingly skilled . . . No liar could carry through a lie to maturity, when the eyes were as singly expressive as her mother's now were; no lie could pass the lips without being betrayed by the merest shadow that would have to come up to protect the eyes.

Madame Koo said, "I loved your Third Sister. And now that she is gone, I love her memory. That is all."

The air in Helen's lungs fluttered out. The eyes were steadfast—the eyes had not changed by so much as a shadow's shadow. For moments neither spoke. But the silence between them was not the charged, vibrating kind. It was sad, rather, and full of longing.

At last, Helen said in a tired voice, "We shall not see her again?"

"Not alive," Madame Koo said. "No, not again."

Helen found a chair and sat down.

"You should not be too much alone," Madame Koo said.

Helen tensed. If her mother mentioned the Majestic Hotel, she would not be able to stand it. But she did not. She said only, "Take care of Little Dog."

When she was halfway to the door, she stopped. "Oh, yes," she said, turning around. Something about her tone—some faintest suggestion of a change about it—pricked at Helen.

"Those sleeping powders—the ones I gave to you, do you remember?"

"Yes," Helen said.

"I will just take them back," Madame Koo said, "the two that are left. I do not want Little Dog getting into them."

Instinct was quicker than remembrance. Before Helen remembered what was at stake, the old flag was going up, the old game was under way: the Mother up to something, Helen matching wits.

"I—do not know where they are," Helen said slowly, watching her mother. "I must have lost them."

"That would not be like you," Madame Koo said evenly.

"Oh, I am very careless," Helen said. "I am awful. Dji-bo is always scolding me."

"I would have them," Madame said.

"Oh, don't bother about them," Helen said, her stomach turning over. "Little Dog will not get into them, I promise. Besides, who knows? Feeling the way I do—I did not sleep a wink last night!—I might just take them myself."

"An excellent idea," Madame Koo said. "I will give you some. These, however, are designed for those who are very ill. They are a bit too strong for your purpose. Where are they?"

"I really do not know," Helen said. "Unless I left them in Leila's court, I haven't the least idea."

"Will you help me to hunt for them, then?" Madame asked. She moved swiftly to a chest and threw it open.

It was difficult for Helen to believe her eyes. There was Madame, her mother, going through her things with fingers that were suddenly as thorough and as deft as a thief's.

"Mother!"

Madame did not turn or desist. "Won't you help me?" she asked politely.

At first, Helen was too stupified even to get up and go through the motions of helping. However, in a few minutes she did rise and—being careful to stay within her mother's range of vision—she pushed at a few objects that were on her dressing table. Then she sighed and sat down, once more, though this time on a different chair, the chair where she had laid down her purse and sweater, eons before. The sleeping powders were in her purse, her sweater was draped over it and hanging over the arm of the chair, at the same time. When Helen had settled herself, had leaned back as if to combat her amazement and fatigue, she began to push the purse around—inch by inch—until it was directly behind her, with the sweater remaining where it had been. The chair's back was to the wall. Her mother was not trained to the purse tradition. It was possible that she might overlook it.

Meticulously, thoroughly, Madame Koo went through Helen's drawers and chests. She looked into the envelopes of old letters, into pockets. She unfolded and refolded linens. She lifted handkerchiefs out of their box, one at a time. She did not miss the trick drawer that was in the floor of her toilet case.

When she was quite through, Helen said in a voice that was struggling bravely to be sarcastic, "You must not forget *me*. Would you not like to go through these pockets of my dressing gown?"

"That might be advisable," Madame Koo said.

Actually, she came. She came and put her hand into first one, then the other of Helen's pockets. Helen thought that when she wanted something, pride—dignity—everything was sacrificed to it. She was examining the sweater. For some reason Helen was very calm, though the purse was digging a hole in her back.

"Perhaps . . ." Helen said. "Do you suppose that, after all, I could have left them in Leila's court?"

"Let us hope you did," Madame Koo said. "I should be most distressed if any of the children got into them. I had no idea you would take your responsibilities so carelessly."

With that, she left, closing the door behind her.

Helen sat motionless, while the old, familiar signals flashed through her mind: an urgency that was out of proportion, persistence, sham reasoning . . . Why was her mother so anxious to have back those sleeping powders? The fact that she did rendered them important. Granting that, how did they fit into the puzzle?

Helen could see herself speared on two horns. The one, the remembrance of her mother's tenderness and of her words that had been true. The other, her mother's relentless search for the packets, her mother the schemer, her mother the liar. . . . *Three packets.* One was gone, two were left. . . .

A scene was re-enacted in her mind: Leila lying on the bed, restlessly moving her legs. Herself, reaching for a tumbler of water, saying, "Take this . . . Sit up a little."

She looked down at her hands which people told her were small and fine-boned and graceful. *These hands.* "Take this." What was innocence? What was guilt?

She could know, now, exactly for what she had bargained. ("The nights can be managed," her mother had said.) In the neatly folded packets—poison. (Why three?)

The perfect plan. To murder, without the necessity of being present, without the need of making use of one's own hands. "Take this—sit up a little." Then the other words that were true, "I loved your Third Sister. And now that she is gone, I love her memory. That is all."

Helen turned her head from side to side. "You have killed me, too," she whispered. But was that so—when her mother had never called her *pau-pei* until today—when she had never revealed until today the innermost depths of her eyes? What was truth, when it was not this or that, a shaft of urgency, a shaft of despair, fear, a lesser love or a greater hate. If Madame loved Leila (and she did) under what possible circumstances could she wish to kill her? If she considered poor, sick Leila a monstrous threat? But to what?

She thought, I do not want to know. My stomach turns over, my hair rises up, I am not able to know, I cannot stand to know.

But slowly, slowly, Helen's hand moved back, closed over her purse that had made such a heap in the small of her back and drew it out. She dropped it in her lap. She bent over it. She undid the clasp. Blindly she felt around inside, rejecting her compact and Little Dog's top, until she found the two packets. The right thing for her to do, of course, was to have them examined—analyzed. She should take them to an apothecary's. She lifted them out and stared at them.

The door opened.

"I thought you would find them," Madame Koo said. "Thank you." She put out her hand.

Helen laid them on the square, flat palm.

"Thank you," she said in a small voice to the one who had been standing just outside, waiting the while.

V

A maid, with natural feet, was flying through the courts. "Madame!" she called. "Oh, Madame!"

"What ails you?" someone asked her.

But she would not stop to explain. She rushed on. "Madame! Oh, Madame!"

"You are going in the wrong direction," someone informed her. "She is with our First Young Mistress."

The maid turned around. She ran straight into a bench but she would not even stop to rub her knee or swear.

Madame Koo came out of Helen's court. "Who calls?" she said. "What is it?"

The maid drew up. "Oh, Madame!" she said. But she was panting so that she had great difficulty about finding words. "Oh, Madame! It is terrible—awful. It . . ."

"Get your breath, child," Madame Koo said. "Begin again."

"Oh, something dreadful has happened."

"Yes?"

"It is the little maid, Tsi-yuen. Oh, she has gone out of her head. She is raving mad. Blabbing at the top of her lungs!"

"Yes? And to what purpose? Why?" Madame Koo was walking steadily toward Old Koo's court.

"Oh, how should I know?" the maid cried. "I could not make it out. Before there was time to turn around, Second Young Master sent me after you. But . . ."

"But what?" Madame Koo said. "Do not shout. Tell me now what happened."

"The most terrible thing. No one could stop her, Madame. Even Fifth Old Master leapt from his chair. I seized the hem of her coat and tugged. But, oh! She did it. She freed herself from me and burst right into Old Master's rooms!"

"You mean . . ." Madame Koo checked herself—checked her anger, checked her foolish questions. Whatever was done was done. She walked faster.

"Right past his closed door she went, Madame! To provoke him to the blackest rage. She is in there now! And Second Young Master is beside himself. Oh, Madame!"

"Yes, yes," Madame said soothingly, but walking still faster. "It was good of you to find me so promptly. Now, go somewhere and rest yourself."

Madame wasted little time with pointing the finger of blame at herself. Providing she had known that the little maid was behaving queerly, she could not have guessed where she would go to unburden herself. There was nothing to be gained now by observing that had she been there, this would not have happened. She was, furthermore, accustomed to the trials that beset the one who found it necessary to be three different places at once. One must either reduce one's importance or accept the consequences.

In the second court from her lord's, a group of family and servants had already begun to gather. They were anxious to maintain a comfortable distance, yet equally determined to be within earshot of this latest development. (Madame Koo never ceased to marvel at the speed with which a piece of news could travel in a big house—almost it was known before it had happened.)

"Go away," she said to them, in passing. "Why are you not about your business? Do not let me catch you here when I come out."

The court itself was deserted. Fifth Brother Koo's chair was upended. Old Koo's door was wide open. She could hear the little maid's voice reaching for heaven—wildly sobbing out her snatches of words.

"Oh, sir—not Tear Drop—must not be flogged to—I got her the—It was—everything!"

When Madame Koo got to the door she saw what seemed to her to be the most unlikely tableau she had ever witnessed. Her lord was sitting in his chair, leaning a little forward, his hands hanging loose between his knees and smiling. Fifth Brother Koo was smiling somewhat stupidly. So was George, though his was a watered-down and sickly variety. So was the steward—out of sheer relief. (But why was he here? Why was he not about some cunning scheme?) Only Tear Drop, who was standing in the threshold, more out than in, was not smiling. Her face was dark and red-stained and full of hate.

"Oh, sir," the little maid was sobbing, "I repeat. Tear Drop had nothing—*nothing*—to do with it. *I* got her the rope. *I* gave her my clothes. That is so! I—I . . ."

At that moment Old Koo realized that his wife was in the room.

"You hear this, Old Woman?" he said in what was almost his natural voice. "We have found the villain. Or rather—she has found us." And—actually—he chuckled. "She confesses everything."

"Oh, Master, sir. Hear me. You *must* understand. Truly, truly . . ."

"She is annoyed," George said, also laughing, "because we do not believe her."

Tear Drop made a sound that was barely audible.

"Indeed?" Madame Koo said, entering into the spirit. "What do you think we should do with her?"

The little maid was confounded. She looked frantically from one to another. Her eyes stopped on Madame.

"Madame," she said, "Madame. *You* will believe me. Why should I confess to something I never did? Why, I even got her the letter she wished to deliver. I had it with me all the time. I helped her with everything. Why should I lie? I will take ten thousand oaths. I . . ."

Old Koo was delighted. "Should we cut off her toes?" he said.

"But, sir—my *toes*? The point is if anyone must be flogged to death, it must not be Tear Drop who is innocent. It must be me!"

"Guilty on all counts," George said. "It is obvious, obvious. When Tear Drop was the one in authority, was supposed to watch her every minute, who was it that bribed her to look the other way? You, little maid?"

The little maid blushed furiously. "No one bribed her. She . . ."

"Oh!" said Old Koo.

George cleared his throat. He very much enjoyed being in tune with his father. He said, "Do tell us how you explain the earrings. How is it that Tear Drop was the one paid in earrings instead of you?"

The little maid launched into what would probably have been a long and involved explanation had not George's laughter drowned her out. All they heard was, "I tell you it was Third Young Mistress who stole those earrings. She . . ."

"Stole them from herself, eh?" George said. "Very logical. . . . And what of the suit of Tear Drop's clothes that's missing? Give us your version of that."

"But *I* have a suit that's missing—the rough, blue country clothes I came in. If you don't believe me, come and see!"

"Oh—oh," Old Koo groaned. "My son, press her no further. Do not, I beg of you, steal *all* the glory from such a mite of a maid. Perhaps she took two suits—so there!"

"She did!" the little maid cried.

Laughter. The little maid turned this way and that.

Seeing Madame, she rushed over to her and would have knelt before her had Madame not held her up.

"Madame—Madame! I call on you!"

"My dear, I am at your service."

"Then tell them, Madame. Make them see. It was only that Third Young Mistress wished Tear Drop to take the blame instead of me. Explain it to them, Madame. The way you looked at me, the way you smiled, the words you spoke. You already knew. Tell them you did."

But Madame merely patted her head. "Do you know where she went?" she said.

"No, but . . ."

"You speak of a letter. What letter?"

"I do not know but . . ."

"Do you know to whom she was taking it? Or where? Or why?"

"No, but . . ."

Madame Koo said, "I hate to so disappoint you, little one. But no, neither can I believe you."

The little maid was crushed. She seemed to wilt before their eyes, while Tear Drop (Madame saw) was gliding over the threshold, was gliding away, was gone.

"It was I who took all the risk," the little maid said forlornly. "It was I who cared. It was I who loved her."

Old Koo's smile faded from his face and eyes. The bloated look returned.

"Let everybody get out!" he said. "Are my orders nothing but chaff on the wind? Did I not say, 'Let no man or woman pass that door again until . . .' What is this! Who dares to clutter and intrude? Get out! Get out and close that door behind you!"

They bowed. They backed toward the door.

"You!" Old Koo said to the little maid.

The little maid started. She clasped her hands. "Yes?" she said, with one last flickering ray of hope about her voice. "Yes?"

"Stay with me for awhile," Old Koo said, the tears suddenly streaming out of his eyes. "I would have you near me."

They closed the door softly behind them.

"Father is much better," George said. He shook his head. "Now, what do you suppose got into that little maid?"

Fifth Brother Koo returned to his chair and stood awkwardly waiting for someone to set it up straight for him. Madame went over at once. She righted the chair and felt of the teapot that was on the table beside it. "If it is too cool," she said, "you must tell me." She filled his cup and saw that he was comfortably settled. "I will call your maid for you directly."

"Look here!" George said. "Where's Tear Drop?" He whirled around and glared at the steward. "She was standing by you. Where did she go? What happened?"

"Why, I . . ." The steward looked all around him.

"She seems to be gone," Madame Koo said.

"She can't do that!" George said. "Good lord!" He hurried across the court and disappeared through the moongate. The steward started to follow but Madame detained him with a gesture.

"And why are you here?" she asked.

"Ah, Madame." He bowed. "I came back to report."

"So?"

"I have a watchman acquaintance or two, you see, to whom I thought it might be wise to put a few discreet questions—what with their being abroad at night and their special knowledge of beggars and such."

Madame Koo nodded.

"One who works in the Ki-tsung district told me a curious tale. I did not have to prod him—he was full of it. He says it is doubly curious because it occurred not long after he had heard the news of what had transpired at a certain funeral—how the blood ran and a coffin was blown to bits. He says that he had this funeral in his mind and was cursing his employer who made him go out on such a night when he met up with a ghost. He swears that she edged up close to him and put her face into his face and said in a strange, unearthly voice, 'Watchman, do you see the Third Koo Girl?' And the watchman said her face was not two inches from his—the Third Koo Girl's, giving him such a fright that he ran for ten li without stopping. . . . And I must assure you, Madame, that he described her perfectly—tall and thin and gaunt. He had seen her at meetings, it seems, although because of his employer, he is quiet about that. But I think there can be no doubt."

"Did he mention how she was dressed?"

"No," the steward said. "He claims he was much too frightened to notice details. All he remembers is that her clothes were poor."

"At what hour was this?"

"At the first watch of the morning."

"And you are having the surrounding area thoroughly combed?"

"Indeed, yes, Madame."

"He was quite sure of the time?"

"Quite sure, Madame. He was beating his gong for the hour when he met her."

Madame Koo was perturbed. She had been very sure—positive, in fact—that the girl had left with the purpose of committing suicide, that the girl considered it her only solution but that she had been too proud to perform the act within the walls of the Koo House which she had tried so diligently to destroy, that she refused her family, and particularly her mother, the satisfaction of witnessing her final defeat. Why else had she torn the lotus picture from top to bottom? Madame had not only felt she understood her daughter's action—she had even admired it. In all her worries, she had not included the girl herself, counting absolutely upon a corpse and hoping for its quick acquisition. But now, this discrepancy in time did not please her. It did not bear out her supposition. According to the officer of the guards, she had been scaling the wall at ten o'clock. The watchman had not met up with her until one o'clock —three hours later. What had the girl been doing? Delivering a letter, perhaps? If so, what was involved?

There was the funeral, too, to be accounted for. Madame Koo had supposed the girl proud and solitary, entering into no conversations, killing herself a good hour before that funeral procession began its way through the streets. Now, she must suppose the girl had heard of it or, even, stumbled across it. It would be unsettling, to say the least. But what particular impression would it have made on her? She would have been at least partially drugged. As yet, Madame had had no time for examining the powders, which of course she would do before destroying them. Was it possible she might consider she had still a few revolutionary duties to perform? Why had she asked the watchman such a question —was it merely delirium or something much more purposeful, much more sinister? The more Madame thought about that mysterious letter, the more she did not like it. If the girl were up to something, if a corpse was not what was to be found, then the entire situation took a new and much darker turn.

"Increase your efforts," Madame Koo said to the steward, who had been standing patiently by. "Let this ghost story be used to good advantage. Let it draw you and yours into conversations, though you will be ostensibly looking for a runaway slave. Do you comprehend?"

"Ai, Madame, I do."

"Tell Lao Liang to pass this word on to the others: that they should readjust their minds, that they should be prepared for either corpse or woman, even while it should yet be a corpse brought in."

"Yes, Madame."

"One thing more," Madame said. "You have been told that she would be dressed in gray cotton, of good grade, since according to our Inventory of Clothing Issued to Maids such a suit is missing. This may or may not be so. She may be dressed in rough, blue cotton which would be, I believe, a deal too short for her in the legs. . . . Now, go."

The steward obeyed.

VI

The door slammed. Andrew, lying on his chaise longue, did not sit up or open his eyes.

"You are a fine lot!" Tear Drop said. "A great towering pillar of protection and strength—that's what you are!"

Andrew smiled.

"You fall all over yourself—don't you?—hurrying—rushing to Madame and Old Master to intercede for me. Oh, son of the devil! Thief's bones! Seed of the most ancient sin! I curse you, I revile you, I call on all the devils and all the gods!"

"Your acquaintance is catholic," Andrew said.

"May you rot in hell for ten thousand generations! May you be tortured for twice as long! May you be reincarnated into a dog that you may know nothing but whip and boot and slow starvation! How I have hated you and your cold, superior ways! How I despise you!" Tear Drop stopped for breath.

Andrew raised his head up on his hand and looked at her. He took in her dirty and discolored face, her uncombed hair and disheveled clothes.

He said, "You do not in any way please me, this morning. Besides, you are upsetting my stomach. Now, aren't you contrite?"

Tear Drop placed a bundle she was holding carefully down on a table. She came up to Andrew and stood over him. She began to cry.

"Stop it," Andrew said. "I like you better in character. I like you hard."

"Oh, yes," Tear Drop said, "you like me hard. You *like* it. You would also like to see me flogged to death. You would enjoy that!"

Andrew shrugged.

"Or could you stir yourself from that sofa? Could you afford the exertion? You like me hard, oh Buddha. As if a slave could live if she were anything but hard! As if she could survive the master's boot and whip if she were not hard!"

"How you go on," Andrew said. "No slave is mistreated in this house."

"Whose virtue is that?" Tear Drop asked. "The slave's? No—it is the master's whim or bounty. And the Old Lady has had her day with slaves here, don't think she hasn't. Madame will not last forever. The other day may come again—the slave never knows. Today the order is that a slave shall be flogged to death. But of course, that is not mistreatment." Tear Drop's sobs grew louder. "Hard and clever, dear Buddha. With her wits her sole inheritance, her security and her means for finding whatever fortune she can snatch. It is not easy, not pretty to have only your wits to depend on. It does make for hardness and for worse. Who says different is weaving fairy tales. How can a slave be generous or unselfish or gentle?"

"If you are going to begin to moralize," Andrew said, "prepare me some earplugs. I am already washed away in your self-pity."

But Tear Drop said, "When I came here, I was three years old. It did not take me long to learn my lot. . . . Oh, I struggled, I worked. I learned to embroider and to read and to sew and to cook. I learned refinement and all the manners and habits of a lady. I begged that my feet should be bound as small as theirs. I learned modesty and polite conversation and all the arts of pleasing. Then when I was older and it became apparent that I would be beautiful, I humbly thanked the gods—not for the beauty but for what it might get me. I saved my coppers and went to the temple and burned incense to the Goddess of Mercy. If I remained desirable and things broke well for me, there was the chance that some son might choose me as concubine and I should not, after all, be wished off to the first brutish farmer that made his appearance when I became of age. I prayed that I might yet earn a place, that I might not be turned out."

Tear Drop laughed bitterly. "I was assigned to you. Old Master said, 'Let the most beautiful slave of the House be assigned to him.' Because you had been expelled from college and he and Madame wished to save your face. How proud I was."

"They made a touching effort, didn't they?" Andrew said. "Remember all the feasts they made to me? Nobody asked me any questions either."

"That day," Tear Drop said, "the day I was given to you, I thought my troubles were over. I thought that I was made. I would forget all the chafing, bitter days with Third

Young Mistress when I, who was dainty and beautiful and embodying all the virtues of gentle breeding, must be constantly with and constantly conscious of the awkward, stupid, big-footed one who had none of my virtues."

Andrew sat up. "And you were proud of the contrast, weren't you? You were so damned proud of being better than Leila in every way."

"Proud?" Tear Drop said. "Proud? Bitter is the more suitable word. Did my accomplishments matter? Was it I who received advantages, love, security, jewels, an education, clothes—through no effort and no virtue? It was not I, my friend. Still, there was a little compensation in being all the things she yearned to be and was not."

"Certainly," Andrew said. "And you laid it on thick, didn't you? You made the most of it. The more graceful you were, the more awkward you made her feel. You reveled in that. You were always—oh, so fragile. Sending her trotting after you, running your errands, while you laughed up your dainty sleeve. . . . I remember. Don't suppose I did not writhe in the days when I used still to writhe. Don't suppose that I didn't hear of the bragging you did to the other servants: 'You should train your mistress as I have mine. She does the fetching and carrying at our place. My feet are bound. My Third Young Mistress's were left unbound that she might wait on me!' "

Andrew reached for a cigarette. Almost—he had got excited. He leaned back.

"Such fine concern for your sister," Tear Drop said. "My suffering does not matter. That it might not have sat so well with me to know that I might toil until I dropped and get nothing while she, without turning her hand, should have it all—everything."

"You bore me," Andrew said.

"I will not bore you much longer," Tear Drop said.

"And I would have you know this—you, at least!" Her lip curled. "I did not help that slut escape!"

"Of course not," Andrew said.

Tear Drop stared at him. "What! You know that?"

"Naturally," Andrew said. "It was I who helped her escape—by keeping you away from her."

"And you—you . . . Knowing that, you do not lift a finger to help me. Oh, this is too much!"

"On the contrary," Andrew said, "I am at your disposal."

But Tear Drop hardly heard him. "You would let that creature undo me—destroy everything I have worked so hard to get—for something I never did. Oh! I call on Buddha!"

"It is too bad you do not have the nature to appreciate irony," Andrew said. "You would be so much more interesting."

Tear Drop's eyes narrowed. "Don't think I am through," she said. "Don't suppose that I am going to just sit around, waiting to be flogged to death."

"Oh, I don't," Andrew said.

Tear Drop turned, walked haughtily into the bedroom and snatched a quilt off the bed. Andrew followed her as far as the door and leaned in it, watching her.

"Give me your knife," she said.

He took it out of his pocket but he did not carry it to her. He made her come to him. She came, she seized it out of his hand and returned to the bed and began ripping the quilt at the seams.

"And are your winter garments lined with it, too?" Andrew said.

"It will be a blessing when I do not have to cower beneath your words again."

"Have you cowered?" Andrew asked.

"Yes, I have."

"Good," Andrew said.

Tear Drop was removing handsful of money from inside the quilt. In her haste she was pulling out shreds of raw silk batting with it.

"My God," Andrew observed mildly. "It's a wonder it didn't crackle when we slept on it." He laughed.

"You did what you set out to do," Tear Drop said, "if you would like to know—if you would enjoy the satisfaction of hearing me say it."

"Where are you going to stow it?" Andrew asked. "Do you want a box?"

"Oh, you did it," Tear Drop said. "I came to you so full of assurance. I was so anxious to please you, to make you happy once more. I was so sure of my beauty and of my abilities. . . . You did it, if that's what you wanted."

"You dropped some," Andrew said. "On the floor—there. Just under the bed."

"Little by little," Tear Drop said, "you did it. Day by day, every day. You sneered. You called me stupid—old-fashioned—a wished-off product of another age, as I believe you put it. An inconvenience that you did not have the energy to throw off."

Tear Drop tore the cloth covering of the quilt halfway down and somewhat less than half across. She began to fold her money into this strip.

"Yes," she said. "You succeeded. You smiled your cruel smiles. You kept me busy fetching and carrying and preparing special dishes of food for your delicate stomach that then you would not eat. You either addressed me with double talk or else you talked to me in English or French—in whatever I could not understand. Oh, yes, you did it. You made me feel the unwanted hag. When I lay in bed, powdered and perfumed, as you ordered me, and waited for you to come, you never did. You made it very clear that you preferred the company of whores or actors or"—she stole a glance at him—"or of yourself."

"You are well paid for it," Andrew said, leaning in the door, smiling. "You are well paid for whatever trouble I have caused you."

"You congratulate yourself!" she said. By folding it carefully, Tear Drop had made the strip of cloth into a sort of money girdle which she now tied around her waist.

"But do not congratulate yourself too soon," she said, "on having remained a stranger to me, this while. It would be a mistake for you to do that. You think that I do not know you, don't you?"

Tear Drop sat down on the bed and took a comb out of her pocket and began to comb her hair. A sly look crept over her face.

"Perhaps you are not aware that you talk in your sleep," she said. "You talk in Chinese then. Ha! I know that you yearn to be an American—modern. I know that in your foreign schools you did all you knew to change yourself. But they would not have you, would they? They asked you what you had done with your queue? Laughed long and loud at you and your efforts?"

Andrew looked out the window.

"You are ashamed of being yellow," Tear Drop said. "You are ashamed of your home and your family and your race. You are afraid—you have nightmares and cramps in your stomach. You hate yourself more than you have ever hated me. You sit around and dream that you are a great figure in history, when all the time you know you will never do anything. So anxious, so ashamed, so yellow. And you supposed that you had kept this secret from me to whom you were so superior."

Tear Drop was combing her hair with rapid strokes, suiting her words to her motions.

"Too bad," she said, "that, after all, you cannot drink

yourself to death. A pity your stomach will not allow you, is it not? Without the fire of drink, your dreams must grow very pale."

Andrew turned. "That's better," he said. "You look much better with your hair combed."

"To the last!" Tear Drop said, standing up suddenly. "To the very end, you refuse to give me the satisfaction of hurting you. Of meaning even that much to you. Of seeing you wince or blush—just once. I do not touch you. Oh, I pity you . . . I do! What runs in your veins—vinegar?"

They heard a noise from the outer room.

"Buddha!" Tear Drop whispered fiercely. "What was that?"

"It is someone knocking, I believe," Andrew said.

"Oh no. Not yet! It couldn't be!"

"It most definitely is," Andrew said, smiling.

"While I have wasted my time—thrown it away on you," Tear Drop muttered, looking frantically around her.

But Andrew's rooms were so arranged that except for the high casement windows and a blind passage, there was no exit but by way of the outer room.

"No," Andrew said, following Tear Drop's frantic appraisal of the windows. "I am afraid you could not make it."

"All right," Tear Drop hissed, standing very erect, very close to Andrew. "Go ahead. Go on and give me up."

"Why don't you get under the bed or something?" Andrew said. "Coming!" he called over his shoulder to whoever was knocking. He reached for the screen which stood carelessly to one side and placed it across the opening. Then he started for the door which Tear Drop had slammed so rudely. But he noticed the bundle that she had laid on the table. He picked it up and dropped it behind his chaise longue, as he was passing. It made a loud, heavy, metallic sound in landing which the knocking fortunately covered.

"Andy!"

"Yes. Come on in."

It was George, looking (Andrew thought) considerably bothered.

"Hello," Andrew said. "What keeps you from work?"

George and Andrew always spoke to each other in English. It was George's idea for self-improvement and keeping in practice. Andrew liked it best when others were around because it attracted attention and made them seem important and mysterious and gave them a bond they would not otherwise have had. He also liked it because he spoke so much better, so much more idiomatically than George.

George was looking sharply around the room. "Have you seen Tear Drop, Andy?"

"No, the little wayward bitch, I have not. But do sit down."

"She did not come here?" George said, his small cold eyes getting smaller and colder. "Good lord!"

"What's the matter?" Andrew said.

"What's the matter?" George considered his brother. "You do know what has happened, Andy, do you not? That Leila escaped? And that it was Tear Drop who helped her escape?"

"Sure," Andrew said.

"Well?" George said. "Now, Tear Drop has escaped—disappeared, at least."

"Oh," Andrew said, "if that's all, don't let it worry you, George. She'll check in here and tap the old cash register before she goes anywhere. You know that. Sit down. Make yourself comfortable. Tag her when she comes through the door, why don't you?"

George dropped into the nearest chair. "You wouldn't be hiding her, would you, Andy?" he said. "Harboring her? Anything of that sort?" His eyes were fixed on the screen that divided the two rooms.

"Cigarette?" Andrew said.

"No, thank you."

Andrew lighted his own and shook out the match. "You know," he said, "I ought to be ashamed. I could have put in a showing. Was the Old Man pretty rough on her?"

"He has ordered her to be flogged to death," George said—announced, really. He waited for Andrew's reaction. When he got none, he went on. "I intend to get a little information out of her before that happens. . . . You're a queer egg, Andy," he added with a mixture of admiration and contempt.

"I'm a queer duck," Andrew said. "Or a bad egg. Which?" He laughed when he saw that George had to check himself from saying, "Both." He noted the fine, horizontal lines that had appeared in George's forehead. They were a recent addition. So were the shadows under his hard little eyes. Was it possible that George who took physical exercise and went to bed at nine o'clock at nights was suddenly suffering from insomnia? "Good lord," as George would say. He could not keep his hands still either. Good lord. What was the matter with George?

"Why aren't you out making the profits?" Andrew asked.

"What a question!" George said.

"Well," Andrew said. "How's the Wang Widow's Bridge Mill making out?"

Andrew did not know why he asked George questions like that, when he didn't give a damn. He did not know why he so often tried to act like a businessman around George, when he despised business. George was pompous and dull. Since Andrew spent so much time making a fool of him and nearly always succeeded, why couldn't he relax? Why was he afraid of him? Why did he care that George treated him with fine contempt when, all the time, it was George who was the first-rate ass? Maybe it was that George would always get there—would sneak up from behind, looking smug and well-fed and smooth, and inherit the earth. Ah, yes. The trouble was that Andrew could not take George seriously, though he was afraid of him, and thought he probably should. George had graduated from the Harvard School of Business. Andrew had been expelled from a liberal arts college whose name gave him a pain to remember.

"Look here, Andy!"

Andrew crossed his legs and blew out a cloud of smoke.

"You don't seem to realize it," George said, "but this affair is serious. Leila has to be found."

"Why?" Andrew asked.

"Good lord!" George said. "If the house was burning down, you would sit around on your . . ."

". . . can," Andrew supplied.

". . . and want to know why. . . . Do you not even know there has been a revolution?"

Andrew thought he probably knew a great deal more about the revolution than George did. It was a rash thing his father had done—particularly when it seemed clear to him that Leila had not wished to return home. He said, "So what? The Third Koo Girl is dead. Didn't *you* hear the commotion?"

George winced. The last time Andrew could remember George wincing was when—at the age of twelve—he had hammered his thumb instead of a nail. . . . Curious.

"That's exactly it," George said. "The Third Koo Girl is dead. Do you think it's advisable to have a second Third

Koo Girl at large? Why, if Leila is recognized, she may be mobbed."

Most curious, when George and Leila had been anything but close that George should care so much about that that he should be getting lines in his face and circles under his eyes! "I have an idea," Andrew said, "that Leila will make that her business. I have an idea she will take care of—that. She's of age, my dear George, and knows a little about the revolution herself. . . . But let's talk about the funeral. I confess . . ."

"Father has ordered her found," George said.

"Let Father find her, then," Andrew said. "Now, that funeral . . ."

But George was not listening, he was apparently not morbidly fascinated as Andrew was; he was drumming his fingers rapidly on the table.

"They take me for a fool," he muttered. "Mother thinks I am a donkey."

"Why, George!" Andrew said, pretending to be shocked.

"It is strange," George said, "how it is always your family that makes you feel that way. . . . Never mind." He looked at Andrew. "Father wants Leila found," he announced. "Well, you are now looking at the man who is going to find her and don't you forget it. It will not be Mother, you understand. Did you ever hear of a steam-roller? Consider that my own particular search is like that—a steamroller. Have you heard about bloodhounds? I have ordered some shipped down from Shanghai." He smiled. "To you I am a fool because I sit here waiting for your Tear Drop who will not come, eh? But keep this in your mind. While I sit here being the fool, my men—the ones *I* have hired—are out all over this countryside, combing it. Right now. They have very explicit orders. They will find Leila. You will see. Mother will see. Why,

I have methods that neither you nor the old folks ever dreamed of!"

Andrew shivered. He did not say again, "But why, George?" Or, "What's this to you?" Temporarily, at least, he was too involved with the chills that were attacking his spine. He said, "You are very efficient, George."

George was standing up, looking at his watch. "I do not count on you, Andy," he said. "I can get along without Tear Drop's help. But if she should come and if you should feel so inclined, keep her here and send a servant for me, will you?"

"Sure," Andrew said, "I'll be glad to."

George straightened his tie, cleared his throat, gave the room a final, appraising look and went out.

Andrew was still looking at the door when Tear Drop came in.

"Oh, hello," he said in English. "What do you suppose is eating him?"

"Where is my bundle?" Tear Drop said.

"I will tell you," Andrew said, switching to Chinese, "if you will promise not to thank me for saving you from the clutches of George."

"Well?"

"It is behind the chaise longue. You will have to lean far over to reach it."

"Bastard!" Tear Drop murmured. But for the first time, that day, she smiled.

"How about your money?" Andrew said, watching her firm little buttocks go up in the air and the sharp drop of her breasts as she bent down. "Did you get it all? Do you think it is safe? I want to be sure you are fortified."

"Do not bother your head over that," Tear Drop said, recovering her bundle. "It is none of your business."

"Oh?"

She turned around. Andrew put out his hand. "Give it to me," he said, indicating the bundle.

Tear Drop went pale. She backed off. Andrew snapped his fingers, once. "Hand it over."

With a sob, she threw it at him. He caught but almost dropped it. He took it to the table and untied the knot. The cloth fell away. A burst of color, a mad, dizzying glitter made his pupils contract. Before him were all of Leila's jewels. (They had to be Leila's. Nobody else in the family had received so many presents from the Old Man.)

"My word!" Andrew said. He touched an amethyst bracelet. "Fortified!" He threw back his head and laughed. "You know," he said, "that's rather good." Quickly, he wrapped them up. Carefully, he tied the knot in the kerchief. He turned to Tear Drop who had been standing like the victim of some witch's spell, bowed, and held the bundle out to her.

"Farewell," he said.

Tear Drop seized it. "You . . ." But apparently she could not find the word that fitted him. She began to sidle rapidly toward the door, never taking her eyes from Andrew, who did not take his from hers.

When she had reached it, when she was slipping out her hand to open it, Andrew said, "Curiosity, that's all, but how will you get past the gates?"

Tear Drop tossed her head. "And so you are such a gentleman," she said, "that you did not know that all these years I have had a beautiful friendship with Siau Liang, the gatekeeper's son!"

Now, her hand was touching the door. Now, Andrew said, "Madame, my mother, approves your escape, my lovely. If she did not, Siau Liang or no Siau Liang, you would never get further than that court out there."

"That's what you think!" Tear Drop cried. She was out of the door, at last.

"That's what I know," Andrew called after her. "So, go slowly, dear."

VII

"She is now on her way to the gates," the servant said.

"Good," Madame Koo said. "And Ah-doo is in his appointed place?"

"Yes, Madame. He is ready to follow."

"Thank you," Madame Koo said. "That will be all."

It was always best to let nature take its course, when that was possible. Tear Drop, with her resources, was to be allowed the opportunity of following her nature—of going to some strange city and posing as some fine lady, on the lookout for a fine life. The fine lady would not be given to telling tales about her slave's past. But since Tear Drop knew too much, it was as well to make sure she did follow her nature and did not, for instance, tarry for so much as half an hour in this city or open her pretty mouth to a single acquaintance she might happen to meet.

Madame heard her Old Crone to the end and the end was this: "Of course, this thug admitted he had been sworn to secrecy but . . . Well, Madame, that fatal name was loud on his lips—the—uh—Third Koo Girl's."

Madame Koo told the Crone to wait and disappeared into her rooms. She who could never afford the heat of anger was livid. In the end she must be foiled by her Second Son? By George? By George, whom she had considered so dull and safe as to be herself the one (in her instructions to Lao Liang) to grant him free permission to come and go through the gates. Fate was to play her such a trick as this? For it must be Fate. Or was Madame losing her touch? No, no. Madame could not have been expected to predict that George (who would not even move in to hear her interview with an officer because he was not invited, who spent his time slapping slaves and the wrong slave, at that!)—that George should *dare* to move without her consent, that George on his own should launch a search! Either Nature itself was letting Madame down or strange forces that were outside the province of Nature were at work.

Clumsy, blundering ox . . . What did he know about hiring men or instructing them! Undoubtedly General Ma at this moment had already heard for whom the Koo Family was searching. This, when Madame was on the verge of abandoning the notion of any large-scale search (so fearful was she of the attendant publicity), even one directed by herself, with every precaution taken. She had examined the sleeping powders, at last, and discovered that the opium was not what the girl had taken, thus diminishing her last solid hope for a corpse, quickly acquired. But in spite of this dark turn of events, Madame had been about to decide to leave everything to her trusted few rather than run the risk of a big search. Now the damage was done. There was only one difference now, only one small way in which the situation was better than if her lord had blabbed: General Ma would have to move more cautiously, that was all. And what would this Colonel Shu choose to believe and do—when he heard?

It was not in Madame to swear or rant. She took the gold-and-jade stickpin out of her hair knot, the one her old lord had given her at the birth of their Second Son, and she snapped it in two.

She stared at it, lying in her hand. Then she laid it carefully on the table and sat down.

For almost an hour she sat thinking. Then she drew a pen and writing materials toward her. She mixed the ink. On a sheet of rice paper she brushed the characters for: "Silence or death that is eternal silence." Upon a second sheet she wrote the identical characters. She did not use the Koo seal. She clapped her hands for her Old Crone who entered without a word.

"Take these," she said, deftly folding each into an infinitesimal square. "One is to go to the keeper of the jail, the other to the guard Old Master dealt with. See them together. Say what family sent you. Keep your evil eyes on them while they examine these documents. The illiterate have reverence for that which is written. Say, 'Silence or death that is eternal silence.' Grin your evil grin and leave. But if you are seen . . ."

"Madame, it will be my business not to be seen. But may I make the suggestion that perhaps a fatal accident to the guard, at this time would . . . ?"

". . . would be most suspicious?" Madame asked, giving her a look.

"Indeed, yes, of course, of course," mumbled the Old Crone.

"Send Lao Liang to me," Madame said. "And ask that Wei-sun come, immediately he gets in. You are dismissed."

Wei-sun, one of the four trusted servants, came before Lao Liang did.

"Wei-sun, we begin a search."

"Yes, Madame."

"I will personally interview all the prospective men. You will bring them to me, one by one, directly after nightfall, and if necessary, throughout the night."

"Yes, Madame."

"This is the plan, Wei-sun. For every five men hired,

three will search for the runaway slave, Tear Drop. These three should be clumsy and loud-mouthed. The other two out of every five search for—the Third Koo Girl, Wei-sun. I think I need not tell you what qualities they should have."

"No, Madame."

"Very well, then. Go."

"I go, Madame."

Lao Liang, the old gatekeeper, came. Madame spoke only one sentence to him.

"The House rules are to be relaxed," she said, "with servants and family to come and go according to usual."

Next, Madame would go with her old servant, Wang-ma, through the courts. To Wang-ma she would make it clear which servants were to be assigned to errands that would take them out to the streets and which were not. In the various courts Madame would see the male of the highest rank, the male in each court who was in authority over all other males. To each Madame would explain that while her lord's House rules were now relaxed, it might be advisable because of the unsettled times and the general need for closed mouths, if only the older and more sober men went abroad.

Thus Madame, who herself controlled all of the women's movements at all times, made sure that while the House rules were to be as usual, with nothing wrong or out of the way at the House of Koo for General Ma or Colonel Shu or other curious souls to hear about (all Houses had been closed these past few days) that nevertheless only those who fell into one of two categories should be the ones to go out—the responsible and the superstitious. Never single-faceted, Madame Koo's policy: if ever there was a time when garbled rumors that were tinged with madness were needed, it was now.

VIII

Throughout the night the Small Gate opened and closed and strange men were noiselessly ushered through the sleeping courts and noiselessly ushered back out again.

George, after having been closeted with his mother, moved his headquarters to the Wang Widow's Bridge Mill. He knew that without saying as much, she had commanded him to cease his activities. She could not outwardly command it, since his father had ordered his sister found and he was within his rights as oldest living son, as filial son. George reimpressed upon his men the great need for secrecy, but that was as far as he could go in the direction his mother asked—it was the first time in his life he had disobeyed her.

When the next day dawned, all over the city, here and there, in this street and that, near the city gates, squatting in alleys, loitering around the railway station, walking on the Big Horse Road, stumping along with beggars' bowls, leaning against walls, glancing into shops and huts and outdoor toilets and bathhouses, there were men scattered about like dots on a map.

"Have you seen a slave with heart-shaped face and willow form?" some of these men would ask.

"Have you seen any woman hereabouts who is thin and tall?" others would say. "Dressed in gray or blue-cotton cloth, aged twenty-three but looking older, and without any scars or birthmarks, with a gaunt face and natural feet. Her hair would attract your attention."

Still others put it like this: "Have you seen a girl who gave you a start? Who made you think that the Third Koo Girl had risen from the dead?"

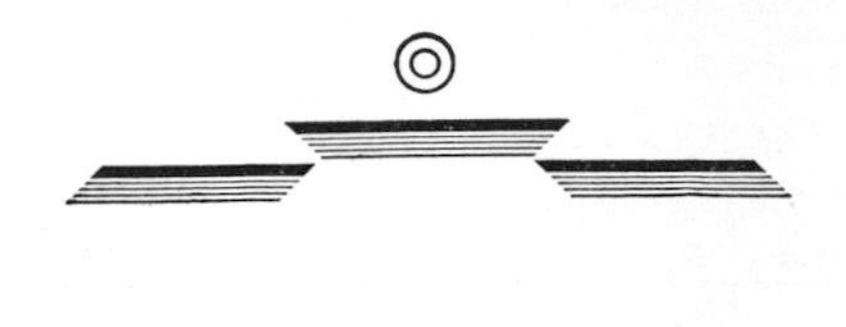

7

I

ON Sin-ss-ka Square, Christopher Blair stopped. He looked in on the shops and listened to the talk of passers-by. He did not hear her name mentioned. Several people spoke to him.

"Greetings, Bao I-sung."

"Ten thousand fortunes, Bao I-sung."

And: "There goes he who killed Old Koo's Number One."

He went into three different teahouses, all crowded and noisy. In each he took a central table. Nothing. Neither she nor the revolution was the topic of any of the conversations that he overheard. He went to the Dzung Waung Miau, the biggest temple, and stood around for half an hour in the principal court where the fortunetellers and the geomancers had their stalls and many people were collected. Nothing. He could understand that they had learned their lesson, but . . .

Deeply puzzled, he started out for Pu-tang Street. When he was going through an alley he noticed a vender, several yards ahead, setting down his portable stove, raising up the wooden lid and peering inside, while he was talking over his shoulder to an ordinary-appearing man who went off as Blair approached.

"That one," said the vender, with a laugh, "seeks a tall, gaunt woman with hair. Will you have a good hot bun?"

"I don't mind if I do," Blair said. And while he was paying, "Whom did you say that one sought?"

"A tall woman with hair. Ha-ha."

"Did she have a name?" asked Blair, laughing too.

"No name. Just a woman with hair."

"Very funny," Blair said.

"I could do with one," said the vender. "Tall or short, fat or thin, eh?"

For awhile Blair followed in the direction the man had taken but he had lost him. He crossed over to the Old North Gate Street and walked its length. He went through Big Market. Nothing. Nothing more. Looking at his watch, he started out once more for Pu-tang Street.

At Pickpocket Bridge a man walking abreast with him suddenly turned and fell on a woman, rather tall and poorly clothed, who was going the other way, with a basket on her arm.

"Take your hands off me!" the woman cried.

Instantly people began to gather around.

"Now what ails him?"

"Is she his runaway spouse?"

"Let's just have a look at you, eh?" said the man, jerking her head back by the hair.

"Thief's bones!" the woman shrieked.

Some of the people laughed.

"Nay," said the man. "You are too old. You are genuinely much too old, old hag. Go on."

"Rape your mother's mother. Rape your . . ." The woman went off, cursing at the top of her voice.

"What was the meaning of that?" Blair said to the man.

"Why is she so genuinely much too old? Whom do you seek?"

The man looked at Blair.

"A woman who might make you believe the Third Koo Girl had risen from the dead—since you are so curious."

Christopher Blair said, "You must be mad."

He was conscious of the faces of the people who were standing around, of the sudden draining of expression at the mention of the name. It was their business to push whatever it was (belief or grief or despair) down as far as their bowels. They had returned to the factories, they would return to the land, business was as usual.

"You seek the Third Koo Girl when the Third Koo Girl is dead?" Blair said. "What on earth ails you?"

"There are these seekers," someone standing close by muttered.

Someone else: "They seek her ghost."

The people were melting away. The man yawned. He said, grinning at Blair, "Ghost hunting or jellyfish hunting—what is the difference, my friend, so long as you are well paid. . . . I pick no bone of trouble with you. Good day."

"But who pays you so well, then, for such an undertaking?" Blair said.

The man laughed. "Wouldn't you like to know?"

"Yes," Blair said, "I would."

He went on. He took a long way to Pu-tang Street but came across nothing more. In Pu-tang Street the pock-marked beggar who regularly worked the street was squatting opposite the shop. Blair hunted in his pocket for coppers.

"Ah, Bao I-sung. If everyone was as generous as you!"

"How's that son of yours?" Months ago the beggar's son had been brought to the hospital, having lost three fingers to a silk vat at Wang Widow's Bridge Mill. The boy was twelve.

"He will go back to work very soon," the beggar said.

"Without his hand?"

"Ai . . . Half wages. Better than nothing. He will try it—he will do what he can."

Blair crossed the street and entered the shop. The beggar looked after him.

II

The door was closed and bolted on the inside. For awhile Leila kept her eyes on it. Waiting was part of her training. She sat on the edge of the bed, slowly and steadily swinging her legs. She would have invoked Christopher Blair's image if she could, but that was not possible, she discovered. The substance of him kept receding and it was futile to try to follow him through the streets. . . . Hers was not the power to re-create him. Sardonic, quiet, accepting his half-caste's estate, long ago, too consciously. He must have felt obligated to love what he should have been free to hate. She felt he was prouder than she was—apologizing for something or other by administering to life, as a surgeon. Cutting it open, though, before he sewed it back.

She thought about the feud between her family and him. He had just moved to the city (she had been away at Vassar) when her brother, Lincoln, had been taken so ill. The city was hostile to foreign medicine—particularly to surgery, the most dreaded of its features. The family had called in Chris because they had already had in all the well-known, old-style Chinese doctors who had failed—because they were desperate. Chris was sure to have known what was at stake, since his training had been in both the

Chinese and American traditions and he was no ordinary foreigner, fresh from the States and greener than grass. He must have known he was on exhibition and he certainly knew that Lincoln was the Number One Son of the Big Man and that unless the chances of recovery were good, he should not have touched the case. But he had touched it—even though he had been quoted as saying it was nearly hopeless—he had operated on Lincoln and Lincoln had died on the operating table. Leila's father had vented his rage and his grief on Chris. He had publicly denounced him, calling him butcher and quack, claiming that his cellar was lined with the jars of pickled boy babies and that he ate the eyes of boy children, every morning, for his breakfast. He took an oath to run him out of town. . . . Through the Board of Gentry he put up every kind of obstacle he could think of, even to demanding that the hospital be torn down because the *foons-s'* were not right and would bring bad luck to the neighborhood. The chimneys, it seemed, were set wrong and attracted evil spirits. Of the older generations only Madame, notoriously conservative and antiforeign, understood that Young Dr. Blair had risked a great deal for the sake of a Koo son. Leila was sure that her mother had frustrated, in secret, many of her father's moves. The feud had stabilized. Old Koo would still ruin Christopher Blair if he could, not so much for the old reasons as that he considered him a good enemy—one worthy of an elaborate defeat. Leila could always follow the workings of her father's mind without a hitch. He would not, for example, be pleased to discover him harboring her. He would use it, with the authorities and the gentry, to achieve his ruin.

She knew she was too afraid to feel that she was afraid. She sat, swinging her legs. Under the pillow was the pistol that he had cleaned and loaded and put there. She wished she had always believed in Fate, so that she would have Fate to lean on now. Fate could be called upon to explain everything. Lincoln had been her favorite brother. Christopher Blair had mourned her, when he had thought she was dead, in the streets. If she had not been so feverish and half out of her head the first two days and nights, for instance. If she had not had to do battle with her memories when he was around. Who knew?

His knock, at last. She went to the door and drew the bolt. First, they smiled at each other. The sight of his face and body so pleased her that all else must fade into the distant past.

"Have I been gone long?" he asked. He took off his coat and threw it on the bed. "I went everywhere," he said.

She walked over to the bed, picked the coat up and hung it on the hanger that was on the back of the door. The room was very small. She was aware of it and so was he.

"Everything is pretty quiet," he said. "The people aren't talking about either you or what's happened to the revolution. And there aren't any speakers or agitators around. They haven't been told you didn't die."

He lighted a cigarette. "So it remains a question—whom you have given the slip to—whether to your father and the House of Koo only or to the whole counterrevolutionary bunch. Whether he got you out with or without their knowledge and co-operation and with or without the sanction of the C.E.C. and Shanghai. If he did it on his own, he would want to keep pretty quiet now."

She nodded. She decided it would be best to look anywhere except at him.

He said, "Even if he did it with official approval . . . Well, the execution may have been so well planned, with God knows what sort of dark Act Two in the offing, that now they are in the embarrassing position of being caught in their own trap—of being unable, without a living, breathing you, to prove that anything was irregular—or to prove what they would probably like best to prove—that you're not the material people's gods are made of. Until they found you, then, they would want to be quiet, too."

"But why?" she said. "What would be the point of going through all the motions of arresting and executing me and then not going through with it?" She remembered the courier who had offered her a quick death—perhaps he *had* been sent by a friend. "It seems more likely that my father, at the last minute, asked for and secured my release. Either that or he didn't ask anybody officially—just bargained with, say, the keeper, and some way arranged for a substitution, since you say a Third Koo Girl did die."

She felt his eyes on her—questioning, brooding, pitying. She had made that word "substitution" sound as anonymous as possible.

"My father is a fabulous man," she said.

"Well," he said, "the city is quiet."

She looked at the floor. "I don't understand. So many people saw me—family, servants. They know that whatever happened at that execution, it wasn't I who was among the ones that were shot. What about them? They are surely carrying tales."

"Not yet, they're not. At least I didn't hear any. Maybe nobody at the House of Koo is being allowed out, to carry them."

"But the counterrevolutionists would have made it their business to have heard plenty by now—even if my father had planned on keeping it a secret. Forty-eight hours have passed. What are they waiting for?"

"For the hope of laying their hands on you," he said. "They're afraid to try to disillusion the people about you, without evidence, I suppose. . . . I don't know."

"I can contact the underground," she said, with an effort, "and thus make it known I did give them the slip but am still on the peasants' and workers' side of this lost fight."

"You can and should," he said, "unless they continue to believe you are dead—in which case you had better be 'dead.' "

"But . . ." (Why did he seem so close?)

"So far they have not been told differently and since it's that belief—that you died for them—that seems to them so moving and so important . . . Don't you see?"

"You are keeping something from me," she said.

"That there are searches—hunts—under way . . . 'Have you seen anyone who might make you believe the Third Koo Girl had risen from the dead?' I wasn't keeping this from you. I was just saving it until last."

She leaned over and picked up a hairpin that she saw on the floor.

"I couldn't find out who was conducting the hunts," he said.

She said, "But the news of these hunts will combine with the rumors and tales that will have to come out of the House of Koo sooner or later. I must go to the underground."

"No. Not yet. They can choose not to believe the rumors—they can even choose to ignore the hunts. You're forgetting the myth, the combination of the execution and the funeral, the history of that day and the curious—downright eery—timing of your disappearance from the House of Koo. . . . They're pretty desperate, these people. They have lost and they may just decide they need their Koo Girl dream undisturbed."

She shook her head.

"We will wait to see what happens," he said. He glanced toward the bed where the pistol lay under the pillow, making her a silent promise. "This isn't a bad place for you to be," he said. "They're not apt to suspect me of harboring a Koo."

"No."

She must work at the hairpin: straighten it and bend it, in turn. She did not see him come. He put out his hand and took the hairpin away from her. He let it fall through his fingers. . . . He tipped up her face, ran his fingers lightly over her lips.

"The sun is shining in your hair," he said. "Did you know that?"

They stared at each other.

"Leila." He said it musingly, almost absently, it was the first time he had called her by any name. He drew her to her feet. As she felt his arms close around her, she remembered the times he had touched her when he was nursing her back to health. Their kiss was full of all the longing, all the need that they had felt.

He held her away from him.

"There's an old saying," she murmured. " 'May my body be fire to your body and my soul window to your soul.' "

He led her to the bed. Then he did an odd thing. He took the watch off his wrist, opened the drawer of the table, laid it in, and closed it.

"Now," he said, turning back to her.

She laughed softly. "But time isn't going to stand still."

"I know," he said, with pain and tenderness, beginning to undress her. "But our time is going to be that time out of time we're always hearing about. I love you."

She said, "I know." And was surprised to hear herself put it like that. "I love you," she said. They were new words to her. She had never used them in her progress from girl to myth to woman. Would he be surprised to find her virgin? To discover that her woman's blood was to stain these sheets?

So strange—so strange: that happiness was theirs for the taking, after all these sealed months, all these sealed years. He was stroking her thighs—she opened her thighs.

"My God!" she cried. "I am yours!"

III

By late afternoon the situation had altered. George Koo's men were still about, opening their mouths loudly, some of them even going so far as to say, "Have you seen the Third Koo Girl?" But the rumors that were tinged with madness were beginning to do their work, since the Koo House rules had now been relaxed for long enough. Also, Madame Koo's slave hunters were even louder-mouthed than George's men. Utter confusion reigned and it was as if the name had been taken out of hiding. Yes, the name began to pass, once again, like chain lightning.

"The Third Koo Girl returned to haunt the House of Koo."

"Good for her. I hope she frightened them well."

"I hope she haunts them for a hundred years."

"But how could the Koo Family be conducting a search for a ghost?"

"That is a question!"

"Nay, it is a runaway slave with heart-shaped face the Koo Family hunts."

"Ghost or slave, there is something strange about it!"

"When that coffin exploded, her ghost stepped forth."

"Ai, her ghost walked."

"It is said she never fell in the prison yard."

"Why, but my fifth cousin saw her himself. What is this?"

"It is said how her corpse was mutilated beyond recognition. Perhaps it was not her corpse. Have you thought of that?"

"What I have thought of is how the traitors must always start some stink—that's what I have thought about."

"Ai! Would that she were more than her own poor ghost."

"Our display of the other day struck fear into yellow hearts, that is all. They would like to bring her alive and smear her. Discredit her memory with us—may they rot."

"They shall not defile her memory."

"Ai, if she is so alive—if she never died for us—then let them produce her. Ha!"

"We carry her in our hearts."

A curious twist was this: the changing attitude of George Koo's men, so much less carefully selected than Madame's. They heard from those "who had seen her fall," they heard all sorts of ghost stories. By this time watchmen, beggars, wizards, priests and any number of others were claiming visions and ghostly visitations. And they heard about the slave hunters. Many of them being of superstitious disposition themselves began to feel that they were the ones being taken in. "What sort of joke is this?" they asked of each other. And it began to appear as if George's men might do less harm than Madame Koo had anticipated.

The searches were going ahead. All the approaches to the city were being watched, as well as the canal traffic. Houses and shops were being entered with the flimsiest excuses. Madame had blocked out the city into areas and she was having each area methodically worked by those "two out of every five" of her men.

George had had to give up the idea of bloodhounds due to transportation difficulties, but in addition to his regular men, he had five modern detectives at work in the city and others in Shanghai. It had occurred to him that his sister might already have quit the city. The same thought had occurred to Madame who, however, believed that in that case there was no real hope of finding her and had therefore dismissed it.

George, who had kept to himself at the Wang Widow's Bridge Mill, even sleeping there, with the primary purpose of avoiding his mother whom he had had to disobey, was on this afternoon summoned to appear before her.

And at the House of Koo, while Madame's men came and went, day and night, they were escorted through passages and were not often seen by the members of the family. "The affair." was of course the topic for discussion and speculation in almost every courtyard, although not in Helen's. Helen, after the scene with her mother, had remained in her rooms and would see no one except Little Dog and her maid, Dji-bo, to whom she made it clear that she did not wish to hear her Third Sister's name mentioned nor anything at all about her.

Old Koo had not left his rooms either. The little maid, Tse-yuen, had persuaded him about the advisability of taking food but nothing he ate or drank would stay in its accustomed place. By his own orders, no one was allowed to see him but the little maid assured Madame that he was beyond caring whether his orders were broken or not. She seemed much worried. She said, "Old Mistress, he has a sickness of the heart that has traveled to his bowels." She gave it as her opinion that a doctor ought to be called in. Madame, therefore, went to see Old Koo and came away disturbed and more determined than ever to get "the affair" over with. It was true that if he did not soon have it out with his nature, doctors would have to be resorted to.

George was waiting for his mother. He was waiting in her court, chewing at a cigar, and feeling vaguely but totally sick with dread. He was kept waiting, of course. When he was at last bidden to enter, he was met with,

"You have not ceased your activities?", before he could bow properly and find himself a chair.

"What is the matter?" Madame Koo asked, with a note of gentleness and a note of mockery that would be quite lost on George. "Were you a revolutionary, too? Is that it?"

George started, swallowed desperately.

"You were very busy in Shanghai," Madame suggested.

A pause that became unendurable.

"I was only helping Father," George finally got out. "As oldest living son, as filial son, he has seen fit to give me much responsibility."

"Of course," Madame said. "And you were therefore, perhaps, on an inside track of this revolution that your sister was not. . . . Did you not spend some time meeting with gentlemen behind closed doors in hotels?"

George fidgeted. "So did Father. There was nothing so secret about it, Mother. We had to secure the family interests. How do you suppose we got back here? Father and I . . ."

"You . . . ? What have you done, my son, that has struck such terror into your heart?"

Madame Koo's ruthlessness was the more effective because it combined itself with perfect equanimity and a sense of timelessness. One fending with her sooner or later gave in, as one must give in to the inevitable. She was not going to let George go until she had had her way with him and George knew it.

"I sent a courier!" he blurted out.

"To what purpose?"

"Ah, Mother! Father and the old ones, the gentry, are only one of the elements in our revitalized revolutionary party. We are another—we young, modern, well-educated ones."

"Including your sister?"

George colored. "No, no, Mother. Hers was the element that had to be purged—got rid of—Left Wing."

"I see."

"We are the New China, the New Democracy."

"So?"

"We are the ones who will industrialize and modernize this nation. We have the knowledge and the techniques. We are thoroughly familiar with capitalism—profit and loss and all of that. Who was it, in Shanghai, who knew how to convert this family's holdings into gold and bank drafts and General Motors and U. S. Steel Preferred stocks that were an ocean away from political trouble? It is I and the ones like me who have stayed loyal to our families."

"Because the families hold the purse strings?" Madame asked.

"Oh, Mother!"

"Yes?" Madame Koo had felt as out of her element, in Shanghai, as Old Koo had. She had not held her family's pulse as closely as usual. However, since her discovery of George's act of disobedience, she had made it a point to take a more backward glance. She had questioned both George's wife and his personal servants. "This courier?" she said.

"Mother," George said. "More and more Father had turned over the factories to me, as you know. . . . It was natural that I should keep myself informed on the Third Koo Girl's career. It was her fault that the factories struck. Cheap labor is that which we cannot make progress without. Therefore, when the purge was planned and I was informed that she was to be liquidated, I bethought myself of the fact that it would be awkward and embarrassing to our family. And I thought, also, since I had kept in such close touch with developments here—I thought that the workers might cause us real trouble if she were publicly executed. They might vandalize, break up the machines and equipment, set fire to the dormitories . . . Who could say? It seemed to me to be an unnecessary risk. It seemed to me there was a much better, quieter, more expedient way."

"Which was?"

"My courier," George said, drawing in his breath, "carried cyanide which he was instructed to offer her."

Madame Koo was silent. Her son's motives were very close to her own, after all. She should be lauding him. He, too, had named her major threat to family—he had been acting solely in the family's interests.

Madame said, "You did not see fit to consult your family or father. . . . You wished to get her out of the way before your father, whose favorite daughter you knew her to be, should have the chance to try to save her. Is that what makes you so busy and pale—your fear that your father should discover, now, your share in this? He has frequently named it, by the way, a family affair."

George stared at his feet.

"And the day that your sister returned to this House must have been a bad day for you. You must have considered her leaving it again both fortuitous and disastrous—to take so bold a step as to disobey me."

George said, "It is true that when the courier reported the failure of his mission to me, I dismissed him angrily, and I have been a little afraid of blackmail. Because, Mother, should there be a mess over this—an investigation, say, by the C.E.C.—I will be suspected, along with Father, of having made the deal to get her out and—yes—the business about the courier is bound to come out."

Madame Koo said thoughtfully, "It amounts to this—a brother having tried to take his sister's life."

"She would have died anyway. She was *scheduled* to die."

"You never suspected that your father might have had plans of his own—to save her."

"And drag the family down to ruin," George said bitterly.

Madame was quiet.

George said, "Before this mess becomes a mess and is brought to the attention of the C.E.C. and is officially investigated . . ."

". . . you feel you must destroy the evidence. You must find and kill and dispose of your sister's body—yes. It all becomes very clear. So that your plan which would have frustrated all other plans will not come to light."

"My plan was best," George said stubbornly.

"For your sake, I hope your father never learns of it."

George stared at his mother. His eyes said, "*You* could tell him!" His mother's face was expressionless.

George rose—waiting for Madame to say, "Call in your men." He would have to obey. Madame, however, said, "Good day."

And it was only after George had reached the court that he realized what she had really said: "If there is an investigation, my son, you will be given the privilege of shouldering the blame for the sake of your family you have so dutifully served, never fear. You are the one conducting a hunt. We hunt for a slave."

The hunts continued.

IV

The trouble was that General Ma did not believe in ghosts, he thought, as he sat at his desk, ordering his thoughts and considering his tapering artist's hands. He had had his little chat with Colonel Shu, who had informed him curtly that he had himself examined that corpse of the Third Koo Girl and whatever this nonsense was about, it was nevertheless nonsense and there was an end to it. Was the General questioning the Colonel's integrity? Certainly not. But the General continued to be fascinated with "the nonsense" and—he did not believe in ghosts. . . . As one psychologist assessing another, he was, furthermore, most interested in Madame Koo's slave hunt. Such a lot of bother about a slave, it would seem. . . . He had had a little chat with the keeper of the jail, who was told that positions, like lives, could be lost overnight, in troubled times, and did more than have a chat with the guard who had attended her—but with no better results. They swore, along with Colonel Shu, that the Third Koo Girl was dead. Yet Madame turned the city over hunting for a slave, and the Second Son of Koo, a graduate of Harvard University, was ghost hunting. *Most* interesting.

The General had taken the trouble to interview two or three of George's men. He asked of these one question, in particular: "Have you talked with any of the Koo servants who claim to have seen her?" And from each, almost the identical response: "Yes, Your Excellency. My woman—(cousin or sister-in-law)—knows one of the Koo maids who swears she saw her." And the General: "Swears she was real, eh?" "Yes, Your Excellency. That is, she was sure or says she was sure of it—until that funeral. But now, she says she is not so sure. She says the timing was so exceedingly strange—the funeral and the girl-or-ghost disappearing. She says that she is confused." Hmmm. And who was not? These men, under questioning, admitted that they had been hired to find the Third Koo Girl, though they were far from happy about it, as the General could tell.

What was General Ma to make of this riddle with its pieces that simply did not fit together? One danger was that Old Koo was instigating some lewd and fabulous joke with its object—revenge—and simply using his Second Son as a front. Ma had been informed that the old man was ill in his rooms, which was not a good or straightforward sign. Furthermore, it did not escape the General that the Koo Family was asking for no official help in its present activities.

The people's reception of the rumors and the news of the hunts was of absorbing interest to the General, in view of what had transpired outside the Koo Gates that night. He had to smile, thinking how differently his thoughts had been geared then: first, to dissipating the queer mood of the people; but, second, to appeasing, making up with, and impressing Old Koo whose daughter had driven such an embarrassing wedge between them. . . . By allowing the funeral, he had intended his "quick stroke of the knife" to cut two ways—to provide opportunity for making a great show of protecting the House of Koo, against sticks and stones, of course, of allowing the people to show it no discourtesy. He had not, however, accurately anticipated the intensity of that mob's passion, not even with that day's history behind it. Had he been on hand himself—Ma was by neither habit nor training a field general—he might have been tempted to delay that rocket signal for a little while. How the Koo Family was hated!

Now, these rumors. Could they be turned to good use? Would the people believe slander of her? Should they be helped a little by agitators? But evidence was needed. And there was the danger, already running below the surface, as the General surmised, of the people assuming that this was an organized smear campaign and nothing but a pack of lies.

For the General was supposing, for the moment, that the Third Koo Girl was somehow alive and that dear Old Koo had somehow managed it. . . . He would hardly bother the high authorities in Shanghai about it, in view of Colonel Shu's story, at least not yet. But let him suppose that she was alive and that she had given her family the slip and that, instead of the family's finding her, it would be General Ma. Here was a sweet vision: of Sin-ss-ka Square, at a busy hour; very well dressed and tended, the Third Koo Girl being escorted by some anonymous hirelings through the Square, on her way to her father's house. And what a prize to parade through the streets after "that day" and funeral. She should be deposited at her father's house, too. While the agitators were busy: "Do you see how true she has been to you—how she died for you? Do you see the one you have held in your hearts? Do you want to guess who sold you out and asked Old Koo to come back?" Let the people build to a second, frenzied climax—to another attack on the House of Koo—with, this time, the troops quartered at too great distance. . . . Sweet vision—with the girl, who had made such fools of them, disgraced and overthrown, leaving behind her—instead of this dangerous idealism—the deep cynicism which the General knew so well how to handle. Possibly the people's hate could be reinforced by Shanghai's cold view of a proved deal to bring the Koo House low. The city without the House of Koo to be bowed to, toadied to, placated, and planned around. Who knew? Houses rose to power and fell. A House of Ma was not so inconceivable.

But the General checked the soaring flight of his dream. The only reliable evidence was the living, breathing girl. . . . Her corpse, for example, even a fresh corpse, would not do. And so General Ma—having already assured the Board of Gentry that there was nothing to these rumors and that all they needed to fear was some token of their dear friend, Old Koo's displeasure—called in a captain of his and having assured him that officially this "Koo Affair" was not to be touched, proceeded in this fashion:

"I do not think it expedient to play with rumors, since we know so little, in the first place, and, in the second place, since the people seem to think we smell. They tend to assume we are liars, Captain, don't you think so?"

"They are suspicious of us, sir," said the captain, who was lean and muscular and young.

"Yes. Therefore, we keep hands off. We do not meddle. We conduct no searches, whatsoever."

"I see, sir."

"Is the Second Son of Koo still hiring men?"

"Yes, General. More every day."

"Excellent, Captain. Suppose we select twenty of our very best men. You and I will instruct them most carefully. We will use some of those veiled hints and threats that we are so good at. We will send them out in ones and twos—to hire themselves to the Second Son of Koo. He needs good men. . . . What do you think?"

"Sir, I believe this plan to be inspired."

"Thank you, Captain. Then, shall you be about it? And it is to remain a closed issue between you and me, of course."

"Of course, General."

The captain saluted and withdrew; the General lighted a cigarette and watched the thin, gray spiral of smoke lift toward the ceiling.

The searches continued.

V

For hours they lay on the bed, with the door bolted. For hours he held her in the curve of his arm and stroked her, kissed her. . . . She stroked and kissed him, passion mounting, passion fulfilled, passion dim. The pistol stayed under the pillow. For hours that they did not measure by clock or watch or sun, they lay in each other's arms. They forgot to eat. When the servant came knocking, he must wait until they had dressed. . . . Often she held his head between her breasts, half-starved but "so beautiful," he said. Desire must mount to crest after crest; once when he entered her, she cried. How quiet it was afterwards.

"This is what love is," she said, like a guide on a tour.

He got so he would watch her face, keeping his eyes on her face. "I must see you needing me," he said.

"I gave them the name in Sin-ss-ka Square," she said. " 'That night.' I gave it freely to them."

He did not suggest that he go back out to the streets, to see what was happening there.

She told him she was saying his name over all the years of her life, since she was six. "I will love you as long as I live," she said. He laughed and when he mounted her, the next time, he held her hands imprisoned in his; he held them down. She struggled, but it was of no avail.

The hours passed—unmeasured, unheeded. Whatever went on outside doubtless went on.

"I'll tell you a secret," she said, rising up out of the bed like a mermaid, with her hair full of the light that it had collected from somewhere, falling down to her shoulders. "At Vassar, I was more interested in the sonnets of Elizabeth Barrett Browning than I was in the Declaration of Independence. . . . 'How do I love you? Let me count the ways.' Remember?"

"Pure corn," he said softly.

Another time she said, "I loved what I rebelled against." Smiling, making it half a question: "It's what made me such an interesting rebel."

Still later. "I was a slave. Painting a flower, one day, I came to that conclusion. I was just higher up in the hierarchy of slavery that we call family than Tear Drop was. I was beloved of the master—that's the slave's highest hope."

"And who was Tear Drop?"

"My slave—but we got our roles mixed up. She ruled me with an iron hand. I was called Little Big Foot when I was little. Tear Drop was everything I wasn't."

"Is that why you left home—because you found out you were a slave?"

"Yes and no. . . . They wished to marry me off to a modern man. Except that I wasn't asked, everything was done to please me."

He laughed.

"Is it funny?"

"Very funny."

"Half-caste," she said, tenderly, mockingly.

He did not punish her for that.

They lay, careless, gay, during the daylight hours, sometimes staring off into space, invoking their long-ago pasts. He had flown kites and operated upon beetles, when he was little, as it turned out.

"You are Li Tuh-ying, my med school mistress," he said.

"I am your life. What are you talking about?"

"Does it make you afraid—that we're not strangers?"

"No. . . . But I wish I believed in reincarnation. There."

"Where is Vassar?"

"Vassar is in Poughkeepsie, New York."

"I will comb your hair." Saying, he was aware, something else, but not caring. And, in fact, he combed her hair.

Night—those unmeasured hours of darkness—they could not lie so carelessly, or play, but must lie closely—in contact, each to the other—the matter of holding and being held. If they lay straight, with their feet touching, the top of her head fitted under his chin.

"You are not so tall."

She could not sleep. Each night was eternity, each night was his life and hers, his death and hers; each night, ghosts walked, her ghost and his.

"The coffin exploded."

"A soldier told me about it."

"There is nothing sweeter than laughter," she said.

"Did you enjoy the speeches?"

". . . I knew how to stand."

"You're bitter."

"Am I?"

"You belong to me, you know, and not to them."

"I mourned you," he said, "by seeking to find the most sluttish slut."

"But of course you didn't find her."

"No, dearest, I didn't find her."

Like a refrain: "You belong to me and not to them."

At some time they would begin to sink down, down, down, into a desperate sleep which they shared and which she was the one to break at six o'clock, pressing her head against his chest, hearing the beating of his heart. They shuttled between six and six, it seemed to them then, but only then.

"We were visited by a rat."

. . . "I love you."

"Huan-li broke out in a rash."

Huan-li's letter was a collection of banalities and clichés, strangely moving to them both.

"He could not have put it worse."

"No."

"How did you ever get into the revolution?" he asked. "How did you manage the transition—from flower painting to that?"

"By accident," she said. "When I left home I went to

Canton where there were lots of Returned Students. We became known as the Bright Young Intellectuals, you know. And we ran up and down the Pearl River in speed boats and lived in cubist flats. . . . Freedom was our teatime topic—freedom was pretty much whether or not to bob the hair. But the revolution was brewing there. And Sun Yat-sen had asked Michael Borodin, the Russian, to come and turn his party into an effective agent for revolution. There wasn't time to indoctrinate leadership from the masses. It was Borodin's idea—to use us, to send us out."

"And so you jumped from a speedboat into the revolution."

"Mmmm. Almost literally. Those of us who had been to Vassar and Oberlin and Yale were for democracy—with drastic agrarian reforms—that was the way we put it—and those who had been to Sun Yat-sen University, in Moscow, were for Communism. . . . Our coalition . . . We argued fearfully about it."

For some reason he must draw her so close that she had trouble breathing, he must love her for ever and ever and ever, he must enter her, thrusting his love so high into her that, "God, God," she cried. "Say it," he said. "Say it, say it, say it." There. Oh, there. "I am yours."

"There will be many eternities."

"The stars, did you know, either explode or die of the cold?"

"No." It made an impression on her.

"I have never loved any man before," she said. "It's—to love and be loved. It must be . . ."

"Yes, I'm sure it *must* be," he said.

"I was their most shining symbol," she said sadly.

"I think you are still their most shining symbol," he said carefully and slowly.

He got up and began to dress.

"I'm going to pay a visit to my uncle," he said. "General Ma."

Still only half-dressed, he went out to the court and spoke with his servant. She heard their voices rising and falling. She followed the design on the counterpane with her finger. He came back.

"He's going to make the arrangements. I can pretend to be negotiating for the return of the hospital property. He will know all the developments—everything. It's a good idea."

She nodded.

"I won't go until the servant gets back," he said, sitting down beside her.

They heard him coughing loudly in the court.

Christopher Blair got up and went on with his dressing.

Both knew, so well, that he had not been able to bear the thought of leaving her. It was the moment in which they understood a great deal, the moment they had had to build toward, in spite of themselves.

"You keep the door bolted," he said. "It's a .45. The best way would be to put the barrel into your mouth."

"All right."

He stood in front of the mirror, knotting his tie.

"It won't be long. Not more than a couple of hours. Shall I wind the watch and leave it with you?"

"Yes."

He pulled on his coat.

"You don't look like yourself," she said.

"I hope I look—like the plate of fashion?"

"You do."

"Good. My uncle is very particular about such."

"Be sure you give him my regards," she said.

He bent over her and kissed her. It was a long and involved and complicated kiss—the only one of its sort, she thought, after he had left, and the outside sounds began to bear in on her.

VI

Deep in conference with her Old Crone was Madame Koo.

"Ai," the Old Crone was saying, "the large doses of these mad rumors have done their work—confused and confounded. The slave hunt, Madame, has done its work, as has that splendid funeral. They do not believe she ever left that prison. They are sure that she died as she was supposed to. Their faith. It is a phenomenon, Madame. How they have believed in her and how they have loved her and how they love her memory. You would think that each mother and each mother's son of them, in turn, had given particular birth to her and cleaned up the mess of after-birth and watched her grow and personally watched her die."

Madame Koo said, and there was an edge about her voice, "They will not believe unless . . ."

"Exactly, Madame."

"And General Ma?"

The Old Crone sucked at her gold-filled tooth which she believed was getting loose. "Very busy, Madame, while officially he is idle."

"How is that?"

"Well, Madame. The jail guard is in a condition which he may not live to tell his children about. The keeper was also questioned but emerged more whole."

"And?"

"Well, I saw a man I know to be his lurking around the Wang Widow's Bridge Mill."

Madame said nothing. Of course, General Ma would use her son.

"It is encouraging that there is no trace of her," the Old Crone suggested.

"Or that we have found no trace of her," Madame said, with that restlessness that was lately becoming habitual to her. "Go back to your spying," she said.

The Old Crone bowed and went out. For a moment Madame Koo sat as she was. She had given birth to the girl, she thought, with a sudden very strange stirring of jealousy and passion. She could never forgive her for what she had attempted to do. She would find her and kill her but . . . Was she ill? Alone? Still battling her terror? ("Mother, you must save me.") No simple act of poisoning could have drained her as this ruthless, far-flung search was doing. She had given birth to the girl.

She rose. With Wang-ma, her maid, who was waiting in the next room for her, she started through the courts on her way to see her lord again. She nodded to the ones who rose and bowed and pretended not to see the ones who would have engaged her in the unraveling of some problem. She heard the rapid clitter-clatter of mah-jongg pieces, dry scraps of laughter, the hissing of some servants' quarrel, and thought how the House was returning to normal. Everything depressed Madame. She was more than depressed about Old Koo's illness, though the family remained unimpressed, since they heard no ranting or raving. . . . It was another reason why the girl had to be found. It was Madame's opinion that a sight of the corpse might help, might serve as the cold hard shock that was needed. It was odd how this reason for getting this terrible business over with began to loom almost as large as the other in Madame's mind. Her dear old tyrant had never been like this before and Madame was at a loss without his bombast to counter.

Wang-ma carried the pale, clear, nourishing broth that Madame had prepared with her own hands and the pity was he might even make an effort to drink it.

Madame had called in some doctors the previous evening. . . . The doctors had said that the disease had started in the hour of the horse and they quoted the famous Wang Shu-ho upon his pulse signs—it seemed there was a great wind in his intestines and they had prescribed horn of rhinoceros and syrup of pears. The announcement of this prescription was the only thing, these days and nights, that had caused Old Koo to rally somewhat. He had told the doctors to remove themselves to the bowels of hell. He had said everyone knew that the syrup of pears had only two functions—the first to ward off the feebleness of age, the second to assist pregnant women in labor.

He had seemed almost himself when he had patted his belly and said to clear room and let him give birth; when he had said of the doctors, "If they cannot do better than that, call in that half-caste."

The little maid had assured him that the half-caste was not in the city. Madame knew he was. She knew he was staying on Pu-tang Street, in the blacksmith shop of Wang the Little. Since the death of her son, Madame had made it a point to keep track of this man. Secretly she held him in high regard and was secretly determined some day, when her lord had tired of his baiting, to rectify what she considered to be a deep injustice to him. But, of course, Old Koo had not been serious. He had merely said what he had to show his disgust. Nor had his rallying lasted more than a few flickering minutes. He had turned his face to the wall and said no more.

Madame had got no farther than the moongate when the

little maid was already crossing the court, to meet her. She announced sadly that so far the medicines had not helped him.

"He gives off at both ends," the little maid said. "He cannot go on like this, Madame."

Madame said, "Should I go in?" And thought it curious that she should be asking permission from this slip of a maid whom her lord called "Big Stupid" for some reason.

"He is asleep," the little maid said, "but he will not sleep for long."

Madame went into his bedchamber and was newly alarmed at his queer pallor and the bloated look. Sleeping, he had drawn his huge body into what—for anyone else—might have been described as a ball.

They returned to the outer room and the little maid whispered, "He does not ask about our Third Young Mistress any more. But last night he cried out, 'I do not *allow* you!' He is not asleep when he says such things as that, Madame. He talks to himself, I think. Last night I do not think he slept at all. He went on and on. . . . 'Seed of my sin,' he would say, 'fruit of my seed, heart of my heart, I risked the whole House of Koo to have you back. I threw it in the lion's mouth, don't you know that?' And then he vomits and he says to me, 'Big Stupid, hold my head.'"

The little maid rubbed her arms up and down. She said, "He lets out these small flat curses, spaced far apart, spaced between his stomach rumbles and his belches and his puffs of gas. Or else, 'Big Stupid,' he says to me, 'life has been warm for me and full and I have known a lust for all its teeming moments. What ails me now? Do you think a stubborn female thing can undo me, Big Stupid? You are wrong, Big Stupid. Tomorrow, I drink, I laugh, I bellow, I lie with my women and slap their buttocks and tingle with joy when their buttocks bounce. Tomorrow, I begin again, do you hear? Why am I sad, Big Stupid? She will not come back, not even that I may kill her. Would I kill her, Big Stupid, do you think? If it gave me pleasure—yes, if it gave me pleasure.' At nights, he goes on and on, Madame. Days, as you know, he says nothing. He sleeps for an hour and then he does not sleep and he says nothing. I am afraid, Madame."

Madame reassured the little maid as best she could. Such a large nature must throw off grief, as her lord, till now, always had. When a large nature absorbed grief, there was too much of the nature and too much of the grief and there was no measuring beginning or middle or end.

And Madame thought that if he did not get better, she might consider swallowing the family's face and asking the half-caste, Blair, to come. Something had to be done and it would bear consideration.

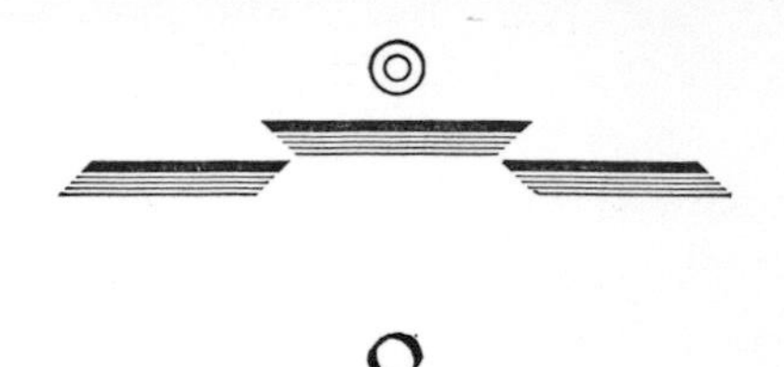

8

I

IN the dug-out cellar of a squalid house near the Old North Gate, some men and women were gathered together. After the execution, the purge and "the taking over" there were those who would have been branded as "Little Communists" and killed had they not gone underground. The only light was cast by a bean-oil lamp that was placed on a table, which was the only piece of furniture in the room. The men and women, thirty-seven, in all, were either squatting on their haunches or sitting very close together on the earthen floor.

One, small and wiry and smooth of skin, was sitting on the edge of the table, swinging his leg. His name was Zia. His shadow was thrown on the wall and some of the people were watching the steadily swinging leg shadow as if hypnotized. The rest had their eyes fastened on Zia himself.

"Well," Zia said, swinging his leg, "we should say, first, that we do not believe in ghosts."

"Granted."

"This is what I say," said a heavy man whose head was bandaged. "The truth need not concern us."

"I agree," said Zia.

"But how so?" several asked together.

"We mean," said Zia, "that if there was something irregular about that execution—if she did betray, sell out, what have you—it is not our worry."

"Then, for the love of your mother, what is our worry?"

"We all knew her," Zia said, swinging his leg. "It is possible. Yang Koh was forever afraid of it. Huan-li, too. Why, Huan-li watched over her like a dog over his bone. It was he who kept her straight. He was the power behind that throne."

"Ai."

"In her position, many tempting propositions must have been put to her."

"But," said one, "if she is living and if they hunt for her, does that look as if she had betrayed?"

"Yes," said Zia. "Betrayed us first. Otherwise, she would have made her way to us. Betrayed us, then betrayed them—for a private life. It was that of which she was so capable."

"I do not follow."

"Why, it is simple. She made a deal with them for the sake of her life. Then she gave them the slip."

"I don't know," several said.

"And what is all this about the Second Son of Koo?"

"It is exceedingly strange."

"It would be nice to get to the root of it."

"It would," said Zia, "but we do not have the resources. Our resources are very limited and we must conserve them. . . . To return to my earlier point: she cannot concern us. It is her memory, only, which we must make our concern. Nothing must smirch that memory, comrades. Truly, the name is our flag. What do we care about her? Let us hope she has gone ten thousand miles away. Providing she does not appear to dispute her memory, I say forget her!"

"Comrade Zia, it seems to me you assume too much. The point is: *if they find her?*"

"Because of our limited resources, that is what we must take our chances around," said Zia. "That they don't have her and that they don't find her."

"But if they do? We must think about it."

"Why?" said Zia. "If they do, then obviously we are ruined. Searches are costly and require manpower—we cannot begin to conduct a good one. We would be throwing away our energies. If there is any finding to be done, we would not be the ones to do it—they would. Let us, therefore, operate as though it were not possible."

"He is right."

"If they have her or if they find her, there is really nothing we can do about it."

"Go on, Comrade Zia."

Zia looked at his own shadow on the wall and noted that it was perhaps four times bigger than he was. He looked away. "Unless you vote differently," he said, "this is what we must do: we must go out to the streets, comrades, and stay out in the streets. We will dispose ourselves here, there, all over this city and we will keep constantly circulating and changing our districts, so that we do not become known. At every opportunity, each time a search is mentioned or a dark doubt is raised, we will say, 'This is the talk of the counterrevolutionists, it is traitors' talk and traitors' filth. Have you forgotten so soon the funeral and how she died for you?' And we will say, 'Do not defile her memory.' And, 'Our display of the other day has struck fear into cowards' hearts. Consider, my friends, had we been armed. It is to their advantage, the cowards, to discredit her memory. Ai, they killed her. Now, they would bring her alive and smear her a little. They do not like this shrine we have built to her.' You have the idea, comrades."

Zia paused. His colleagues nodded.

"And if," Zia went on, "it is ghost stories under discussion, why, we will aid and abet. 'Ha-ha,' we will laugh. 'So the Koo Family is reduced to ghost hunting, eh? What a fat scare her ghost must have thrown into them! May she haunt them for a thousand years.' "

Zia's great shadow was agitating the crumbling, earthen wall. He said, "In other words, everything we can do to preserve her memory intact, we must tirelessly do. That is my opinion. Shall we do it, comrades?"

"Ai."

"Very well," said Zia. "Let us not waste a moment."

"Just one question, Comrade Zia. What if she should yet contact us? It is not impossible. What then?"

"Living, she can no longer serve us," Zia said. "She is only valuable—dead. Do I make myself clear? If she contacts us then it becomes our duty to destroy her." He raised his voice a little. "Comrades, the Third Koo Girl is dead."

II

"Nothing?" asked General Ma of one of his men who had hired himself to the Second Son of Koo and who was now reporting.

"Nothing definite yet," said General Ma's man. "But there is fresh hope of a sort."

"Yes?"

"Yes, sir," said the man. "This Second Son of Koo has methods. He has these five so-called detectives down from Shanghai who go about sprinkling white powder upon various objects and looking intently at this and that through a round glass on the end of a stick."

"Interesting," said Ma.

"One of the things they did was to investigate all pawnshops and in one they discovered a gray cotton suit of woman's clothes which the Second Son of Koo is most excited about. He swears they are the ones she left the House in."

"Good."

"Yes, sir. And now, these detectives will locate the one who pawned them and question him or her."

"Excellent," said the General. "You must return to the Second Son of Koo, at once. And be sure to be on hand when this person is located and questioned. Do you understand?"

"Yes, sir."

"And if the questioner does not know how to question, then . . ."

"Yes, sir."

"If, say, he or she has 'forgot' where and how those clothes were come by . . ."

"Yes, sir. But, General. If it should be she herself who did the pawning?"

"Do not worry. Your duty is to remain with the Second Son who will probably feel that he who is most astute should do the questioning and demand that whoever-it-is be brought in. But I will take care of the detectives. I will put some men on them to detect and intercept any untoward possibilities. I do not think, however, that we shall find she did it. Do I make myself clear?"

"Yes, General."

"Good chap. Return, at once, then."

"Sir, consider that I am already there."

The General smiled. He tapped the bell for his aide. "I will now see my maternal nephew," he said.

Christopher Blair had been kept waiting for quite some time. He had already been over what he was going to say and do. It seemed to him that the whole thing was according to form, and the most natural development possible. Since the hospital was ostensibly his object for coming, he must talk about everything else before mentioning it; that was custom. According to custom, they would begin by polite family questions, move on to small talk, the news of the moment, and finally arrive at their destination—the hospital.

On his way to the headquarters, Blair had kept his eyes and ears open. The rumors were running, now—rumors, ghost stories, garbled accounts of searches—he heard of the one for the slave and of another being conducted by the Second Son of Koo. It seemed to him that the rumors were not being believed. He thought he would have heard plenty without trying. He kept seeing Pu-tang Street in his mind—the door of the shop . . . Leila, as he had left her. He looked down at his clothes. His early, polo-playing, woman-keeping reputation was much more acceptable to his uncle than his later one. He hoped to suggest it.

The booted and buckled aide appeared.

"The General will see you, now," he said.

"Thank you."

"Uncle?"

"My dear nephew!"

They shook hands instead of bowing.

"Sit down, sit down."

"I'm sure I need not inquire whether my aunt is as beautiful as ever?" Christopher Blair asked. "How is she, Uncle?"

"Splendid, my dear chap. Putting up with life—at the Majestic—just at the present."

"And my elder cousin?"

So began the questions about family. And the appraisal, each of the other. Christopher Blair was impressed, in spite of himself, and as he always was, by his uncle—by the trim and elegant figure he cut, his grace and subtlety of movement. It was never difficult to see why he had earned his nickname of "The Gentleman General." He was a devilishly attractive man, with deep-set mocking eyes that held you, preferably, against your will, and his famous hands upon which condemned men were reported to dwell.

"And your parents?" he was saying now. "When do they come back from Manila?"

"I haven't the foggiest notion," Blair said. "But I expect as soon as they hear that this liberation of the liberation is accomplished."

The General smiled. "I say, politically we are not on speaking terms, you and I, are we?"

"I should say not," Blair said, also smiling.

"Well, you look superb!" Ma said.

"Thank you, Uncle. May I return the compliment? And suggest that perhaps this counterrevolution agrees more with you?"

Far from displeased, Ma laughed out loud. "Look here. Are you miffed at me for keeping you waiting? My dear boy, nothing but the most urgent business, I assure you, could have provoked such rudeness."

"Rudeness, Uncle? You embarrass me by assigning to my head such a thought. You could never be rude."

The General produced cigarettes. While they went through the ceremony of lighting them, Blair said thoughtfully, "Urgent business . . . I was out in the streets myself this morning, Uncle."

"So?" said Ma.

"Yes," said Blair. "Tell me, Uncle, have you seen the Third Koo Girl?"

"Ah, a wit, a wit," the General said, highly delighted. "My nephew has developed into a wit. I must write your mother of this."

"So she turned into a typical Koo, after all," Christopher Blair said, leaning back in his chair and blowing his smoke toward the ceiling. "As the sworn enemy of that fine family I do not know, quite, whether to be pleased or displeased. . . . Uncle, what is this you pull?"

"My dear boy—that I pull!"

"Well, who pulls what, then? These rumors—these searches. What am I to think?"

"Don't worry your head about it. It will blow over. Matter of fact, she died when she was supposed to."

"Really?" asked Blair. "You expect me to accept the ghost theory? That the Second Son of Koo—a Harvard graduate, isn't he—is ghost hunting? Where is she, Uncle? Has she given you the slip? Or are you saving her for some dark psychological moment that you prepare for now? Will you pull her like a rabbit out of your hat when that time arrives?"

"You're damned curious," said the General, lifting an eyebrow.

"I'm damned curious," Blair said, lifting his eyebrow in almost exactly the same way his uncle had. "And you know which side I am on, Uncle. And you know what I hope has happened."

"Hmmm," laughed the General.

And Christopher Blair could see that, like most sadists, his uncle was intrigued by what he would consider his nephew's audacity. He held his cigarette well below the level of Ma's desk, that his unsteady hand might remain invisible.

"I hope she *has* given you the slip, Uncle."

Ma leaned a little forward. "What would you say if I told you there was nothing irregular about that execution, that Colonel Shu examined the corpse of the Third Koo Girl himself, with many eye witnesses to the fact that the

Third Koo Girl was brought in alone, was brought in last, and breathed her last breath at six o'clock upon a morning we both remember. . . . What would you say to that?"

"I would say you were lying, Uncle, of course, if I were less well reared. I would either say you lie about that or else that you and the Koos have dreamed up a whole pack of lies to slur her name. One or the other."

"Neither," said Ma. "I give you my liar's word."

Blair studied the ashy end of his cigarette. "Young Koo hunts for a ghost."

The General shrugged. "The trouble with your reasoning is that you are assuming Old Koo and I are in league. If it had been left to me, my dear boy, not a hair on her head would have been harmed. You are right as far as you go. I would have been the first to suggest we take her as our very own. Trouble was, you see, with Shanghai. Shanghai wanted her dead."

Blair nodded.

"It was not left to me. To be perfectly frank, nephew, I could not please Old Koo at the risk of displeasing Shanghai. I am as much in the dark about this aftermath as the next one. If you will work it out for me, I will set you up in a governor's yamen."

"Almost," Christopher Blair said, smiling, "you convince me."

They looked at each other.

"Officially, this curious aftermath is not being touched."

"My tongue," Blair said, "is in my cheek."

"It improves your diction."

"Thank you. You would like to find her, wouldn't you?"

"If she is to be found, I might look down, were I to stumble over her in the middle of the road."

"Well, you know, I hope you don't. Or do you have her

in your keeping this while? You see, after all, I find it hard to decide."

"You have become refreshingly brash, my boy. What is it, a metamorphosis or a throw-back to a young man I once thought I knew?"

"It's probably brain fever," Christopher Blair said, "or boredom. This city has proved depressing recently. I'm leaving for Shanghai very shortly. Anybody you wish me to say hello to? Your taste, if I remember correctly, leaves nothing to be desired. And I'm the least bit out of touch."

"So!"

"I want to get this place out of my system for awhile, perhaps until . . ."

"Until?"

Blair hesitated. He was afraid he had played his cynical, teasing role a little too well to switch, now, to the traditional and courteous beating around the bush that preceded the asking of any favor—the systematic dropping of hint after hint. He sensed that his uncle would find such a switch flat and disappointing and unworthy of their meeting of minds.

"Until," Blair said, "you might find it convenient, Uncle, let us say, to get back that hospital of mine for me."

"Oh!"

For a moment Blair was afraid he had really overstepped the bounds of propriety. But Ma was, instead, appreciative. "So that's what we're getting around to, with all this talk of the Koos. That thing of a hospital, eh? Old Koo might not be very co-operative, eh?"

"Well. But wouldn't you imagine Old Koo would be a trifle distracted these days?"

"Mmmmm. I wouldn't want to fret Old Koo, these days."

"No, indeed. But if no one had the hospital officially, with all this changing of hands, couldn't I—uh—just take it?"

"That will require considerable thought, my dear boy. And while I deeply admire the spirit in which you have asked, I must warn you that such a transaction might have the gravest consequences. But I will keep it in mind, you can depend on it."

"Good," said Christopher Blair. "With a man of your talents, that's all I want to know." He rose. "And I must take up no more of your time, Uncle. In Shanghai, I'll be staying at the Astor. May I look forward to hearing from you?"

"Without fail," Ma said, coming around the desk and putting out his hand. "And incidentally, where have you been burying yourself?"

"Oh, in a blacksmith shop on Pu-tang Street. Why don't you come and see me before I leave?"

"I'll just wait, if you don't mind. I have never had any particular fondness for the blacksmith's trade or lodgings."

"I have developed an acute distaste for them myself. . . . Well, Uncle? Thanks awfully."

"It's been a pleasure."

"I'll let you know where the Third Koo Girl is," Blair said.

They laughed.

"You know, we must renew our acquaintance."

"Yes," Blair said. "We must."

III

He hurried. He reached Pu-tang Street in seven minutes. No use to inquire about the trains (they were probably not running regularly to Shanghai and anyway they would not be safe). He knew the proprietor of a boat *hang*—a boat would be best. He would have one tie up outside the city and they would leave, after dark. She could dress as his manservant, he decided.

"Greetings, Bao I-sung."

The beggar . . . Blair found a copper. "How's business?"

"Dull, as usual, Bao I-sung."

"Mmm." He crossed the street. His servant, who let him into the shop, gave him a searching look.

"Well?"

"He must think about it," Christopher Blair said.

"Who must think about what?"

"I assumed you were asking about the hospital and my uncle?"

"You look very pale," the servant said. "Neither you nor the woman has eaten lately. I will prepare food."

"Oh! Uh—yes—thanks."

He was aware that his servant kept looking at him, waiting for him to say more, but he went on through the shop and across the court. She had already opened the door. He could not wait to get her into his arms.

"Good God," he breathed.

She was smiling, but it was a smile that probed him like a scalpel.

"Is it all that bad?" she asked.

He laughed shakily—sat down on the bed and drew her down beside him. He rested his hand on the small of her back.

"It's time we got out of this hole," he said. "It's a bit past time."

"Hadn't you better begin at the beginning?" she asked, leaning a little toward him.

"Yeah . . . My uncle is in it up to his neck but not

officially. Your father did do whatever he did independently. . . . Shanghai politics."

"The substitution," she said. "I've been pondering that while you were gone. Remembering how it was the keeper and a guard who took me out to torture me. 'I' need not have been brought back till the very last minute—mutilated, maybe, and maybe already blindfolded. My father must have got hold of a girl who could disappear without causing a ripple. Maybe one of the factory girls—that's what I have been thinking. Those girls are country girls who are bound over by their families that are too poor and too many *li* away to come investigating the disappearance of a daughter, providing they cared enough. Factory girls are forever getting sick or dying or running off. Many of them lose touch with their families entirely. It wouldn't have been so hard. They lived in the dormitories after they struck. Somebody died what was probably a drugged and mixed-up death in my place. Somebody who happened to be the right height."

She got up, crossed the room, sat down on a chair. "What else?" she said, after a pause.

"The searches. They seem to be well organized and far flung. They're breaking into shops and places. One of them seems to be conducted by your Second Brother."

"By George?"

"Yes—if that means anything."

Why George, when neither her father nor mother would trust him with anything except profits? Had George been busy in Shanghai? She remembered the courier.

"What else?" she said.

"Another hunt is for a slave with heart-shaped face and willow form."

"For Tear Drop," she said, nodding, "who is made like the eel. Go on."

He found a cigarette and lighted it. He had never seen her like this—had never seen her when her passion was directed toward anything other than him. For the first time he saw her as a leader, as the Third Koo Girl, with her eyes and proud bearing. It was as if she had to reveal herself to him, at this time, as the lost and tragic figure she had seemed to be to them.

"There is no need for you to report to the underground," he said.

She started.

"The rumors are running but they are not being believed."

"They want me dead?" she said.

"Yes."

"They will have me dead?"

"They will believe no slander about you."

"Which makes me the only evidence against myself. I am the evidence. Is that correct?"

He watched her closely. "Yes. I love you. . . . It's finished—here. The curtain's come down, if you like. . . . It's time we removed the evidence."

"You are so right," she said.

He pulled hard on his cigarette. "This city isn't even a dot on the world's map," he said slowly. "We will go far away. . . . Some place like Hilo or Los Angeles."

He waited. She didn't say anything.

"There's nothing more that you can do here, Leila. . . . Come away with me. I can change my name, too, if it seems better that way. . . . We have to go, now." He pulled at his cigarette. Their destiny was in a bastard, twilight hour—their love.

"I would abort life," she said in a low voice. "I would vomit it, Chris. I'm sorry. The world isn't large enough."

He started to speak but she went on, without looking up.

"We took our time out of time, dear Chris, you remember. . . . Dead, I am the symbol that alive I can only destroy. I am so sorry, Chris."

He reached over and put his cigarette out. The silence between them mounted. They could not help it—they were both listening for outside sounds.

He said, "The people created the Third Koo Girl but nobody has ever created a name for their suffering. You became the Voice of the Peasants because you felt they had decreed it and you were powerless. In the face of their suffering, you were overcome with pity and had to comply. . . . Well, I know a little about that suffering. I didn't choose this city to work in for no reason at all. And I know it has been a class war, with the interests of a few thousand pitted against those of hundreds of millions and that it's been that way for too long to think about. And that some day, before too long, it will break wide open again—and whoever doesn't understand their misery can go on offering these false choices between freedom without food and food without freedom. . . . You mustn't think me unsympathetic or suppose that I don't know what I am asking in asking you to leave with me. . . . You haven't been a typical rebel and so you have felt you didn't belong anywhere. But the condition of not belonging is very well known to any half-caste."

She said, "There hasn't been any future for me, Chris. I thought you knew."

"I do know," he said. "There couldn't be when you weren't a leader who was going to go on leading—when there wasn't any place for you in the very system you were advocating. Everything you were advocating intellectually you were fighting with your heart."

She raised her eyes, "I was the sacrificial offering, Yang Koh said. He said I could have died for them all."

A pause.

Christopher Blair said, "I wouldn't be asking you to leave with me, if I didn't think the world was large enough for two people who understand they don't belong anywhere but do belong to each other and together to find a place. . . . You came to me that night. Trust me. You can. Don't make a foolish sacrifice—because you have to learn how to live with yourself all over again—when the issue doesn't demand it. If you like—you can't do this to me when I love you as I do and when I know you love me."

"I belong to the people," she said, breathing very deeply and unsteadily.

He saw his watch lying on the table, reached for it, looked at it, put it on his wrist.

"As far as the people are concerned," he said, "you have already made the supreme sacrifice—at the crucial hour—indisputably and unforgettably. You died that morning at six o'clock in somebody else. They have already repudiated tales. At the very worst, only a tale—a hint—of your being alive and of your whereabouts could ever get back to this city, and that is unlikely. . . . Don't be so afraid of the strange accident that has released you from your responsibility to them. You had no control over it. . . . Is it so inconceivable to you, poor darling, that there could be some little left-over part of your life that you can make yours?"

He stared at her and she at him. The silence stretched and strained.

"I—can't do it, Chris."

"All right."

"So what are we to do?" she cried. "Wait here until they break the door down—climb over the walls? No!"

Her eyes went to the pillow under which was the .45.

"We will eat something," he said. "I think the servant's fixing it."

IV

Christopher Blair's servant left the blacksmith shop, after he had offered them the food that they would not eat and had cleared the dishes away. He failed to exchange his customary greetings with Yeu-ding, the proprietor of the hot-water shop, or with Ah-san, the peddler. He walked woodenly, with an air of remoteness.

"Have you seen one who would make you think the Third Koo Girl had risen from the dead?" some fellow asked him, at a street corner, where he was waiting for a rickshaw to pass.

The servant barely heard him. His mind turned in solitary fashion around his own problem. . . . He knew his master inside out. He knew of his blood that flowed two ways in the search for a formula that could blend. He knew of his generosity that was placating and of his tenderness that Madame Bao, his mother, had worked so hard to knead out of him. Of how, as a boy, he had worn himself away over kites and the catching of butterflies because the other boys would have none of him, except as they were ushered into the house by invitation, with many things upon a table to eat and games arranged for them to win. . . . Of the great calm of his home which no amount of a child's foot stamping could blast. He knew what kind of tutors his mother had hired to have him taught. And he had watched his father, from whom the boy had contracted his strain of tenderness, read him books and take him upon long walks. But Madame, his mother, had had great ambitions for her son. Therefore there was the friction between the father and the mother over the son, with the father never knowing of it because of his love of the woman and his love of the son who was out of the woman, expending himself upon a cloud of love that was at a safe distance from the woman's scheming. The father, a gentle and foolish foreigner, with a mind for his books. The mother, a woman. As a slave, which she was in her heart, she would have done well enough. The mistake was the foreigner's: to make her a ruler.

Sometimes the servant thought he knew his master better than he knew himself and he knew that his master's life had reached its crisis. Never in earlier years, when he had kept so many, had he opened his heart to any woman. Nor did the servant remember any talk by the other servants that might lead him to suppose that it had been any different with the one, Li Tuh-ying, whom the master called Leila, whether milk-name or love-name.

Well, many years had passed since he had kept her in the house on Soochow Hutung, in Peking. The servant understood that his master's heart was a lonely heart when Li Tuh-ying came knocking in the dead center of that dread night. She had invaded his heart—no doubt about that. Ill and gaunt and badly dressed—but still there was a stamp of breeding about her, a sadness about her, a something about her that the servant was hard put to define.

The crisis was this: here was the woman fashioned to complete his master's purpose on earth. The servant felt it. He felt the power of it and its beauty. She was obviously his master's lost half, that half that reconciled his blood and gave him life, and the servant would have chosen to welcome her if—if she had not brought trouble in with her.

Yes. Trouble hung like a pall over the blacksmith's shop. It was no ordinary trouble but a trouble so dark and so oppressive that the servant was caught staggering beneath it, without knowing what it was. They could not eat, though the woman was half-starved; their eyes sank deeper into their heads; they were not sleeping, and their hands shook. Everything they said and did and did not say or do communicated this trouble that they would not name to him.

Why had love and trouble walked in together? What was this trouble, when its intensity and magnitude matched the intensity and magnitude of their love? What did it mean? That it was political, the servant felt almost sure, considering its timing and the hints his master had dropped. He sent Wang the Blacksmith away; he did not want her existence mentioned; he visited his uncle. But what political trouble was there that was so charged with doom? Indeed, what political trouble was there that his master's uncle, as a favor, could not fix? For this trouble was doom, the servant knew. He knew his master well enough to feel that certainty. The trouble was poised to strike—to destroy. And what was it? What was it? What could it mean? Was there nothing, nothing to be done?

The servant, in his preoccupation, jostled a small group of people who were standing in the door of a shop.

One was saying, "And do not believe the traitors' filth. Have you forgot how she died for you—the Third Koo Girl?"

The servant went around these people. He had thought to do a little tardy marketing but he was in no mood for it. What was the use, when they would not eat? He made the turn toward his teahouse. It was the one where he always went and it would be a better place than most, he thought, to sit and brood.

V

At the House of Koo:

Andrew was in need of an audience. He had lain for hours and hours on his chaise longue and given himself over to a line of the most brilliant deductive reasoning and had thus arrived at a major discovery which, however, was not precisely the kind he could share with his actor friends and his whores, even were he allowed out. He would not have told Tear Drop about it, had she been around, because Tear Drop did not appreciate irony. Besides, he was miffed at the mere idea of her, because he missed her. He thought about Helen and decided Helen was the best audience that the House could provide him.

Now, Helen had remained secluded in her rooms, all this time. And it was hardly surprising that her voluntary seclusion had annoyed everybody, most of all Little Dog who had been reduced, in his desperation, to hiding a tiny green snake in her bed. But not even that had succeeded in returning Helen to the bosom of her family where she belonged. She was not ill, like Old Koo, but simply depressed and unable to take an interest in anything. She sat about carelessly dressed, with her hair uncombed, and sometimes she wept but more often she just sat about, forgetful that her function in life was to please and charm, feeling vacant. Since she had forbidden Dji-bo, her maid, to say anything to her concerning her sister and since she had only seen Dji-bo and Little Dog's nurse and Little Dog, she was in ignorance of everything that had happened since that day when her mother had left her.

Andrew, who had heard about his sister's seclusion and who was sensitive to all things at once and who was therefore in constant danger of coming apart, dressed carefully in his newest and loudest sports jacket and armed himself with a whole tin of Capstan cigarettes and his newest and finest cigarette holder and went to Helen's court. First he conversed with Dji-bo, Helen's maid, and succeeded by stroking her thighs in sending her off in a panic. Then he knocked on Helen's door and entered her sitting room and called out, persuasively, that he was there. He received no answer. He repeated himself.

"Go away," Helen called back.

Andrew settled himself in her best chair, placed his tin of cigarettes on the table beside it and said, "You're missing all the developments. Come on out, like a good girl, and I'll catch you up."

There was no answer from the bedroom.

"They haven't found her," Andrew felt more or less obliged to call, so that Helen would be sure to hear him. "Or didn't you even know they were hunting? Between them they've got damned near every thug in the city out looking for her and they haven't laid their hands on her yet. Don't you think that's good?"

Andrew felt sure he could now afford to fit a cigarette into his holder and that before he was through getting the cigarette out of the tin and into the holder, Helen would be out. He was not wrong. She came, but looking so pale and drawn that Andrew was unable to enjoy his triumph. He found himself stammering.

"What are you talking about, Andy?"

Andrew told her. He was both relieved and gratified to see her reacting with intense excitement. Her eyes began to shine and the color to flood her cheeks—it was almost a metamorphosis.

"Mother and George both hunting?" she said. "But Andy! Then she isn't dead!"

"Well . . ." Andrew said, flipping his ashes into a vase. "She may be, you know, but then again she may not be. *They* don't seem to think so."

"But, I mean . . ." Helen stopped short and stared at him. Then she handed him something that vaguely resembled an ash tray. Then she said, "Now, Andy, you wait right here. Don't go away. Don't even move."

And she disappeared into her bedroom. Before Andrew had smoked four cigarettes, she re-emerged looking like a picture in a flowered silk dress and high heels and even earrings.

"Well, I'm damned!" Andrew said.

Helen assured him that it was not possible for her to think when she looked such a terrible fright. She could now think without impediments, she said. She drew up a chair with an air of great conspiracy.

"Now, Andy," she said. "The foul deed is yet to be done, is that right? It is still in the future, is it, when I thought . . . Now, Andy, tell me all. Everything."

Andrew did—omitting, however, his major discovery. That he was building toward.

"Leila really must have climbed the wall," Helen mused.

"Well, of course," Andrew said. "What did you suppose?"

"Never you mind," Helen said. "But why? Why did she leave? Where did she go?"

Andrew shrugged.

"Well, why are they after her?"

"Dear," Andrew said, "you are ignorant."

Helen was so excited and eager and lovely to look at that Andrew had a great time with her—giving her information little by little and making her beg for it. When he gathered that the psychological moment had arrived, he laughed mysteriously and said, blowing an elegant smoke ring, "Georgie was a revolutionist, too."

This did not get the desired response. All Helen said was, "Oh."

"But not," Andrew said, "for the same reasons Leila was."

"Why was Leila?" Helen wanted to know.

"Oh, good lord!" Andrew said, disgusted. It was

George he wished to explain. He asked Helen whether she did not remember how busy George had been during their refugee period in Shanghai. George, he said, had turned himself into a revolutionist. He explained that George had got on an inside track of the revolution that poor Leila didn't even know existed until much later. While Leila was starving and sleeping with bedbugs, Andrew said, George was having conferences with gentlemen behind closed doors in hotels that were in the French Concession.

Helen's reactions, so far, were positively medieval. She said that naturally George, as the oldest living son, had to look out for the family interests. She said he was expected to determine the prevailing political winds so that he could know just when to jump on the bandwagon. She said she didn't understand what Leila had done but she certainly understood about George—it was a tradition and time-honored. He would have been unfilial had he behaved any differently. She said, getting back to her wind metaphor, "The family must always be sure to blow comfortably in the right political direction. Even I know that. How else could the family survive?"

"A family affair," Andrew mused. "Truly. Pop paying tribute to Chiang and promising this and that. George and his sort—these smart, streamlined Western products—now, they're the ones to watch out for. They're the coming thing. They're the *new* democracy. They understand humanity. Doesn't it make your blood run cold?"

"No," Helen said, "it does not. And Andy . . ."

"A family affair," Andrew said. "Except that Leila's the villain. Leila's the threat. Leila doesn't want to make a profit out of democracy. Can you imagine that?"

"Andy!"

"Dear sister," Andrew said, waving his holder at her,

"George is very, very busy hunting for Leila . . . Why?—Darling, not to please Father. He wouldn't get lines in his face and circles under his eyes if it were that! George wants Leila dead—because—who knows?—he was involved with those who ordered her executed! I ask you—why else?"

"Andy!"

"Well! Why else?"

Helen stood up and teetered around the room on her high heels—almost as badly, Andrew thought, as the old ones did on their lily feet. "Oh, Andy," she said.

"I would be willing to bet my worthless life that that's it," Andrew said. "And George never expected Pop to turn up with Leila. He must have thought it was all settled. Whew! That must have been a bad day for George. But isn't it fortunate that he has Father's order to hide behind? He's looking, spending all these thousands of dollars to find her, dead, for Father. . . . It's a family affair, I tell you. Mother's looking, too. Supposedly for Tear Drop. Isn't *that* a laugh? Maybe she's looking because Father wants her found and maybe not. I've wondered."

Helen was lost in thought.

"What's the matter?" Andrew asked. "Are you going to start?"

"Start?"

"Start hunting for her."

"Oh, no," Helen said. "I do not have the capital."

"Nor I the energy," Andrew said. "It's really too bad."

"It is," Helen said.

"Particularly when we're so talented and imaginative and could probably outsmart them."

"Mmmmm," Helen said.

They looked at each other for a minute. Andrew said it was time for tea.

Helen had got rid of Andrew as soon as she tactfully and safely could. She said not a word to him regarding her suspicions about her mother. She would not have thought of taking Andrew into her confidence. But as soon as he was gone she went into action.

First, there was the quite considerable problem of capital. One could do nothing without "talk" money. She looked over her jewels and sent Dji-bo's nephew, who was allowed to leave the House whereas Dji-bo was not, Helen discovered, quite in the dark as to reasons, to the pawnshop with enough of them to raise a tidy little sum. Then she told him to fly over to Wang Widow's Bridge Mill, George's headquarters, and contact two or three of George's men and to bring them to her that she might proposition them. They should be her "ears and eyes" instead of George's.

So far so good. The intrigue and the planning were like a restorative to Helen. But now she must give herself over single-mindedly to the problem of getting next to Madame, her mother. Madame's men, as Helen quite well knew, would not be so easy to approach, much less bribe. Helen was not nearly so impressed with George as Andrew was. She rather thought Madame, her mother, was the chief enemy. And she almost automatically assumed that if Leila were found, it would be one of Madame's men who would do the finding, barring freak or accident. . . . What to do, then?

Helen had an acquaintance with the steward and succeeded in waylaying him. This was his second day of grace. He was to be given one more. If "the person" were not found by that time, he would be discharged. He behaved more like a burrowing mole, Helen thought, than a human being. Helen tried to sound him out but she dared not try to bribe him, any more than she would have dared it with the Old Crone or any other of her mother's retainers. All she discovered from the steward was that the city was blocked out into districts and that it was the poor districts that were being concentrated upon. He only told her that because she fooled him into thinking she was in her mother's confidence. She did not learn that Madame's order was, "Whatever it is you find, let it be a corpse that you bring." Had she done so, she would have given up on the spot, since what she was counting so heavily upon was the possibility of interception. Of a man coming and reporting that "she" was at such and such a place and waiting for orders.

What next, Helen wondered. She had to infiltrate with spies since she could not go about hiring any hundred or two hundred men and send them beating about after the ones who were already beating about.

It was at this point that Helen thought of Siau Liang, the gatekeeper's son. Siau Liang seemed an immediate hope. He was in a strategic position. He could not help but be able to see a great deal and he would necessarily be among the first to know of Madame's men's comings and goings. . . . Siau Liang was certainly a thought.

Helen was not unaware that Siau Liang might be just a sop that she threw to herself—to fend off the awful lethargy and vacancy of the past few days. She was more than half-aware that she snatched at Siau Liang because it made her feel that at least she was doing something and thus did not have to confess that Leila might as well be dead, after all, since she was so powerless to save her. Helen wished to leave none of her poor little stones unturned.

Well, then, Siau Liang. But Siau Liang was not to be bribed. His old father would discover the money lying around somewhere and with his old arms he would beat his son to death and then die himself from the exertion and there would be the House of Koo without gateman or gateman's son. Never mind, Helen thought, she could at least handle Siau Liang without bribing. Unlike Andrew, she knew all about the friendship that had existed between Tear Drop and Siau Liang. She knew that Siau Liang was quite foolish about beautiful women and she was not unaware of her own standing in the House: she was held to be the most beautiful woman in it. Far more beautiful, for instance, than Tear Drop who had, anyway, left it.

Dji-bo's nephew had not yet come back. Well, then, let her proceed with Siau Liang. She sent Dji-bo immediately to the gates to fetch him and spent the time while she was impatiently waiting for his arrival at her toilet table. Not that Helen considered for a moment doing the least thing that was improper with Siau Liang. Not at all. She merely intended to be beautiful; she merely intended that Siau Liang should see she was beautiful and be so overcome that for the mere sight of her, he would agree to crawl on his hands and knees from earth to hell, that was all.

Helen gave her hair a final pat and smiled at her reflection in the mirror. Guile made her feel so at home with herself. . . . Leila was not dead yet.

VI

But as it happened, Siau Liang was not at the gates when Helen's maid, Dji-bo, went after him. Siau Liang, the one who had learned to take his pleasures as they came, had had no pleasures for so long that he had done an unpardonable thing. He had asked his father, while his father was asleep, for permission to leave the House of Koo and because his father had nodded his head, in his sleep, Siau Liang had taken this as due permission and left it. Now, according to Madame's categories, Siau Liang was superstitious enough, but the trouble was that because of his strategic position, he knew too much—he knew, for example, about the true nature of Madame's hunt—and he had therefore not been allowed out. But Siau Liang's reasoning had run something like this: it was he who had helped Tear Drop escape, was it not? And Madame, who knew everything, had not punished him, had she? Therefore, as the night followed the day, he must have risen high in Madame's favor, and therefore if he disobeyed his father's orders which he knew perfectly well, in this case, reflected Madame's orders, he would not be punished either, would he? And the truth of it was, Siau Liang was "restless to death," as he put it. He had been in that state ever since Tear Drop's departure.

It was a fine day, Siau Liang thought, with the sun shining sweet and soft and a bit of a breeze fluffing out his coat, as he walked. He intended to visit a house of whores he knew about which was a positive wonder, but it was a bit too early for that—whores were best after sundown. He thought he would just go to his teahouse, first. On the way, he bought a three-inch pocket mirror from a peddler, to take back to his old man, as a present. Siau Liang always went to the same teahouse, the one indeed that most of the servants who considered themselves "of good family" preferred. He went through the doors and into the central room.

Now, Siau Liang did not always take wine in the afternoons; he more usually took tea. But he found some of his friends who were drinking wine and Siau Liang, sitting down with them and finding them so hospitable and genial, decided not to be different. Besides, as a Koo servant, he had his face to make—they must not suppose he could not afford it.

"Siau Liang, we have not seen you since the monkeys wore the hair off their asses. Where have you been?"

Siau Liang grinned.

"Call the waiter," one of his friends said. "Tell him to bring Siau Liang his tea."

"Tea," Siau Liang said with a sneer which he followed with a particularly good and foul oath. "The wine in this place is dismally weak but I suppose I can put up with it."

"Ha!"

"That's the spirit, Siau Liang."

The wine was brought. Jokes were swapped. Siau Liang noticed that the servant of Blair, looking about as cheerful as a swindler swindled, was taking up space at the next table. But since the servant of Blair and the servants of Koo were not on speaking terms, Siau Liang contented himself with observing loudly that someone, very close at hand, was smelling up the atmosphere. His friends laughed but, of course, that thing of a Blair servant went right on sitting.

Two of Siau Liang's friends were playing the finger game in which each decided in advance how many fingers he would hold out. One called the guesses, the point being to guess correctly. And it was the loser who must drain his wine cup at a single swallow. This game could be played very fast, even with time out to swear and laugh when you won or lost. Siau Liang had never played it before but he had watched it, often enough, at feasts.

Before he realized quite what he was doing—and perhaps because he simply could not remember jokes to tell and was ashamed to be forever horse laughing and hitching about on his chair without contributing his share—he nodded and gestured to the fellow sitting across from him. He raised his hand and waggled his fingers. The fellow grinned.

"Ah, Siau Liang, think twice. I shall be your ruin."

"*Tan sen,*" Siau Liang called, ignoring this, starting the game off.

Siau Liang lost—over and over. He discovered his fingers were more like blocks. He was drinking so many cups of wine that his head began to spin and his tongue to thicken up. He was getting the worst of it, all right. He was afraid he was calling "*Tan sen*" again and again, which meant "Hands alike," when he should have been calling "*Liang hau,*" two gold flowers (two fingers), or something else. Anyhow, he knew it was not his place to call a stop.

"*Tan sen,*" he shouted and doubled over with laughter before he drank.

When he raised his head he asked his companions to notice, please, that unsavory character—the servant of Blair. He told his friends he had thought it over and decided that it was their duty to throw this scoundrel out. His friends glared at the servant of Blair and hurled some epithets at him and swore they would certainly do it, the Blair servant paying not the least attention. Then everybody—including Siau Liang—promptly forgot his existence.

Later Siau Liang's companion called a halt to their game. The others also stopped—those who were playing, as well as those who were merely drinking. They all sat back in their chairs and yawned and looked about. Siau Liang looked, too, but he did not even see the Blair servant this time. They yawned and belched. They had reached that time when they could not even think of any more improper jokes to tell.

"My little whore has left me," Siau Liang said, leaning on his elbows.

"Who—the slave?"

"Yes, the slave."

"Poor Siau Liang," they said, snorting with laughter. "So that's who has left the House of Koo!"

"Shall we help you find her?"

"What do you think," Siau Liang said, with dignity, "that she is the only whore in heaven?" That did not sound just right. "There are others, my lads, there are others."

"Siau Liang is a tiger."

"He is a wolf with fangs."

"Never mind," Siau Liang said, who nevertheless enjoyed being the center of attention. "What you don't know! What all has happened at our House! I tell you I have shouldered responsibilities!"

"Oh, yes."

"Sure."

"Siau Liang is a lion with shoulders."

Siau Liang shook his head. He leaned hard on his elbows.

"Well?" said one. "And who stole your pretty whore?"

"Nobody stole her," Siau Liang said. "She became involved. Everybody has become involved at our House. Involved." He liked that word.

"Ho!"

"You hear him!"

"He is involved with his groin."

"What about it, Siau Liang?"

"It all began four mornings ago," Siau Liang said. "Or was it five? No, I think it was four."

"Four, five, five, four. Perhaps it was six."

"Yes, it was six," Siau Liang said. "She appeared—like a ghost."

"Who—your pretty bitch?"

"No, no," Siau Liang said. "My bitch left. Don't confuse me. She came."

"Don't confuse us. Who?" Two friends nudged each other.

"Why, the one who is known to me as our Third Young Mistress, the one who is known to you common trash as the Third Koo Girl."

"And the one who is known to her father as her mother's bastard ch——"

"As Leila!" Siau Liang sternly interrupted. "If you must know her by all her names."

They heard a teacup crash and break.

"Look at that servant of Blair—he cannot hold a cup in his hands. Go on, Siau Liang."

"We never heard of her, Siau Liang."

"It is all right to be coarse about my slave," Siau Liang said. "But I will not allow it about the family that I serve."

"Oh, all right, Siau Liang. We beg your humble pardon. Go on."

"Yes, Siau Liang. Let us hear your version. Only make it new and different. We weary of the others. Make it juicy, Siau Liang."

Siau Liang was mollified. He leaned forward. He leaned so far that he fell right off his elbows. "Come closer," he said. "Can you keep a confidence? Because what I am about to tell you is no idle talk—it is all in the deepest confidence. My father would behead me if he ever found out. . . . Well?"

"Siau Liang, do we not look like men of staunch heart and sealed lips? Are we not your bosom friends?"

"That is true," Siau Liang said, after he had thought it over. "Let us put our heads together."

They all leaned far over the table, putting their heads together, touching their heads, bumping them a little, and

Siau Liang began his story. At first he spoke in a whisper. But then, as he went on, his voice got louder and louder. He rather played up his own part. He said that he had let her in the gates and that she had stopped and spoken with him at length in a mysterious, unknown tongue. When he came to the fatal night he said that he had seen, out of a perfectly clear starlit sky, a great three pronged burst of lightning fork through the heavens and meet just above her court. He was so intrigued with these embellishments that he immediately believed them. He ended by saying, "The next morning she had disappeared. Evaporated. Gone, my friends, entirely. Was she a ghost? Did she take her own life and then dispose of her own body? Was she carried off by the unnatural lightning that struck at exactly the time her funeral was passing? Who knows, who knows? Who can say when there is one search that is organized by Madame, our mistress, and this other by Second Young Master?—But never mind. If she is living, the family wants her dead. I know. I am no blockhead. But is she living? Or was she pierced to the heart by that lightning? I say, what happened to her when no one can find her—when she is quite, quite gone, leaving this whole tempest of trouble behind her. Is it not exceedingly strange?"

"Good grieving Buddha!" one of his companions said. "The same old drivel."

"We have had enough of this!" said another.

Siau Liang wished to elaborate on the tempest of trouble. He wished to so describe Tear Drop's plight and her appeal to him as would leave his friends smacking their lips and sitting all over their chairs. But they would not let him go on.

"This boy is wine coated," they said. "He is drunk. He takes a silly ghost story and tries to blow it up."

They said he was a fraud and they suggested to him that

he tell his ancestors about it. "Hush, Siau Liang," they said. They said it was time to depart. They scraped back their chairs. They were solicitous about Siau Liang—they helped him up, although he did not want to go. They pushed a waiter out of the way. They advanced. They steered him across the room and out the door and down the steps.

The servant of Blair sat on.

Much later that night Siau Liang was staggering home in his ripe, wine-coated condition, having had his fill, even of whores, when Dji-bo's nephew stopped him (coming out of the dark and scaring him near to death) about twenty paces distant from the Gates of Koo.

"Siau Liang," Dji-bo's nephew said. "Before you go through those gates and your father beats you to a pulp, let me tell you this."

"What?" asked Siau Liang, getting worried, remembering foggily that he had left the House of Koo with questionable permission and that he had perhaps opened his mouth too much in a certain teahouse. His father might beat him, poor old feeble thing.

"It is this," said Dji-bo's nephew. "After your father has let you in and beaten you and scolded you for all your sins and has fallen to sleep once again, you should come to the court of First Young Mistress. She would have a word with you. On the quiet, Siau Liang, do not forget."

"Murder!" Siau Liang said.

But Siau Liang was so dazzled by the beautiful young mistress and her apartment and the soft lights and the late, intimate hour that he promised lion-like feats. He promised and promised until he promised that he would find the Third Young Mistress himself.

Helen was already discouraged by the fact that she had been unable to get hold of any of Madame's men—more accurately, that she dared not try—and that she had learned nothing from George's men. And she was now so discouraged by Siau Liang's condition, feeling sure that he could not have found a rickshaw had he been sitting in it, that she sent him off and herself retired in the lowest spirits she had felt since she had placed two sleeping powders in the outstretched hand of Madame.

VII

Christopher Blair's servant had long since left the teahouse and was squatting, like a beggar, in a temple square. It was very late and there was no one about. He was looking at the stars and turning over many thoughts in his mind. The first shock of realization had passed. Her name was Leila. . . . The name, the starved features, the stamp of breeding, the hour of arrival, the trouble that hung like a pall—all had closed around the teahouse tale he had heard, like the petals of a touch-me-not flower that has been touched.

He squatted there under the stars and knew sorrow.

A watchman passed somewhere near and beat his gong for the second watch of the morning. Almost, the servant wished back the time of his own helplessness. His master's lost half was also his master's undoing. The woman was indeed doomed. Death had laid its cold hand on her and she could be only the dust of his master's dream.

Was there nothing to be done? Ai, there was this to be done—there was his master to save, there was the catastrophe to be called off before those who hunted found. Before Old Koo discovered who it was that was harboring her. And since the pall of trouble had in no way eased after his master had paid his visit to his uncle, the servant must also suspect where the uncle stood in this.

The Koo Family wanted her dead, and the people believed she was dead and that only her ghost had risen and he dreaded to think if they should hear otherwise. He remembered how she had come—in the wake of her own funeral. He shuddered. He turned his head toward the stone screen, in that temple court, where the Buddhist hells were depicted. And all he saw were the shadows and the darkness and not the hells.

"Have mercy on her," he muttered.

He poked at the ground with his fingers. Death was the woman's fate and his master had been drawn into it. If he understood that to get his master out meant that the woman must be pushed toward the fate that already claimed her, there was no help for that. By her living a little longer or a little shorter, he would yet have his master's heartbreak to handle. But a little longer and he would also have his master's ruined reputation, which had once before suffered a mighty blow at the hands of Koo. She must be got rid of. Let him sheath his heart and mind in hardness and coldness and consider how.

The watchman beat his gong for the third watch of the morning. He had turned over plans and abandoned one after another, as being riddled with possible pitfalls and complications. One in which he must kill her himself and dispose of her body in the nearest canal. One—where he would merely force her to quit the blacksmith shop for the streets, allowing the ones who hunted to do the rest. One in which he would take the matter to General Ma but that was the least good and born out of desperation, since he could not tell how displeased the uncle would be with the nephew, due to the Koo angle. The one he was examining now was much better and it could serve two purposes. He would contact Madame Koo who was conducting a search and who would be far nearer the heart of the matter than the Second Son. He would tell her the truth. He would tell her his master was gone on the woman and was keeping her at his place. Hoping that Madame would not believe this truth. Hoping that she would believe it was only a way for saying that the master was holding the woman prisoner and was ready to give her up—for a consideration that the servant would name. . . . The consideration would be the cessation of the feud and all baiting and all publicly derogatory statements concerning the half-caste; it would include the return of the hospital and a guarantee that the local gentry would not hereafter interfere with its operation in any manner or way whatsoever.

The reason the servant considered it necessary to tell the truth was that he would not be able to tell how his master would behave, afterwards, if the subject were ever brought up or even if it never was brought up. If he should, at any time, let it be known that he had loved her, then the truth would take care of it.

And the reason the servant would name a consideration, a price, was so that in the first place the transaction would look real and genuine. But in the second place, why not be practical if it could be handled so discreetly and quietly that his master need never become aware of it, need never realize that any sort of bargain had been struck? His master was to assume, simply, that Old Koo had tired of his persecution, what with the war and other interests.

As for that, his master was to know nothing about any part of it. He would tell the Koos they could come for their daughter at a certain hour, no sooner, no later. At that hour he would arrange with a friend of his for a medical emergency which would take the master away from the shop for long enough. He intended to explain his own prolonged absence in terms of that emergency. And indeed, he would not go back to the shop at all until everything was in readiness. He would say that his friend was acutely ill and that he had been with him, this long while, and he would ask his master to come. His friend must be properly ill, some way, too. He would have to think that out. When they returned, the woman would be gone, with the servant knowing no more than his master. But if the master made him stay with the woman, not wishing her to be left alone? Well, he could say that some ruffians had stormed the place and hit him over the head, so that he did not know what happened after that.

This plan seemed better to him than the others, being two-faceted as it was. And based upon a factor as predictable as his master's medical honor. Nothing else might succeed in prying him away from her.

He squatted there, turning over the plan, when he ran onto a small practical difficulty that had not occurred to him. Because of the feud, he was not on speaking terms with any one of the Koo servants. How, then, was he to contact Madame? Was he to call in some third person to act as go-between? He did not like the thought of that, not when he had already decided that he would not even take into his real confidence the friend who was to be ill. Not when he had already gone over in his mind his roster of friends and selected as the most likely one—a consumptive—to whom he had only planned to say, "I have been unjustly accused by my master of loose living and thieving and need an alibi, since he is out for my skin. As my friend, I ask you to be ill and to say that I have nursed you this whole night through and to moan and to spit up some blood if you can, that he may see for himself when he comes." No, the idea of a go-between, of any third person, did not sit well with the servant. He pondered. Then he himself should do it? Yet he could not get past the Koo gates without bringing down a storm of speculation and comment. How should he get annonymously past those gates? But then, he asked himself, why should he get past them? Why not have Madame Koo meet him somewhere to talk things over? That would be much better. Ah, there! This thinking of gates reminded him that that one who had blabbed in the teahouse was the gateman's son. What could be so wrong with using him? He was foolish and loud-mouthed, true, but as the bearer of a message to Madame he would make himself automatically responsible to her and she, it was safe to predict, would know well how to seal his lips. . . . Nor had he been so drunk that he would fail to remember having blabbed. Ai, he would be uneasy in his mind. And if the servant went at dawn and knocked softly, so that no one's attention was apt to be attracted unless the old gateman's, which would be all right, too, keeping it thus in the family. But wait. What if Madame knew where his master was living? It was a danger to pause over but he felt quite sure she would never guess that her daughter was just there—negotiating or no negotiating—for the taking. No, not with all these elaborate trappings. He would phrase his message most carefully. She would find it advisable to abide by the rules of negotiation that were laid down. It looked all right. Siau Liang should do. He would sit here until the dawn that was not so far off. Then he would go and deliver his message through this Siau Liang.

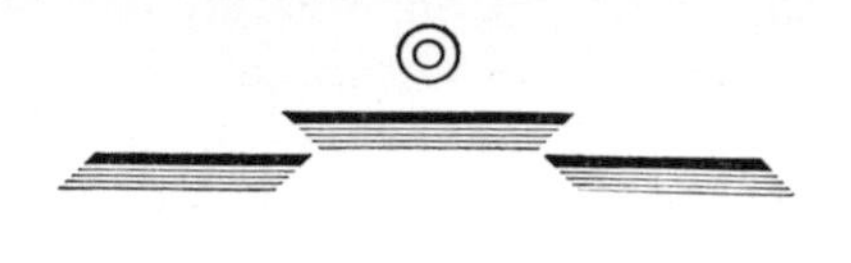

9

I

THE light scatter of sounds meant it was dawn; the rose light was against the window. She recalled how the House of Koo had seemed to her to be, that morning, the component parts of a dream that she was walking through. The pistol was under the pillow and she was in his arms. It could not go on. She shifted her position, a little, so that her head was against his heart and she could hear it beating. How long had the expectancy of death hung over her, dictating the terms of courage, of all her thoughts, of, even, her love? How long had she been operating on, I am finished and what I do I do on a margin? She had wanted to tell Little Dog there wasn't any password.

Six o'clock.

Yang Koh: "Do not be proud any more."

Huan-li: "Heart of our heart, we give you our permission to forget who you are."

But what about the dreamlike faces that are arranged in tiers, with their mouths slightly open? She turned restlessly. He put his hand in her hair, buried it in her hair, drew her head back until their eyes met, and hunted, and held—oh, what? Did she, in the last analysis, know? Did she know anything?

"I will decide it for you," he said.

She was trembling. "How did you know?"

Their kiss was the long and involved kind.

"Then," she said, "let's go."

They were silent a moment.

"I wonder if we dare wait until tonight," he said. "We need the cover of darkness. I'll have the servant arrange for a boat."

He swung his legs over the side of the bed and was gone.

She closed her eyes. The prospect of life was frightening—more frightening than the other. How wobbly and uncertain it made her feel! Had she changed her mind because love and life were worth waking up and dying, every morning, for? Or because she could not leave him now? Or because she was ready to fight it out with herself—with the memories and the guilt? Or because she had served them and could no longer and therefore dared . . . Or because she trusted him to find a place that was far enough away? She wasn't sure. She was putting love above everything—she understood that. That and the fact of her faith in him—that he would manage to get her out of the city without her being caught; that he would manage—if anything should go wrong—to blow her face off.

He came back.

"He isn't here," he said, frowning.

She sat up. "The servant?"

"Yes, and it isn't like him. I wonder . . ." He looked at his watch. "We damned near have to wait until tonight." He smiled wryly at her. "I should have decided for you sooner."

II

There was a knock at the Small Gate of the House of Koo, a cautious yet forthright knock. Siau Liang heard it. Indeed

Siau Liang had been up most of the night. The strange knock was repeated. Siau Liang would not have climbed out of his bed on any account whatsoever had not Lao Liang, his father, commenced fretting and muttering. He got up and made his way with great care to the gate and said, "Who's there?"

There was a pause.

"If," said a voice from the other side, "that is the blabber of tales in a teahouse, open."

Siau Liang's head whirled. He was all thumbs drawing the bolts but at last he got the gate opened a crack and peered straight into the face of the servant of Blair.

"Name of a name," Siau Liang said, "what do you want?"

The servant of Blair looked past Siau Liang.

"Carry this word," he said, "to your mistress, Madame Koo." Again he must pause. "Tell her," he said, "that if she desires some news of a toad, she herself and no other should be in the third hall of the Waung Dzung Temple this morning at ten o'clock. Four hours from this time, no sooner and no later. Go straightway and tell her that."

Siau Liang gaped.

The Blair servant, having slowly repeated every word of his message, turned and walked woodenly up the street and disappeared into the first alley he came to.

"Siau Liang!" Lao Liang, his father called.

Noiselessly Siau Liang closed the gate.

"And why do you beat your gums at this hour?" his father wished to know.

"I was not beating my gums, Father," Siau Liang answered. "Too much wine, Father," Siau Liang said. "I was heaving."

Helen was half asleep (in that depressed state that is almost sleep) when Dji-bo came and announced that Siau

Liang was waiting to see her. Remembering Siau Liang's condition and of how he had kept her waiting up for him half the night, besides, Helen was badly disposed toward Siau Liang. She was nervous and cross. She was thinking that if he started bringing her each little nothing, with great elaborations, just for the excuse of seeing her, it would be too much.

"But it is according to your own orders," Dji-bo was saying, while she was helping her dress. "You told him to come at any time, day or night, if he had news."

"Well, he had better have news, then," Helen said. "Hand me my shoes, Dji-bo, and for Buddha's sake, go fetch some tea."

In spite of this grumbling, however, Helen dressed with considerable care. She found it necessary to make up her face completely and to dabble on a little perfume and to give a touch or two to her nails. Dji-bo was back with the tea before she was ready to go out to Siau Liang.

"Ah," she said, "Siau Liang, most vigilant servant, good morning."

Siau Liang was so unsteady that when he tried to bow it was almost his undoing. Helen waited the proper time for him to speak. He only sputtered and stammered. Finally Helen said, "You have news, Siau Liang?"

Siau Liang clutched at the door frame. "I have news, First Young Mistress," he said. "I am on my way with it to Madame. I merely thought to stop here. . . . That is, in view of my oath . . ."

"Yes, Siau Liang?" Helen sipped her tea and studied the fingernails of her left hand.

"Well!" Siau Liang burst forth. "Here he comes, then, this odious character!"

"Who, Siau Liang?"

"Why, the servant of Blair!"

"The servant of Blair?" Helen set down her cup. "Our House has no dealings with him or his."

"That's what I say," said Siau Liang, not at all wishing to get himself embroiled on the teahouse end of it.

"And so?" Helen asked. "And what did this one want?" Helen had always been mildly intrigued with the handsome half-caste. She had once considered his move to Lingchow in a somewhat dreamy light. However, the feud had put an end to all that. Still, she thought him an attractive enemy, even now. "What did this servant want, Siau Liang?"

"Well," Siau Liang said. "This is what he tells me. He instructs me to go straight to Madame. And his message is this: 'Tell her that if she desires some news of a toad, she herself and no other should be in the third hall of the Waung Dzung Temple this morning at exactly ten o'clock.' Then this relic turns about and walks off."

Helen was out of her chair. "Good merciful Buddha!" she said. She forgot her manners and stared hard and straight at Siau Liang. "A toad . . . The third hall," she murmured. "Ah, Siau Liang! Siau Liang, Siau Liang!"

Siau Liang was overcome.

"This is it," Helen said, "this is it! We have outfoxed them, Siau Liang, you and I. Ah, Siau Liang, I will give you the sun and the moon!"

Dji-bo coughed loudly and thoroughly disapprovingly. Helen sat down.

Chewing at her underlip, the way she did when she was really thinking, Helen at first found only the name—the servant of Blair—repeating itself in her mind. The servant of Blair was Dr. Christopher Blair's servant. Did this mean that Leila was ill and that Dr. Blair had been called in, perhaps, by the people at whatever place Leila was hiding? One of those unfortunate accidents? Did it mean that he had heard tales of a search her family was making for her and was ready to turn her over—or point out her hiding place? Helen had not even known Christopher Blair was in the city. Suppose, in some way, Leila had fallen into his hands. She could imagine a worse fate. But why was he opening negotiations? It did not sound as if he had Leila's welfare at heart. Ah, he did not love the Koos, that was certain. This must be gotten to the bottom of.

"Siau Liang," she said, "you must not deliver this message to Madame, my mother. I shall go to the temple for her."

"Oh, but Mistress!" Siau Liang was beside himself. "Mistress, I must deliver that message. I must!"

"No, Siau Liang, that is exactly what you must not do. Put your trust in me, Siau Liang. No harm will come to you, I swear it."

Still, Helen was speaking mechanically, absently. The message was: "Tell Madame that *she herself and no other* . . . Ah! . . . Did Dr. Blair intend to send his representative to the temple or would he be there himself? That was the question, the vital one, Helen thought. She looked at her watch. It was ten minutes until seven. If it was the servant of Blair who was to be at the temple, the prospects were dark. Not knowing the first thing about him, she had no idea in the world she could handle him. But if it were to be Christopher Blair himself—then that was a different matter. At Lincoln's bedside, if she remembered correctly, Christopher Blair had not failed to both notice and approve her, even when, in view of her brother's condition, he had had no time for her. It was, Helen felt, safe to assume that Christopher Blair was not impervious to a woman's charms, to a beautiful woman's entreaty, no matter what his present designs. Helen felt she could so put the life-and-death stakes of this business to him, that he could not but resist seeing her side of it and agree to abandon his plan.

Whatever the outcome, Helen felt it was Christopher Blair she must deal with. For an additional thought had just occurred to her: suppose that the servant was not representing the master but himself? It was most unlikely, but in that case it was doubly urgent she reach Christopher Blair and get him to use his influence on his man before the proposed time of the temple rendezvous. Yes, the more she thought about it the more convinced she was that it would be the servant at the temple. Because of the feud, it would almost have to be the servant. It was tradition. Oh, Buddha, certainly. And she would be sharply rebuffed—and it would be too late.

Meanwhile, five more minutes had passed. If she were increasingly certain that the wrong person was going to be at the temple, would it not be advisable to forget about the temple entirely? *Wouldn't it?* Just to go to Christopher Blair's house? At once? This moment? To surprise him? To take him off guard and . . . Oh, but there were all sorts of risks in that. He could refuse to see her. Or perhaps he would not be there. Or perhaps . . . She must stop this or she would talk herself out of everything!

"Siau Liang," she said. "I forbid you to deliver that message."

Siau Liang gulped. He had been explaining all this while that he must.

"I forbid you, Siau Liang. If it should come up later, say that you mistook the instructions and understood him to say First Young Mistress instead of Madame. I will take full responsibility, I will protect you, Siau Liang. I swear that. And now you must swear to take the message no farther. Will you swear that, Siau Liang?"

"Yes," Siau Liang said, feeling unjustly treated and persecuted and noble, at the same time.

"Now, Siau Liang. Where does he live?"

"Where does he live?"

"Where does Bao I-sung, the half-caste, live since the war?"

Siau Liang scratched his head. He had to admit that he did not know.

"Think, Siau Liang."

Siau Liang thought but nothing productive came out.

"Oh, heaven," Helen said, turning to her maid. "Dji-bo, where does the half-caste live?"

"Now, how should I know?" Dji-bo asked. "Anyway, 'tis probably a secret. Did he not move from his big foreign house because they wished his half-foreign neck? Who knows where he lives, is what I say. And who cares?"

"Ah, Buddha!" Helen said. "Buddha, Dji-bo, go at once. Put a few discreet questions to whoever it is you are forever gossiping with. Go on, Dji-bo. Quickly. Find out."

Dji-bo, grumbling, took herself off.

"And you, admirable and faithful Siau Liang," Helen said. "Do you go back to the gates and stay there. If I should come, you and not your father, must be there. You must let me out, Siau Liang. And you must get rid of your old father some way, Siau Liang. That is what I ask. Send him forth to his teahouse—anything. Only he must not see me leave. Can you arrange it, Siau Liang?"

"Yes," Siau Liang said, rolling his eyes around. Sadly: "I—I could bolt him into the back room." Then, brightening: "He will still be asleep if you will come soon."

"Soon or a little later, it must be the same, Siau Liang, do you understand?"

"Yes," Siau Liang said.

Helen went halfway across her court, thanking him. Some minutes later Dji-bo returned with the news that the Koo servants did not make it their business to know where the half-caste was staying. Some insisted that he was not in the city at all. One was sure he was staying in the teashop of Ching the Pock Face, on the Little Horse Road but admitted he had it on hearsay when his brother reminded him that Ching the Pock Face's shop had burned down three years before. The upshot was that nobody really could say.

"Of course," Dji-bo said, with a wry smile, "if there is one in this House who knows with certainty . . . There is one in this House of whom it is said that she knows everything."

Helen was furious. "Then, Dji-bo, why are you wasting time? Why do you not . . . ? Oh! Madame, my mother."

"The same."

Helen could have cried. Here, time was passing and she was stopped cold by the most trivial obstacle. Who would know? It was quite, quite true. If anyone knew, her mother would. . . . She who was trying so desperately to forestall her mother should . . . But wait! Father was ill, according to Andrew. He had not left his court, according to Andrew. And Helen had not yet done what custom called for—she had not yet paid *any* "daughter's duty calls" on her mother, to inquire about his health, almost unpardonable negligence on her part. If there was no other way . . . She searched her mind clean for any other way, since it seemed such an awful waste of time, but found none.

"Dji-bo, is my mother up at this hour?"

"Dear Mistress, your mother is always up at this hour. She has breakfasted and no doubt she has already sent out her orders of the day to the cooks and to the . . ."

"Very well, Dji-bo. Go and announce me."

"She will die of the shock."

"You just go and announce me, Dji-bo."

Helen hurried back to her bedroom. She sat down at her toilet table and began to take off most of her makeup. She rubbed the top of her head with her hands, mussing up her hair some (but not too much). She inspected herself closely. Then she rubbed in the tiniest bit of eye shadow under each eye. She changed into one of her oldest and most unbecoming gowns.

Little Dog turned over in bed and mumbled something in his sleep. Helen bent over him and kissed his ear. "Meat dumpling," she whispered, "wish me luck."

She hurried out.

But by the time Helen reached Madame's court she was walking slowly and there was a vagueness about her walk and about her manner and particularly about her eyes. She looked, indeed, as though she had not slept all night and saw no real prospects of ever sleeping again. How fortunate, she thought, that she *had* remained in seclusion since Leila's departure, that she had had that hysterical scene with her mother, that even in her little burst of activity the afternoon before, she had not left her court; how fortunate that she really had worried and lost sleep.

She wandered into Madame's sitting room, bowed, and said, "Mother, good morning."

Madame looked up from some ledgers which were on the table before her. She said, "Sit down, my dear."

Helen sat down obediently and said nothing. Her eyes wandered aimlessly about the room and when she felt her mother's eyes on her, she smiled a weak and watery smile and continued to say nothing at all.

"Would you like some tea?" Madame asked her.

"I don't know, Mother," Helen said. And then, as if rousing herself. "Of course, thanks. That would be nice."

Madame poured her a cup. Helen took a sip and put the cup down.

"You are up early," Madame said.

"Yes," Helen said, offering no further explanation.

Madame looked at her daughter. "You are keeping too much to yourself," she said. "You must not get ill. There is enough trouble in this House."

Madame seemed as sad and troubled as Helen was pretending to be. And for a moment Helen felt a guilty pang of conscience to be taking her mother in.

"Mother . . ." She let her voice trail off. "Nothing seems . . . I wish . . ."

"What is your wish?"

"Ah, nothing," Helen said. She raised her eyes and gave her mother a look that accused, that begged, that said, "Call in your men!" Her mother looked away.

"I do not understand," Helen murmured.

"I do not ask you to understand," Madame Koo said.

They sat.

Helen said, "And I. Well, I have forgot why I came. It seems to me that the days have turned into nights."

"I know."

Again, Helen was sorry that her motives could not be what they seemed. She fingered her teacup.

"And why did you come?" Madame asked her.

"The nights and days are all alike," Helen said. "I have been negligent. It was not until yesterday that Andrew told me of Father's illness. How is he, Mother?"

"He is ill. Quite ill."

"I'm sorry."

"It is no ordinary bilious attack."

"Have you had doctors in?"

"But they did not help."

"Whom did you ask?"

Madame told her. Helen nodded thoughtfully.

"You know," Helen said. "It may be the fault of my Shanghai education but . . ."

"Yes?"

"I know what doctor I wish we could have in."

"The half-caste?" Madame Koo asked. "I have thought of him."

"Have you?" Helen said, pushing at her cup. "The feud. It is too bad. . . . But there. Of course, he is not to be reached, anyhow."

"As for that," Madame began.

"He is in Manila," Helen said.

"You have been misinformed," Madame said. "He is still with us."

"Really?" Helen said. "Surely not at the compound?"

"No," Madame said. "He is at a blacksmith shop."

"A blacksmith shop! Mercy! What blacksmith shop?"

"One on Pu-tang Street."

"Well!" Helen said. "He has moved down in the world." That was enough. She dared not ask the name of the shop. She would pray there was only one. At this point, the old signals must not be allowed to go up. "If Father does not improve," she said. "What do you think? Would he consent? Would the family, do you suppose?"

"I cannot say about your father, he behaves so strangely. The family would have to be convinced that he is very ill indeed before it would be agreeable to swallowing so big a pride. We shall have to see. If he is no better by tomorrow I may suggest it. But it depends on your father. The family, of course, can be managed."

"Of course," Helen said.

They sat on. Every nerve in Helen's body was throbbing. But she waited for her temporary interest in her father's illness to vanish, she waited for the return of her listlessness, for the vacant look to come back to her eyes.

"Well," she said, "I should go, I suppose, and see to Little Dog. He will be waking."

"Do not neglect him," her mother said.

"No," Helen said, rising. "Well . . . Good morning, Mother."

"I will send you over a tonic," Madame said.

But when Helen was out the door and slowly crossing the court, Madame looked most thoughtfully after her. Her masterpiece. The work of her brain and years. How nearly perfect she was, too. Had it not been that her hands were most exquisitely manicured, had there not been the unmistakable hint of perfume about her which did not somehow go with her wan and wandering ways, Madame might not indeed have noticed that slender shaft of urgency.

She closed her ledgers and began to reconstruct the scene which had just passed between herself and her daughter in her orderly and meticulous mind.

III

Helen fairly flew. She did not know whether she should go dressed beautifully or badly. Badly, not to attract attention. Beautifully, if she was to persuade the doctor. She decided upon a compromise: a quiet but beautiful blue silk. She decided to go without Dji-bo, though she had never in all her life been out of the House alone before. She changed and made up her face as fast as she could, much relieved that Little Dog had gone off somewhere with his nurse, put all her money in her purse, and took a devious way to the gates.

Siau Liang was there. Helen gave him a deep look and slipped out the Small Gate. She had to walk over two streets before she found a rickshaw. She ordered the puller to put up the hood and draw the curtain so that she would not be seen. For ladies, riding, that was customary enough. She got hastily in.

"Pu-tang Street," she said.

IV

"Put some money in his hand," George Koo said. "Give him five silver dollars."

The beggar, slouched there, on the other side of George's desk, in front of the row of green metal filing cabinets, made George angry. It made him angry and nervous just to be forced to look at his dirt and rags. The detective counted out the money and gave it to the beggar who surely should have been overwhelmed by such riches. There were several of George's men standing about. One, by the window, was yawning. George told him to stop.

He looked back at the beggar. He had already asked him all sorts of questions but the beggar stuck by his story: that he had found the clothes and picked them up, but could not remember just where.

"Now, my good fellow," George said. "With all that good money in your pocket, I am *sure* you can remember where and how you came upon those clothes. In what section of the city was it?"

"Well, sir," said the beggar, scratching his neck. "I believe . . . Yes, sir. I think it was in the Old North Gate section—that's where it was."

"That's better," George said.

"They were made into a bundle," the beggar said.

"Ah, fine!" George said. "And now. Surely, you can remember the street. A street is not so hard to remember, after all."

The beggar's hand traveled up to his head, which was probably ridden with lice, George thought.

"Well?"

"Well," said the beggar, "let me see. I believe—yes. It was that small street—what is the name? That crooked one? Oh, let me see. Feng-tsau Lane. That was it."

"Good, good," said George.

"And it was just outside that apothecary's shop, I found it."

"Fine," said George. "Fine. I know exactly where that is."

He waved the beggar out and turned eagerly to his detectives. "We will have that district thoroughly combed. We will raid that shop."

"And what makes you suppose she is in either the shop or the district?" one of the detectives asked. "A person can wad some clothes into a bundle and throw them anywhere. The chap was obviously telling the truth. And obviously he knows no more about her than we do. And obviously we are right back where we were."

After the beggar had crossed the Wang Widow's Bridge and was walking along the Big Horse Road, a man, rather poorly dressed, caught up with him.

"He had you in, too, did he?"

"Ai," said the beggar.

"And I see you did what I did, eh? Well, it is always better to lie. On principle."

"Ai," said the beggar, "always. It is the first lesson the beggar learns: if called in by officials or high-ups, lie about the earth and lie about the sky and lie three times about your mother's eye."

The man laughed softly. "And what a fool that one is. One can afford to use one's poorest lies on him."

The beggar snorted. "And get the biggest pay!"

"Ai, ai," laughed the man. "And you will not have to beg for three whole months. And I will not have to strain my back at a rickshaw for half as long."

"So that's what he had you in about."

"Ai, he did. Wished to know—had I pulled a tall,

gaunt woman. I had, you know. And I knew where I had pulled her. So you know what I said?"

"That you had only ever pulled short fat ones in all your life."

"Exactly," said the man. "And did he try to involve you with this tall and gaunt one, too?"

"Of course."

"And had you—like me—seen her?"

"Nay," said the beggar. "Never. I do not see ghosts, if that's what you mean, though I thought we were talking talk. But I will tell you—I have not worked that Old North Gate section for a decade. I must work the Ki-tsung section, now, and it's poorer."

"Too bad."

"Well, it is the Beggars' Society ruling. I sit on Pu-tang Street all day and knock my head for a copper."

"You must have been overjoyed, then, to fall over that bundle."

"I was."

A laugh. "And did you fall over it?"

"I did—believe me or not—right there on Pu-tang Street. How is that for luck?"

"It is fat luck."

"It is," said the beggar. "But, you know, it is a curious thing. I would have lied, anyhow, on principle, as we were saying. But this time I also lied to protect a gentleman."

"How is that?"

"Well, now. I have been begging for three score years. And I must squat in miserable streets from morn till night and never, in all these years of days and nights, has any man ever been so good to me as this one—tended my son, he did—and never passes me without a "Good day!"—that's it!—and alms. And so, since he is living in Wang the Little's blacksmith shop, and I remember that it is just outside that door that I picked up that bundle, I keep it all in my mind when I am called in by this Koo oaf. And my old lies take on new purpose. For who knows? He has done me favors—a beggar. Well, maybe it's a favor I do for him."

"Yes," said the man. "And a good way to think of it, too. . . . But you said he was a gentleman, did you not? What, pray, is he doing in a blacksmith's shop?"

"Oh, well," said the beggar, giving the man a look. "What does that matter?"

"You are right," said the man, "it does not matter. . . . And here is where I turn off for the rickshaw *hang*. Good morning, beggar, and may you eat well."

"Good morning and the same," said the beggar, walking on.

The man could have hoped for a more fruitful gleaning, he thought, but perhaps his august employer could extract something out of it. He made a second turn toward the headquarters of General Ma.

V

A blacksmith shop, at last. The shop of Wang the Little, Helen saw by the sign, but it was closed tight. She stood there, trembling, uncertain. She had let her rickshaw go at the head of Pu-tang Street and walked down it. Was there another blacksmith shop or not?

She raised her hand and knocked. Nothing happened. She knocked again and louder. Then she thought she heard a sound from within.

"It's me!" she called out stupidly. "Helen. Please let me in."

A bolt was shot—another. The door creaked back. Helen covered her mouth to keep from screaming. She fell in over the threshold and slammed the door behind her.

"Leila!" she sobbed. "Oh, Leila. Leila, my God!"

Leila had to hold her to keep her from falling. Helen could not stop crying; the shop was dark after the street and full of shadows. She laid her head on Leila's shoulder and wept. Then, through her tears, she saw the half-caste standing close by and she stopped her tears. She stood off from Leila. She looked from Leila to Christopher Blair and back again.

"So!" she said.

They said nothing but they did not need to say anything.

"You bring news?" Christopher Blair asked her.

His voice was tense and quiet. Helen looked sternly at him.

"Did you or did you not send your servant to our House?"

"No," he said, his eyes going to Leila's. "So that's it."

"Yes," Helen said.

"Then, everything is up."

"Not yet," Helen said. "At least, I hope not." Suddenly she was intensely angry. "Dear Buddha!" she said. "What have you two been doing? Why haven't you left this place before this? Or don't you even know there are men all over this city hunting for Leila? I simply do not understand."

"We were waiting until tonight," Christopher Blair said.

"Till tonight, oh, Buddha! What have you been doing all these days and nights!"

They did not answer.

"Merciful Buddha," Helen said. "You cannot wait till tonight. You must leave this place at once!"

"You have made us understand that," Christopher Blair said. "But how? I can't take her out there."

"There must be a way," Helen said, chewing at her lip. "Because there is no more time. It is now twenty-five minutes past nine. Your servant thinks he is to meet Madame, our mother, at the Waung Dzung Miau at ten o'clock. When he does not find her there . . . Well, I leave it to you to imagine how long it will be before he again attempts negotiations. One hour? Two?" Helen did not speak of the other fear that was at the back of her mind. "We must think up some sort of disguise," she said. "The right disguise . . . Come. Quickly. Take me to your rooms. I must see what clothes you have."

They hurried out of the shop and across a small court.

"In here," Christopher Blair said.

They went in. Helen looked around at the dark and dingy room, when suddenly an idea hit her. It was the room, a poorer one than she had ever been in, which was the negative source of her inspiration.

"Never mind disguises," she said.

They looked at her.

"It is the poor districts that are being combed," she said, "the poor canal traffic that is being interfered with, the poor people who are being bothered—I have it all from the steward."

"Yes," Christopher Blair said impatiently, "of course."

"You make your mistake by being poor," Helen said, with an air of finality. She looked critically at Christopher Blair. "Don't you have a better-looking suit than that?"

"Certainly. But . . ."

"Then get busy," Helen said. "Change into it. Change into the best and most conspicuously foreign suit you have. Hurry."

Christopher Blair continued to look at her for a moment. Then he went to the back of the door and ripped a suit off a hanger.

"You have to leave first," Helen said to him. "You have to get a boat and have it tie up at the Zau Jau landing. Is that the nearest to this place?"

"Yes," Christopher Blair said. "But I'm not leaving without her."

Helen's heart contracted. "Listen to my plan," she said gently. "Then, if you can think of a better one, you need not follow it. But mine is dependent upon your leaving first—leaving now. So keep dressing while I explain it to you."

"All right."

Leila was helping him. She was kneeling in front of him and changing his shoes.

Helen said, "You must go immediately to a boat *hang* and hire a large, fine houseboat—the best and most expensive you can get. You must walk boldly out of this place, you must be lordly about it. You are tired of the war and you are hiring this boat to go to Shanghai in, since train travel is so irregular and difficult. Good. And those who know you know also about the feud and will not suspect you of taking aboard any Koo passenger."

Christopher Blair nodded.

"Very well. You arrange for the boat. Then leave your boat and go to the East Water Gate and bribe the East Water gateman to let you speedily out of the city when the time comes. Be lordly with him. Tell him you are planning this trip and delay of any sort irritates your digestion. Tell him to watch out for your big boat and to raise his gate up, well in advance. Then take your boat and tie it up at Zau Jau and wait there. Those are your duties."

"Go on."

"Leila, no elaborate disguises for you. The main thing is for you not to be seen. But you will change clothes with me. This gown will be a trifle short for you but it is obviously expensive. Let's trade, now, Leila. Here."

Helen began to unbutton it. Leila began on her jacket.

Helen said, "How long would it take you, Dr. Blair, to hire that boat and see the East Water gateman?"

"An hour—on the outside. I know a boat *hang*. There will be no trouble about it."

"Good," Helen said. "Then, you leave by the street. I leave, at the same time, by the alley, in these clothes of yours, Leila. Throw me the trousers. And I hope there *is* an alley. . . ."

"There is."

Helen pulled the trousers on. "While Dr. Blair is arranging for the boat," she said, "I am arranging for a rickshaw—no common, ordinary street variety, such as I rode in just now. But a fine, black and shining one," she said. "And perhaps there will be a second rickshaw—who knows?—with a lady's maid in it." If she could turn herself into one fast enough. "At any rate, one hour from the time we leave, not one minute sooner or later, a rickshaw will draw up in front of this shop, with top up and curtain closed. They have their eyes out for a poor and humble person. Well, Leila, you merely step from shop door into this rickshaw which is going to be so obviously the equipage of a lady of wealth. The puller will carry his fine lady straight to the Zau Jau landing where the fine boat will be waiting. . . . Zau Jau is only two streets north of here. The entire transaction will take maybe five minutes. . . . Well?"

"Does a lady emerge from a blacksmith shop?" Leila asked.

"There will be no time to tell," Helen said. "It is all over before even a beggar can get time for a second look. You go to the door a few minutes early and open it a crack and be ready. The rickshaw comes up, as the lady steps in. Then it is gone. The puller, maybe, bent down, just there, to scratch his leg."

There was a pause.

"By my watch," Christopher Blair said, "it is twenty-two minutes until ten. Here." He handed it to Leila.

"Have you thought of a better way?" Helen asked him, hoping terribly that he had.

"No," he said. "It's the only way."

Helen knew it was. She said, "If I could see to both boat and rickshaw, I would. As it is . . ."

"I know," he said. "Check your watch with hers."

This was done. Leila sat down suddenly on the edge of the bed. Christopher Blair said something in a whisper to her and pointed toward the pillow. Then he bent over her. Helen looked away. When she looked back, he was gone.

"Show me the way to the alley," Helen said.

VI

One hour—lacking seven minutes. Well, it was almost time. She was sitting on the bed, with her hand under the pillow, touching the gun. She would wrap a large silk handkerchief of Chris's that she had found around it, to conceal it, when the time came that she must leave the shop for rickshaw. She had it folded neatly—in her pocket. Seven minutes. She decided to wait in the shop. She rose, with the gun in her hand, to open the door. . . . With her other hand on the bolt, she must remember how the stars had followed one another tightly, down the sky, that night. She must remember a temple out of her childhood with a blue roof and old-gold walls. She slid the bolt—opened the door. It did not surprise her that a Koo Family servant was standing motionless on the other side.

"Wei-sun," she said, jerking the gun up. He was one of the ones who had carried her from the jail.

"Third Young Mistress," Wei-sun said, with courtesy.

"Madame ordered me to follow your sister. I climbed the wall and have been biding my time."

"I see," she said. "And what does my mother want, Wei-sun?"

"Second servant and basket are in the alley, Third Young Mistress. Madame wants a corpse brought home."

At which moment they heard loud knocking out front and a voice raised: "Open, Nephew."

She nodded, as if she might also have been expecting it. It would be General Ma. To the servant she said, almost sing-songing her words, "And what is to be the fate of this corpse, Wei-sun?"

"It is to be destroyed, Third Young Mistress, I believe, with the news of it never to reach anyone."

He inclined his head in the direction of the knocking, out front, which was getting louder.

"Well, then, Wei-sun," she said. "Get me out of here." She smiled, thinking he must consider it an odd command, since she was the one who had the gun trained on him.

She said, "But be sure you tell my mother, Wei-sun, that I did it myself."

She saw a section of blue sky behind him. She raised the gun to her mouth in one, long, convulsed motion and pulled the trigger.

And while Wei-sun was dragging the corpse through the court, while the shop door was being beaten in by heavy blows, some beggar in some alley was singing:

"Third Koo Girl, Third Koo Girl,
Tall Girl, Tall Girl . . ."